KV-701-510

SPECIAL MESSAGE TO READERS

THE ULVERSCROFT FOUNDATION
(registered UK charity number 264873)
was established in 1972 to provide funds for research, diagnosis and treatment of eye diseases. Examples of major projects funded by the Ulverscroft Foundation are:-

- The Children's Eye Unit at Moorfields Eye Hospital, London
- The Ulverscroft Children's Eye Unit at Great Ormond Street Hospital for Sick Children
- Funding research into eye diseases and treatment at the Department of Ophthalmology, University of Leicester
- The Ulverscroft Vision Research Group, Institute of Child Health
- Twin operating theatres at the Western Ophthalmic Hospital, London
- The Chair of Ophthalmology at the Royal Australian College of Ophthalmologists

You can help further the work of the Foundation by making a donation or leaving a legacy. Every contribution is gratefully received. If you would like to help support the Foundation or require further information, please contact:

THE ULVERSCROFT FOUNDATION
**The Green, Bradgate Road, Anstey
Leicester LE7 7FU, England
Tel: (0116) 236 4325**

website: www.foundation.ulverscroft.com

Alison May was born and raised in north Yorkshire, but now lives in Worcester with one husband, no kids and no pets. There were goldfish once. That ended badly. Alison studied history and creative writing, and worked as a waitress, a shop assistant, a learning adviser, an advice centre manager, and a freelance trainer, before settling on 'making up stories' as an entirely acceptable grown-up career plan. She is a member of the Society of Authors and the Romantic Novelists' Association, and won the Elizabeth Goudge Trophy in 2012. Her novella, *Cora's Christmas Kiss*, was shortlisted in the Love Stories Awards, 2015, and for the RoNA Rose, 2016.

You can discover more about the author at alison-may.co.uk

ALL THAT WAS LOST

In 1967, Patience Bickersleigh is a teenager who discovers a talent for telling people what they want to hear. Fifty years later, she is Patrice Leigh, a nationally celebrated medium. But cracks are forming in the carefully constructed barriers that keep her real history at bay. Leo is the journalist hired to write Patrice's biography. Struggling to reconcile the demands of his family, his grief for his lost son, and his need to understand his own background, Leo becomes more and more frustrated at Patrice's refusal to open up. Because behind closed doors, Patrice is hiding more than one secret. And it seems that her past is finally catching up with her . . .

ALISON MAY

ALL THAT
WAS LOST

Complete and Unabridged

CHARNWOOD
Leicester

First published in Great Britain in 2018 by
Legend Press Ltd
London

First Charnwood Edition
published 2019
by arrangement with
Legend Press Ltd
London

A catalogue record for this book is available
from the British Library.

ISBN 978–1–4448–4091–9

Published by
F. A. Thorpe (Publishing)
Anstey, Leicestershire

Set by Words & Graphics Ltd.
Anstey, Leicestershire
Printed and bound in Great Britain by
T. J. International Ltd., Padstow, Cornwall

This book is printed on acid-free paper

For my parents — thank you for not being at all like parents in novels

1

'I've lost my place.' Patrice scowled at her manager, who was fussing about, rummaging through the wardrobe at the other side of the hotel room. Barney was always fussing. She could very well do without it. Georgios had never used to fuss, but Georgios was . . . The thought slowed and somehow slid away from her. Georgios was . . . Across the room, Barney slammed a drawer shut. Georgios wasn't here anymore. Of course. Patrice turned her attention back to the local newspaper and pack of index cards spread across the bed in front of her. 'I need to concentrate.'

'If you'd wear an earpiece, you wouldn't have to remember all that.'

She shook her head. Earpieces were for amateurs. Patrice considered herself rather more gifted than that. She glanced through the notes on the cards in front of her and then shuffled them into order. Dead certs went first and last. She'd risk a couple of cold reads if she had to, but not until the audience was warmed up. She'd seen too many people die on their feet because they'd tried to read an uncooperative punter. She turned back to the six-month-old local paper. It was a good story — the deaths were tragic, senseless and premature. For a second her fingertips lingered over the picture of the two mothers. 'You're sure these two are coming?'

Barney nodded. 'They picked up the tickets last night.' He was still riffling, ineffectively, through the wardrobe. 'What am I actually looking for?'

Patrice sighed. The man was an imbecile. 'The lilac jacket. It goes with this skirt.'

He stopped. 'The jacket I picked up from the dry cleaner's this afternoon?' He strode over to the door and lifted the jacket, still wrapped in plastic, from the hook. 'I told you where I'd left it.'

Patrice bundled her index cards together, stood and relieved him of the hanger. 'That will be all for now.'

She waited until the door to the suite clicked closed before she slumped back down. The jacket, wrapped in its pristine cover, taunted her. According to the tag it had been sent to the cleaners two days ago and picked up today. Logically she must have taken it, or asked someone to take it, to be cleaned, and then told Barney to pick it up. She didn't remember doing any of that.

Patrice took four deep breaths. It was what she always did before a performance. It calmed her, 'centred' her she supposed the newer spiritualists on the circuit would say. It helped her to remember who she was right now, and all she needed was to keep hold of right now for a few weeks more.

There was a sharp rap at the door. 'Miss Leigh! It's time.'

*　*　*

2

'I can't find you.' The girl on the box office desk flicked through her file of tickets.

Normally Leo would have charmed his way through this type of tiny mishap, but tonight was different. Tonight he was so close to finding what he'd been missing, and he was struggling to keep the tension out of his voice. Only his wife knew exactly why he was here, and she thought it was a dreadful idea. Leo forced a smile. 'Somebody called Barry ... no, Barney something was supposed to have arranged it.'

The girl frowned. 'Miss Leigh's manager?'

'Yes!'

She sighed. 'Well, you didn't say that, did you? That's guest list, innit?'

Leo swallowed down the flippant answer he wanted to give, and accepted the newly discovered ticket. He took his seat towards the back of the stalls and looked around. It was a traditional sort of theatre with red velvet chairs and not enough leg room. It was big though, and pretty much full. The ability to reunite lost souls with their loved ones must be a bankable skill. The woman to Leo's left leaned towards him. 'Are you hoping to hear from anyone in particular?'

The woman looked to be in her fifties, no more than five or six years older than Leo, but she could have been a different generation. Lank grey hair clung to the side of her face, and she was dressed in a too-small polo shirt, leggings and trainers, with a stripe of greying sock at her ankle. She shifted her weight in the seat, spreading her coat over her knees, before turning to look at Leo.

'So, anyone in particular?'

'No. No one in particular.' That was a lie, but what Leo was looking for was none of her business. He opened his notebook and tried to look engrossed.

The woman failed to take the hint. 'I'm here for my Dennis.'

Leo paused. He was also supposed to be working. He swallowed. 'Right. And Dennis was your . . . '

'What, love?'

'Dennis? He was your . . . ' Leo waited, but the woman didn't fill the gap. 'Your husband?'

'No, dear.' The woman gave a big throaty chuckle that rippled with Benson & Hedges and good humour. 'Dennis was a Pekinese.'

'A dog?'

'He was with me sixteen years.'

'Really?'

'That's a long time for a Peke. They have terrible problems with their insides. All the toy breeds do.'

'Okay.' Leo didn't quite know what to ask next. He glanced at his watch. 7.27 p.m. It was going to be a very long three minutes.

'Do you have dogs, dear?'

Leo shook his head. The woman shook hers too. 'Oh.'

This was a room full of believers. For most of his life, Leo hadn't really thought about what came after you died. But these days, he was sure. When people were gone, they were gone. You just had to find a way to accept it.

Leo looked around the theatre again. He'd

never been to anything like this before. Among the usual hum of pre-theatre chatter there was something else. Here and there he could see the odd person sitting alone, staring straight ahead. And there were couples, heads bent towards one another, waiting to see if tonight would be the night.

The house lights went down and an announcer's voice filled the theatre.

'Ladies and gentlemen, please welcome to the stage, Patrice Leigh.'

Applause. The curtains opened. The stage was empty apart from a stool and a small high table, with a jug of water and a glass.

As Patrice Leigh walked onto the stage, some people in the crowd stood and cheered. For a moment, the room took on the feel of an evangelical rally, but Leo's eyes were fixed on the woman on stage. He'd watched clips online, of course, and read interviews, but this was his first time seeing her in the flesh. A breath caught in his throat, but his brain wouldn't provide the language to make thoughts about the moment. He didn't even know what word he ought to ascribe to her. What had he hoped to feel? Some sort of connection? Some spark of belonging? Leo forced himself to breathe. The idea was ridiculous, of course. The woman on the stage was a stranger. He tried to look at her like a journalist. What would he write in that all-important opening paragraph to a Sunday supplement interview? He was the king of the opening paragraph, the description of how the waiter's head turned in recognition of the starlet approaching the table, or the summary of the superstar's dressed-down shirt-and-jeans combo. How would he describe Patrice Leigh?

The woman on stage could easily pass for a decade younger than her sixty-seven years. She's stylish, but never threatening. She could be the mother of the bride at an elegant country wedding, or the wife of the mayor of any of a hundred market towns, but she's not. She's Patrice Leigh, the woman who's built a fifty-year career on the claim that she can talk to the dead.

Leo shook his head. Not *claim* that she can talk to the dead. This wasn't going to be a job where doubt was encouraged, and it was a job. Whatever else it was going on, it was still a job.

On the stage, Patrice bowed slightly in acknowledgement of the cheers and smiled at her audience before raising her hand for quiet.

'Good evening, everyone.' Her voice was warm and somehow homely, the kind of voice you'd expect to offer you a nice cup of tea. 'It's really lovely to see so many of you here tonight. Now tell me, raise your hands, who's come along this evening hoping to hear from someone in particular?'

Hands shot up all over the room, including from the bereaved Pekinese owner next to Leo.

The woman on stage nodded. 'Yes. Yes. I can feel that there are a lot of people in need here tonight'

She stood silently for a minute. 'You know I can't promise that everyone who's hoping for contact will find exactly what they're looking for, but there are already a lot of spirits trying to

6

come through. There are some incredibly strong feelings there in the spirit world. And that's why I do this.'

The woman's voice cracked ever so slightly, and she continued more quietly. Leo shifted forward in his seat.

'I do this to try to give people some peace, not just to all of you hoping to hear from a loved one tonight, but also to all the spirits who do me the honour of sharing themselves through me. It's a real blessing to be able to bring these two worlds together.'

The applause started again. The woman smiled.

'Shall we make a start? I can already feel spirits desperate to come through. This is where I'd be overwhelmed without my spirit guide. I made contact with Stanley the first time nearly fifty years ago now. He's been my constant guide in the spirit world.'

Another burst of applause, apparently, for the long-departed Stanley.

'I do need quiet though, just for a moment, while I establish my link with Stanley.'

She closed her eyes.

The woman next to Leo nudged him hard in the ribs. 'He was killed at the Somme, you know.'

Leo nodded and obediently noted *Stanley — Somme* on his pad.

On the stage, the woman staggered slightly. Some members of the audience gasped, but she held up her hand for calm.

'Stanley is telling me there are so many people waiting to come through, but there is one that feels particularly urgent. I'm getting a name. Paul. No. Sorry. Phil. Phillip. Is there anyone here who that name means anything to?'

There was quiet from the audience. Patrice turned slightly towards the wings. 'Can we have the house lights up a notch?'

The lights came up.

'Thank you. So I have a Phil or Phillip coming through very strongly. He's right here besides me.'

Two hands went up at opposite sides of the theatre. One of the hands stood up towards the front, and the woman on the stage moved towards her.

'The name means something to you?'

Leo peered forward. The person standing was a woman. Leo could only see her profile but he guessed she was in her forties.

On stage, Patrice staggered slightly, putting her hand out towards the stool to steady herself. 'Oh. There's a lot of emotion here. Phillip really is desperate to be able to speak to you.'

She paused and turned her body towards where Phillip was, apparently, standing. She held up her hand and nodded.

'He's very anxious that you know that he's okay. Phillip was your son, wasn't he? Carole? He's telling me that you're Carole?'

In the audience, Carole nodded. 'He was my baby. When he died . . . '

The woman on stage shook her head. 'Don't tell me. It was very sudden, wasn't it? I'm seeing a flash of red, very strong red. A red car? An accident, a car accident.'

8

Another nod from the audience.

'The other car was going too fast, wasn't it? Phillip was driving his new red car, wasn't he? But it wasn't his fault.' She turned again to 'Phillip'. 'Oh, darling!'

Back to Carole. 'He's worried that you're cross with him. He wants you to know it wasn't his fault. I think Phillip needs to know you're not cross with him.'

Leo could feel himself getting drawn in, straining to see Carole's reaction. She was shaking her head.

The woman on the stage spoke again, more softly this time. 'I think Phillip needs to hear you say it.'

Carole's voice was quiet. 'I know it weren't his fault. He was a dead careful driver. That's why we let him have the car.'

'Phillip hears that. That's so helpful for him. Already he's so much more at peace, and . . . oh no. I see. I see.'

Patrice's voice tailed away.

'It wasn't just him, was it?'

Carole shook her head.

'I know. He's telling me. Tariq, was it? The lad that was with him.'

Someone gasped loudly further along the row from Carole. On stage, the medium turned towards the noise. 'Is that Aisha? He's saying Aisha to me. Stand up, my love. You're Tariq's mum?'

A second woman stood alongside Carole. 'And you came here together tonight?'

The women nodded.

'That's wonderful. Oh, your two boys were such good friends, weren't they? And I can tell that you're feeling they went too young. Far too young.'

She paused again listening to the spirit. 'Tariq wasn't quite eighteen when he went, was he?'

'He would have been eighteen last month.'

'I know. He's telling me. Your boys are both here. They're together. They're telling me they had a wonderful celebration for Tariq's birthday in the spirit world. That was just last month, he's telling me. They are both safe now. They're both at peace.' She took a couple of steps towards the front of the stage. 'They're here. Is there anything you want to say to them?'

The second woman, Aisha, spoke. 'Just tell him I love him.'

'You can tell him, dear. He can hear you.'

The theatre held its collective breath as she spoke. 'I love you, Tari.'

'He hears you.' Patrice paused again, listening to the spirits. 'He loves you too. And he's asking you to give his love to someone. Fatima? Yes. Fatima. That's the name he's giving me.'

'That's his sister. She's only a baby.'

The woman on the stage held out her hand. 'She's so young. Tariq wants you to remember him to her, and he wants you to know that he's going to be watching over his little sister.'

Leo could hear Tariq's mum crying now. The other mum put an arm around her, with her eyes fixed resolutely on the stage.

'I'm feeling so much contentment from your boys in the spirit world. They're telling me that

10

they don't want you to put your lives on hold. That's what they're saying to me.'

Both mothers wept, holding onto one another as their sobs bubbled upwards and echoed around the auditorium. Leo turned his attention back to the woman on the stage. She stared at the two mothers, and nodded very gently to herself.

'The boys have to go now. Our time with friends in the spirit world is, sadly, limited, but they're well. They're at peace.'

The two mothers retook their seats. On the stage, Patrice Leigh turned to her audience.

'I think we've all shared a very special moment there.'

The applause was loud and lengthy. They'd come here to see Patrice consult with the spirits, and they were getting exactly what they'd paid for.

Leo stared for a second longer at the woman on the stage before making his way up the aisle and out of the theatre. He headed onto the street. Leaning on the wall of the theatre, he pulled a cigarette he rolled earlier from a holder in his pocket, lit it and took a long drag. He'd been meaning to give up for ages. He'd been going to give up when he was thirty, and then forty, and then definitely forty-five. He'd promised his mother — God rest her soul — that he was quitting. He pulled his phone from his pocket. A missed call from Marnie. He touched the screen to ring her back.

'Leo?'

'Hi.'

There was silence for a second. His wife hated

the telephone. Leo could chat for hours to a friend on the phone, but Marnie detested the thing. She only ever made brisk, purposeful calls.

'What's she like?'

Leo didn't answer.

'I mean, have you talked to her yet?'

'No. I just saw the start of the show.' He listened to his wife breathing on the other end of the line. She had a way with silence that Leo didn't share. It made him want to explain, to justify, to make her approve. 'I'm going to take the job though.'

More silence.

'I mean the money's decent, and the freelance stuff's dried right up.'

'That's not the reason. Is it?'

'It's part of it.'

'Fine.' He could hear the irritation. He could imagine her whirring through the counselling sessions in her head. *Leo needs to work to be more open. Marianne needs to work at not pressuring Leo to discuss emotions before he's ready.* Everyone was working on something. 'Grace phoned this evening.'

Leo relaxed. They could talk about Grace in safety. Beautiful Grace. His children were the best thing, by far, that Leo had ever done. 'How was she?'

Marnie laughed. 'She was Grace. She's fine. She thinks we should be giving her more money.'

They talked for a couple more stilted minutes before hanging up. Leo followed the conversation with a quick message on his agent's voicemail. If he was treating this as work, he really ought to go back in and watch the rest of the show. There was pub across the street. He succumbed to temptation.

Inside, he sipped his pint in a quiet corner. It was too quiet. He should have gone back to the theatre where there were enough people to drown out the silence between his ears. Everywhere was quiet these days. His parents' house was abandoned since his mum and dad had gone within a few months of each other. Home was him and Marnie, no Grace or Oliver to yell at for wasting water and talking on the phone too long. Just him and Marnie being polite to one another. They never used to be polite. He remembered Marnie when he first met her. She'd been wearing a mint, green jumpsuit and bright blue mascara. When he'd found out her name was Marianne, he'd thought of Marianne Faithful and Marie-Antoinette. She'd bullied him into introducing her to his mate, on the grounds that she fancied him more and Leo was a stupid name. There'd been nothing quiet about her. She'd been loud and colourful and gloriously, infectiously rude.

Leo was at the bottom of his third pint by the time the audience came out of the theatre across the street. He watched the people bustle away. He wondered if they'd found what they'd been looking for. Eventually there was only one person left. Leo recognised her as the woman with the departed Pekinese. She stood for a long time outside the theatre, staring back at the building as if she was expecting something to happen. Nothing did.

13

2

Louise decided to make a cup of tea. She couldn't quite remember when making and drinking a cup of tea became a distinct activity to which she felt able to allocate an identifiable chunk of her day, but it was now, and she felt a stab of relief knowing that the next twenty-five minutes were accounted for and she would never have to live through them again.

She stood and walked to the kitchen. Standing up and walking to the kitchen — that in itself had filled nearly thirty seconds. Filling the kettle — another thirty seconds. While the kettle boiled, Louise leaned on the worktop and simply allowed the time to meander by.

She put a teabag in her mug and added milk, and then water. That was the order she always did it, but she suspected it might be wrong. She carried her tea back to the lounge, turning her head to one side as she passed a particular door in the hallway. Louise didn't allow herself to open that door during the daytime. She went in once first thing in the morning, and once before bed, but her rules for herself were clear: Not During The Daytime. She didn't count the afternoons spent weeping on the floor next to the bed. And she hadn't done that today. Not yet.

The letter box clicked and she heard the free paper drop onto the floor. She could look at that while she drank her tea. If she waited until her

14

tea was finished that would be another whole section of the day accounted for though. Louise decided to wait.

She sat on the chair in the corner of the lounge. It was an old chair, faded from years sitting in front of the window, with one wobbly leg at the back. It used to be purple but now the arms were yellowed. She looked at the fabric and wondered when that happened. Gradually, she supposed, not a definite instant change, not one moment when everything splintered and the following moment was unrecognisable from everything that came before.

She could sit on the sofa. It was more comfortable. You could see the telly better. You could stretch out. There was only her here. No one would mind if she stretched out and took up all the space on the settee. No one would moan at her lack of consideration. No one would tap her feet to make her budge up. Louise never sat on the sofa.

She sipped her tea and let the minutes slip by. She glanced at the clock on the shelf, out of habit rather than intent. The ticking had reminded Louise how slowly the time was passing, so she'd taken the batteries out weeks ago. She looked around the rest of the room. Familiarity made it hard to take in, but she had a sense that the room had changed. There were no shoes lying on the floor, no iPod discarded on the arm of the sofa. The remote controls were lined up neatly on the coffee table, rather than tossed wherever they landed and left to burrow their way under cushions or magazines. The room looked greyer than she felt it should, less inhabited, less alive.

Louise finished her tea in silence. She carried her mug to the kitchen and washed it under the tap. She walked to the hallway, steering her gaze away from that door, and picked up the paper from the mat. She carried it back to her chair in the living room, and turned the pages in front of her eyes. Louise tried not to read too much. The free paper was useful because it filled a period of time, and it was mainly innocuous fodder. Shops closing; other shops opening; ring roads being discussed, delayed and debated. Nothing that mattered. Sometimes, too much thinking could be dangerous. Just after it happened, she'd accidentally read a story about two teenage boys who were killed by a speeding driver. They'd printed a picture of one of their mums, a tired-looking Asian woman clutching her new baby. Louise shouldn't have read that. Other people's anguish didn't make her sad anymore, but she'd felt anger rising, as if they had no right to try to bring their suffering into her bubble. Louise's suffering should have been enough for a whole town, a whole country, a whole world.

She turned to the jobs page, and looked at what was available. Louise used to have a job, in the chip shop at the bottom of the estate. She'd quite liked it. There were always people around to talk to, and she'd been able to bring chips home for Kyle. She'd had the idea of doing deliveries to the sheltered flats, because the old folk didn't like to come out in an evening. It'd brought Alan a lot of extra regular trade on the quiet weekday evenings, and he'd put an extra fifty quid in her pay to say thank you. Louise had quit her job three months ago. Or maybe she hadn't quit. She didn't think she'd been sacked. She didn't go there anymore, anyway.

Maybe she should look for a new job. That would probably make her mum and Mrs Hardiman, who lived next door, and Sukjinder, in the Spar shop, happy. Mrs Hardiman kept telling her she was looking brighter. Probably getting a job would help maintain that illusion. Louise knew it was an illusion. She knew that however much she managed to get out, and put make-up on, and even look for a new job, she'd still be grey inside. She was going to be grey inside for ever.

Other people didn't tell her she was looking brighter. Kyle's dad had been round twice since it happened, which was twice more than in the previous five years. He hadn't said anything much at all, but he'd wanted to fuck her. She remembered reading, a long time ago, that some people in her situation found themselves feeling incredibly horny, like their body was trying to overcome the numbness by making them feel something else. Louise didn't understand that. She was feeling every single second passing as a stab into her guts. She didn't have the space to feel anything else. She'd told Kyle's dad to sling his hook.

Even though her mum told her she was looking well, Louise could look into her mum's eyes and see that they both knew that it was a lie. She kept popping around though, every day to

17

start with, and even now at least twice a week, and she put the kettle on, and they sat in silence, with her mum's hand clasped over Louise's, in what Louise supposed must be solidarity. When Mum said anything, it usually started, 'I can't imagine . . . ', which was true at least, but still meaningless. Louise couldn't remember her mother holding onto her hand before. She assumed she must have, when Louise was tiny, to cross the road or keep her close. When she tried to think of holding hands, her head filled with Kyle's sticky toddler fingers held tightly in her grip.

Louise turned back to the jobs page. Care home worker? She could remember being taken to visit her grandmother in her care home, when Louise was a little girl. They seemed like places where death was always close. No.

Administrative assistant? Louise could manage Facebook and email and eBay on the computer, but that was about it. They wanted typing and spreadsheets. No.

Louise closed the jobs section and went on to the Local Events. There was a psychic appearing at the Alexandria. Louise looked at the clock. It hadn't moved on, but she thought it might be afternoon by now. She folded the paper and took it with her into Kyle's room, where she sat on the floor and read for a moment. Then she stood up, opened the wardrobe and took out an oversized hoodie. She pulled it over her head and wrapped her arms around herself in an imitation of a cuddle. She sat back down on the floor and waited for the crying to begin.

3

'Are you quite sure about this, Miss Leigh?'

Patrice nodded. Barney was fussing again. It was tiresome at the best of times, let alone now. She pursed her lips. 'Just bring him up. And some tea. We should offer him tea.'

That gave her a few minutes alone at least, while Barney went downstairs, found this journalist that had been talked about and brought him back up. This book was something she'd wanted to do. It had been there in the plan Georgios had written with her in one of his last lucid moments. *Legacy.* That had been the word he'd used. Patrice took her seat in the tiny lounge area that meant the hotel got away with terming her room a suite, rather than simply another room. The hotel was the best the town could offer, and it wasn't so much bad, as simply forgettable. Patrice settled back and took four deep breaths.

There was a sharp rap at the door. Show time. 'Come in.'

Barney came in followed by a stranger. Patrice stood to greet him. 'You're Mr Cousins.'

He hesitated, stumbling slightly over the words. 'L . . . Leo.'

She nodded. 'And I'm Patrice Leigh. Which of course you know. Call me Patrice.'

The man swallowed. Patrice held the frown she was feeling back from her face. He seemed nervous. Why on earth would he be nervous?

19

She'd been told that he'd worked on books with footballers and one of those glamour model reality TV people. Something didn't seem quite right. Patrice filed the thought away for later. For now, she needed to put him at ease. She glanced around the room. Barney was fussing around with some poor room service attendant in the doorway. That would do. 'For goodness sake, leave it on the table.'

Barney took the tray from the waiter and placed it on the table between Patrice and the journalist. Patrice waved him away. 'I'm sure we can manage.'

She leaned forward and started pouring the tea as Barney backed out of the room. As the door clicked behind him she caught Leo's eye. 'What do you make of him, Leo?'

'Barney?'

'Yes.'

Leo accepted a cup of tea and paused. 'He seems efficient.'

Patrice smiled. 'The Third Reich were efficient. What else?'

Another pause. 'Maybe a little dull.'

That was more like it. Patrice laughed one of her earthy throaty laughs, and clapped Leo on the leg. 'He is, isn't he? I'm wondering about letting him go.' She snapped her hand up to her mouth and gasped. 'Sorry. Shouldn't have said that.' *Share a confidence or ask for help with a problem to build rapport.* Patrice sat back in her seat and sipped her tea. Time to get down to business then. 'So you're the one who's going to tell my life story?'

'That's the idea.'

'And how do you do this?'

'Well, it's partly up to you. Normally I'd do interviews over a couple of weeks, and then go away and write a draft, and then come back for follow-up interviews to fill in any gaps.'

He continued straight away. 'Of course you have final approval on the manuscript.'

Patrice scolded herself. The doubt must have shown on her face. That wouldn't do; she was used to being more careful than that. But he thought it was concern about the content not the timescale. That was manageable. 'Very well then. Where shall we start?'

'Well, erm . . . the beginning.'

Patrice forced herself not to bristle. It looked like she was going to be taking charge of this as well. 'The beginning of what? My birth? My first experience with the spirit world?'

'Yes. That. Tell me about your first psychic experience.'

He didn't actually draw air quotes around the word psychic but Patrice could hear them sitting there in his tone of voice. 'You're a sceptic?'

'I wouldn't say . . . '

She held up a hand to wave away his discomfort. This was familiar ground. 'Scepticism is fine.' She took a sip from her tea — milky with two sugars. 'Scepticism is sensible. There are a lot of charlatans. If something looks too good to be true, any sane person would be sceptical.'

She watched Leo jot down response on his pad. 'Okay then. Let's start with your first psychic experience.'

A rather obvious place to start, Patrice thought, but at least they were getting going. She allowed her gaze to wander slightly to the side of Leo's head, and let the tiniest of sighs escape her lips. This was a story well-crafted by telling and retelling, her own little quirks and foibles layered over the bones that Georgios had come up with nearly fifty years before. 'It was all through my grandmother. My mother's mother. She was the only person I knew in my family who had the gift. My mother had no abilities.' She shifted her gaze to meet Leo's. 'That's not unusual. You hear of these things skipping generations and suchlike. Anyway my grandmother was married to my grandfather for many years, but he died before I was born. The war. I never met him, but one day I was at my grandmother's house and I saw, quite clearly, just as I see you now, a man standing in her hallway.'

'Were you scared?'

Patrice shook her head, picturing the scene she was conjuring as she spoke. 'Why would I be? He wasn't brandishing an axe or anything. And it was a different time. Neighbours often popped by, delivery boys from the grocer. My grandmother had a man who came and worked in the garden. I assumed he was someone like that. Anyway he didn't say anything to me, nor I to him, and I went through to the back room to ask my grandmother who the man was.' Patrice glanced away into the middle distance. 'I'll never forget her reaction. She was doing her knitting and the whole thing, needles, yarn and

22

everything just dropped out of her hands. She jumped to her feet and rushed into the hallway, and she started shouting at the man. I followed right behind. I must only have been about four or five.'

Patrice watched her interviewer closely. She'd read an article by Michael Parkinson once, where he'd said he could always spot the moment where a celebrity really engaged with an interview question — the change in their expression, the shift of their body, the rise in their tone — there was always something. Leo leaned forward. 'Go on.'

A smile broke across Patrice's face. 'I remember him staring at me and then staring at her and muttering that he didn't know I could see him. He'd never really left her, you see. They were very lucky. They found the right person, but then when he died he couldn't move on, so he stayed hanging about the house. Getting under her feet, my grandmother used to say.'

Leo checked the light on his recorder and nodded. 'Did you tell anyone else? Your parents — what did they make of your gift?'

Patrice closed the smile down. She never really talked about her parents in interviews. That was going to be difficult in an autobiography. She stuck to the script. Brief, but not evasive. 'My parents never really understood my gift. I mean, I can see it from my mother's point of view. She'd had my grandmother talking about spirits that my mother couldn't see for years. The last thing she must have wanted was her own daughter going the same way.' She leaned back in her seat and folded her hands on her lap. *Closed body language to close down a conversation.*

'I'd really like to hear more about your parents.'

Oh. 'Well, there's really not much to tell.'

'Anything at all?' His fingers tapped against his pad, and for a second his leg twitched before he stamped his heel down on to the floor. He was anxious about something.

'Why so interested in my parents? There's really not much to tell.'

'Well, for the book.'

The book? Of course for the book.

'Anything you can think of might be useful. The more detail I've got the better.'

'I don't know. My father was a pharmacist. My mother was a housewife. They were very normal sorts of people.'

Leo didn't respond for a second. 'I'm sorry, Miss Leigh. Er . . . you look tired.'

'I'm fine.' Was she?

'Well, I didn't really expect to make a proper start today to be honest. Maybe we should arrange to meet up regularly for the next couple of weeks and take it from there.'

Patrice nodded without making eye contact. 'Barney manages my diary. He'll be . . . ' She flicked her eyes around the room. 'He'll be somewhere.'

Leo showed himself out, and Patrice sat back in her chair. She could go and lie on the bed. She could let herself drift away, but she wouldn't. Not yet. She had a show to prepare for, people coming expecting her to raise the dead, and she always gave the people what they wanted. It was what she did. It was who she was.

4

Louise was standing outside the supermarket. It was the big supermarket, which meant that she had to walk into town and then get a bus to come here, but it was better than going into Sukjinder's on the estate. People knew her there and they asked questions and offered sympathy. Here she was anonymous. Here she could stop in the middle of the frozen pizza aisle and think about the way that Kyle would painstakingly pick the peppers off his pepperoni feast but complain when she bought any other kind. When she stopped and stared at the frozen pizzas in Sukjinder's, someone would come and see if she was okay. She preferred to be places where no one cared.

She stopped next to the nappies and looked into her basket. She had bananas and oranges. She preferred the tiny satsumas to the big oranges but she always bought the big ones. Apart from that she hadn't managed to pick up anything else. She forced herself to retrace her steps. Bread, milk, teabags, sugar. She couldn't think what else she might need.

'Miss Swift!'

The voice forced Louise to raise her eyes from the floor. It was Katy. Katy had been Kyle's girlfriend. She lived up this end of town. Of course she did. Her parents had one of those big houses at the posh end of the new estate. Louise knew she was supposed to think of Katy as a nice girl. She remembered hearing the approval in her own mother's voice the first time she'd met her grandson's new friend. Kyle had done well for himself. He was dating up. That was the implication, but somehow Louise had never seen it. She remembered girls like Katy from her own school days. Pretty, popular, clever enough to get to where they needed to be on their own efforts, but lazy enough to prefer to drift from Daddy's little girl to some popular boy's sweetheart to some rich man's little wife. Louise supposed she was being unfair.

She nodded at the girl. 'Katy.'

Neither of them spoke for a second. Louise stared into Katy's face. The younger woman swallowed. 'I wrote you a letter.'

Louise frowned. She didn't remember a letter, but lately she didn't always open the post.

'I didn't send it. I wasn't sure if I should.'

'What did it say?' Louise wasn't sure if she cared. It just seemed like the thing to ask.

'Just about Kyle. Some stories and stuff from school that you might not have known.'

Louise's stomach clenched. More information about her son. Stories she'd not heard before. That would almost be like having a few new moments with him. 'I'd like to see it,' she blurted.

Katy nodded. 'Okay.'

'And how are you?' It was a horrible question, one Louise had no idea how to answer herself, but Katy was a kid. She was probably onto her fourth boyfriend since the funeral by now.

Katy shook her head. 'I dunno. Mum sent me for milk to get me out of the house.'

Louise barely heard. 'And how's college?'

The younger woman shook her head again. 'I dropped out. What's the point?'

The mother in Louise pushed to the fore. 'You should get an education. It's for your future.'

The girl shrugged. 'What future?'

Louise didn't have an answer for that. She started to walk away.

'Wait.'

She stopped.

'I wanted to say something else.'

'What?'

'I wanted to say sorry.' Katy was staring at the ground. 'For the night it happened. Sorry I couldn't do anything.'

'The police said you weren't there.'

'But it was my fault. I made him walk me to the taxi. If I'd let him go straight home, or if I'd been less mardy and we'd gone to a club or something . . . then . . . '

Louise didn't need to hear the end of the sentence. It was a game you could play a thousand ways. If she'd given him a stricter curfew he'd have been home with her rather than where he was that night. If she hadn't given him a curfew at all then he'd still have been in a bar and not outside the bus station at that precise time on that precise day. If she'd let him go to boxing back when all his mates had had that phase of being into it, then maybe he'd have been able to defend himself. If she'd stopped letting him hang around with that bloody

Brandon the first time he'd got them dragged into a fight when Kyle was six. If, if, if. She shrugged at Katy.

'Can you forgive me?'

Louise nodded. Why not? Forgiveness didn't change anything anyway.

She finished her shopping and got on the bus. There was a discarded newspaper on the seat. Louise thought about folding it carefully and taking it home with her to fill some more time, but she needed a distraction right now. Her head was full of Katy. Seeing the girl had pulled Louise back to that night. It had been such a normal Friday evening. Louise had worked the lunchtime shift at the chip shop, so she'd been at home. She'd done a frozen pizza for Kyle before he went out, but nothing for herself. Then later she'd watched *Coronation Street* and had a poached egg. Then, later still, just as she'd been thinking about going to bed, the intercom had buzzed. She didn't usually like to let people in late at night. Normally it was someone wanting to visit one of the other flats and pressing all the buzzers until somebody let them in, but she'd thought it might be Kyle saying he'd lost his key so she'd answered. It was the police. None of what they'd said had seemed possible. A fight. A knife. Not Kyle's knife, they'd said. Kyle'd been trying to break it up, they'd thought. Might have been a racial thing, they'd muttered. Or had they? Maybe that had been later. That night Louise had frozen. The words had come into her head but they'd made no sense. Kyle had gone out with his mates and his girlfriend. He couldn't be dead. His dirty plate was in the sink. There were episodes of his programmes unwatched on the Sky+. His basketball top was still hanging over the radiator waiting for him to need it the next day. There were too many signs of his absolute, glorious, mundane aliveness for Kyle not to be about to walk back through the door.

Louise opened the paper. She would think of something else. Or at least, she would paint a layer of other thoughts over the top of the immediacy of Kyle. She flicked through the pages until she came to a review of the medium show at the theatre. Patrice Leigh. Louise paused. The name rang a bell. She was the woman who used to turn up on one of those morning talk shows. Not *Jeremy Kyle*; one of the ones that was on before he appeared. One of the ones with a woman presenting who did an understanding voice and had big sympathetic eyes. The review was glowing. Patrice Leigh, the reviewer opined, was not just another two-bit fake. Time and time again she'd demonstrated her abilities so even the most dedicated sceptic would be won over. Patrice Leigh was the real deal. Patrice Leigh, the paper said, really could talk to the dead.

5

Leo leaned on the bar in the hotel lobby and scrolled through the email from Patrice's manager. The show that Leo had observed was the first night in a two-month residency. It was unheard of, apparently, for a medium to be so well thought of as to sell out such a long run of shows in one location, but Patrice was something special. The residency also presented the perfect opportunity for Patrice to get her life story down on paper, or rather, for Leo to get Patrice's life story down on paper, as Patrice wouldn't be travelling so would be available to meet regularly in the daytimes, when she wasn't giving private readings to individual clients, of course.

It also meant that Leo had no excuse not to go home. He'd justified staying overnight after the show because he was unsure what time he would finish, but actually his own home was only an hour or so from Patrice's hotel. There was no reason at all that he shouldn't drive over to meet with her and be home in time to have lunch with his wife. Leo tried to feel happy at the prospect.

He stuffed his phone back in his pocket, and pulled his pad and digital recorder from his bag. He ran through the questions he'd scrawled on the pad and checked the battery on the recorder. This was work. He was good to go.

Upstairs, the suite was just as he remembered it, but for a vast flower arrangement taking up the whole of the small side table. Patrice waved a hand at the floral overkill. 'From a grateful client,' she murmured.

Leo peered, as surreptitiously as he was able, for a card or note with the bouquet, but found none. He took his seat at one end of the coffee table, accepted the offer of tea, which Barney was dispensed to fetch, switched on his recorder and swallowed. 'Shall we make a start?'

Patrice arranged herself on the settee and nodded. 'Where were we up to?'

'Well, you'd told me about your first psychic experience. I was wondering if we could focus on your earthly relationships.'

Whether Patrice liked or disliked this idea was impossible to say. She gave a small nod; the expression on her face didn't shift.

'So, to help me get an overview, maybe you could tell me about the most important relationships in your life?'

'The characters one ought to include, you mean?'

Leo nodded. That certainly ought to be what he was thinking about. He shouldn't be yelling inside about one particular set of relationships. Maybe one man in particular. Maybe one love, or simply one fling. Maybe a child. Leo fought to stop his thoughts making the transition to his voice. 'Exactly. It's useful for me to get an idea of the big picture of your life.'

Patrice closed her eyes for a second. 'Well, my grandmother, of course. That's where everything started for me. My parents, although they didn't really understand. Apart from that I supposed I'd say Georgios.'

32

Leo flicked back a few pages in his notebook. 'That's Georgios Stefanini?'

Patrice nodded. 'Without him I would still be a northern girl, probably married to a perfectly nice man, with children, grandchildren even. I wouldn't have had a career. That wasn't something that was expected of me.'

Leo had found pictures of Georgios Stefanini in newspaper archives. He was a big man, dark-haired and olive-skinned, decades older than Patrice though, and apart from a few snide comments on internet forums, nothing had implied anything other than a professional partnership. He pushed his own black hair back. 'How did you meet?'

There was a second of hesitation before Patrice formed an answer. 'I worked for him. Just a summer job in the café at one of his arcades. He was quite the local entrepreneur. He owned arcades, a restaurant, a couple of clubs, I think, as well.'

Leo smiled. 'So how did you get from the café to filling theatres?'

No hesitation this time. Immaculate Patrice took over. 'His wife had passed over. It was her that came to me actually. I remember her quite clearly, standing in the middle of the café and telling me to go and talk to him. 'Tell Georgios that Thea knows he's not eating properly.' That's what she said to me. Of course, I ignored her. Even hearing her calling him Georgios felt disrespectful. He was always Mr Stefanini to the staff. Always. But she wouldn't go away. Eventually I crept up to his office and told his secretary I needed to see him.'

'What did you say to him?'

'Exactly what she'd told me to. I thought he'd be shocked, or upset or angry, but he roared with laughter. Apparently it had been a joke between them when she was sick, when they knew she was soon to pass over. She'd said she would find a way to nag him from beyond the grave.'

Leo paused. He wanted to change the subject. If Georgios was Patrice's Brian Epstein, who was her Yoko Ono? 'You never married, yourself?'

'No.'

'And no children?'

'No.'

Had there been a hint of a pause before she answered? Leo suspected he'd end up playing this section of the recording again and again, listening for the slightest hesitation. He also knew, if he was honest, that it wasn't there. They talked some more about Georgios Stefanini and Patrice's early days as a medium in spiritualist churches and meetings in the north of England, before Leo made his excuses for the day.

★   ★   ★

Patrice was left alone in her suite, wondering why she was doing this. The man asked so many questions, and the answers were becoming more and more confused in her mind. Had she told him that she worked for Georgios? She thought she had. She'd told him the story about his wife bringing them together from beyond the grave. Was that what she normally said? For a moment,

34

she wasn't sure. Hadn't Thea only died a few months before her husband? Patrice sat on the edge of the bed and pulled off her court shoes before lying down on top of the duvet. She could remember the story of how she'd met Georgios very well, and then in another part of her brain she remembered the actualities. Stories and truths were different things. They had to be kept separate, each in their own little drawer, neatly labelled and permanently tucked away. Somewhere inside Patrice's mind, she feared, the walls that held the different realms apart were getting thin. She rested her head on the pillow and closed her eyes.

6

1967

Pat sat on the hard plastic chair and wondered why Mr Stefanini wanted to talk to her. He had never spoken to her before, although she'd seen him walking past the self-service café, where she cleared tables in the summer holidays and on weekends. He was usually swinging his shiny black briefcase by his side; shiny black briefcase, shiny black hair, shiny black leather shoes. Shiny blackness was her overwhelming impression of Mr Stefanini, but, as he walked across the café and squeezed himself into the tiny moulded chair opposite her, she was also struck by his size. He was fat and tall, but, rather than looking oversized, he managed to make everything around him seem too small. In her own imagination, Pat was shrinking, until she was sure that he would be able to pick her up between forefinger and thumb and pop her neatly into his top pocket.

'So, Pat, I'm told you're doing a wonderful job in our little cafeteria?'

Pat nodded. She cleared tables and sometimes did the till, if Barb was on her break. She wasn't really sure how wonderful it was possible to be within those constraints, but agreement seemed to be what Mr Stefanini was looking for, so she provided it.

'I was thinking, it might be time for you to develop your career further.'

Pat didn't respond. This time it didn't feel like any response was needed.

'Have you heard about Gypsy Nadia?'

Barb had told her, with great excitement, that Nadia had run off with Keith, who did the dodgems on the seafront, and taken most of the weekend's takings with her. Pat didn't think Mr Stefanini would approve of gossip, so she shook her head.

'Unfortunately, she is no longer with us, so I need a new fortune teller. Barbara says you're good with customers, and you're a plain little thing. That's what I need. Folks don't trust pretty.'

Pat wasn't offended by this comment. Even at sixteen years old, she knew it to be true.

'I'm not psychic though.'

Mr Stefanini laughed.

'I'm not even a gypsy. I live on Northcliffe.'

'You can live on Mars so long as you fit in the frock.' Mr Stefanini laughed some more. 'No one's bloody psychic, love. If they're married, you tell them you see children. If they're single, you tell them you see love. And if they're married with kids, you tell them you see riches and independence. Work out what they haven't got and tell them they'll get it. Can you do that?'

Pat nodded.

'Good. You'll need a name. Pat's a bit plain.'

'My proper name's Patience.'

'That might do to get you going. You'll start after school on Monday.'

7

The theatre was busy. *Sold out*, the sign said. The ticket Louise clutched in her hand was a cancellation that she'd queued for when the box office opened. She stood in the corner of the foyer and tried to press herself against the wall. There were too many people here. She scanned the crowd in front of her. There was a mix of ages, but not so many men as women, she didn't think. She recognised a woman queueing outside the ladies, and turned her head away. The woman was Yvonne or Yvette or something. She'd been at the bereavement group they ran at the community hall. Louise had only been once. Her mum had suggested it and come along with her. She didn't see how knowing that other people were sad too was supposed to help her. Louise had hated it. That kept happening. Her mum kept coming up with ideas to make Louise feel better and Louise kept hating them. She should have phoned her mum before she came here; maybe today she was sounding more hopeful. Her mum might have been happy about that.

'Are you here for anyone in particular?' The man that went with the voice was in his forties, pale-skinned and insubstantial-looking. Louise shook her head and looked away until he moved on.

The bell rang, followed by a voice instructing

them to take their seats in the auditorium as the show was about to start. Louise hung back for a minute before she followed the throng into the theatre, so that she found her place just a few seconds before the lights went down. Less chance of anyone else trying to talk to her that way, she thought.

The show was almost too much to bear. People were reunited all around her with long-dead grandparents and parents. Louise had to force herself not to scream out loud. Everyone had a dead grandma. Grandmas were supposed to die before you. That was right. What she'd been through wasn't right. These people didn't deserve their murmurs of comfort from the other side. Louise did. Louise needed it. She needed to touch Kyle's face. She needed to see him roll his eyes at her overprotectiveness, like he had done that night when she'd yelled at him to take a coat with him when he went out. A woman along the row from Louise was told that her uncle was at peace. An uncle. Louise had two uncles — her mother's older brothers. One had died when she was seventeen. The other lived in Alicante, and sent a postcard once a year. An uncle wasn't the same as a son.

Every time the spotlight focused back on the woman on the stage the knot in Louise's belly tightened again. Maybe this time. Maybe Kyle would manage to push his way to the front of the queue. Maybe the next message would be for her. But it never was.

When the lights went up at the end of the show, Louise stayed in her seat. She was still waiting for Kyle to come through. Eventually she realised that the place was almost deserted, with the last few stragglers making their way towards the exit. There was one man left in his seat, right at the end of the back row, next to the aisle, immediately in front of the main doors. He had short black hair, and his head was bent forward over a notebook, revealing a thinning spot on the top of his head. He wore leather jacket over a linen shirt. He looked up as Louise passed him. 'Did you hear from anyone tonight?'

Louise couldn't answer. She shook her head mutely and walked straight by. She couldn't give up. Seeing Katy had put the idea in her head, and now it wouldn't leave. She could have more of Kyle. There were things about him she hadn't experienced yet. He didn't have to be so utterly and finally gone. All Louise needed was the right way of getting contact with her boy.

She walked out into the evening. It was warmer than she expected. She'd somehow lost track of the seasons. The middle of summer versus the depths of winter — it made little difference inside the flat. She walked to the rear of the theatre. There was a back entrance, half concealed down an alley away from the street. This was where Patrice Leigh would come out, wasn't it? If Louise could talk to her, one-to-one, that would be the best thing. Then Patrice would be able to talk to Kyle and everything would be better.

She waited, leaning against the wall. There was a pub across the road. Louise remembered going in there before she had Kyle. It'd been a place with a reputation for not bothering too much about how old you were in those days. They'd serve anybody who could reach the bar. That had been the joke. She'd met Wesley in there. He'd worked behind the bar. Before that he'd had a job at some old codgers' pub on the other side of town, but someone had had their hand in the till, and they didn't like to single Wesley out but they still thought he'd done it, so he'd been moved to another bar in the chain. He probably had done it and all.

Louise's mum hadn't been keen on Wesley, and when he'd done his bunk, she'd been almost jubilant. 'I told you his kind couldn't be relied on,' she'd said. Wesley's unreliability wasn't anything to do with his kind, Louise knew; that was all Wesley.

A taxi pulled up in front of Louise, and a moment later the door down the alley swung open. Patrice Leigh, accompanied by a pale, forgettable man in a suit, swept down the alley towards the taxi.

'Miss Leigh!'

The pale-faced man put his body between Louise and Patrice. 'Miss Leigh is on her way home.'

Louise spluttered her words. 'I just wanted to — '

'Miss Leigh is very tired. She does not have time for — '

'Don't be so officious, Barney.' Patrice Leigh stepped out from behind her minder and smiled at Louise. There was warmth in the smile and understanding. Louise felt the tension in her

41

neck ease fractionally. 'Were you at the show, pet?'

Louise nodded.

'And your loved one didn't come through?'

Louise nodded again. 'My son, Kyle — '

Patrice held up a hand. 'You don't need to tell me. I can sense your sadness.'

'Is Kyle here?'

Patrice took a step forward and took Louise's hand in her own. 'I'm sorry, pet. Like Barney said, I'm very tired at the moment. But look,' she glanced sideways at the pale-faced man, 'Barney will take your details and we can arrange a private reading, when I'm rested and more able to sense the presence of those who've passed over.'

She dropped Louise's hand and strode to the waiting taxi. Louise blurted out her telephone number and email address, and let Barney's words wash over her as he promised to be in touch. 'Of course you could come to the show again. There's a few single tickets for some of the weekdays. Different spirits come through each night.'

Louise let them go. It wasn't what she wanted but it was a step closer. Soon she'd be able to talk to Kyle again. Soon.

8

Leo sipped his coffee at the island unit in the centre of the kitchen, staring at the laptop screen in front of him. 'I hope that's decaf.' His wife was leaning on the doorframe. She was in her pyjamas. Leo tried to remember when Marnie stopped going to bed naked. He wasn't sure. Was it before, or after?

He shrugged. 'It's only one cup.'

'It's late. You won't sleep.'

Leo pointed at the computer. 'Not trying to sleep. Trying to work.'

Marnie pursed her lips.

'What?'

'Nothing.'

Leo wondered if Marnie felt as trapped in the conversation as he did. Both of them being polite, both tip-toeing around one another, neither one saying anything that might offend.

She walked past him to the fridge and got a glass of water from the filter jug in the back of the door. 'Are you out again tomorrow?'

Leo nodded. He was seeing Patrice in the afternoon. 'Not until after our appointment.'

'Good. I'm going to go up then.' She bent and kissed his cheek too quickly for him to respond before she scurried away. She paused in the doorway. 'I thought I might air out Olly's room tomorrow.'

'Marnie.'

43

'What?'

'Nothing.'

She stood for a second. 'If you want to say something . . . '

Leo shook his head.

★   ★   ★

The counsellor's office was uninspiring. Leo wondered if that was a choice on the part of the organisation. Did they decide not to make the surroundings too palatial so as not to reaffirm any suspicions the clients might be harbouring of a better, more exciting life beyond the confines of a failing marriage?

Ruth, their counsellor, got things started. 'I thought we might try something different today.'

'Different how?' Marnie answered quickly, as she always did in these meetings, trying, it seemed to Leo, to get Ruth on her side by playing the more engaged party.

'Well, I feel that we've talked a lot about the symptoms of the issues here. Your communication. Your sexual relationship. But I'm still wondering about the underlying causes.'

Marnie jumped in. 'Well, we said, since Grace went to university . . . '

Ruth nodded. 'And that might be all there is. I'm wondering if it would be helpful to delve a little more deeply.'

Leo felt his wife tense beside him. Something they still had in common then — a reluctance to delve too deeply into what was going on here.

'I thought,' Ruth continued, 'that I'd start by

asking you about . . . ' She flicked back in her notes. 'About Oliver.'

'Olly.' Leo heard himself make the correction before his brain knew what was happening. 'Nobody called him Oliver. Olly. Always Olly.'

'Okay. Olly. Do you want to tell me about Olly?'

Marnie jumped straight in. 'Well, he's twenty-four now.' She shot a glance at Leo, who said nothing. 'Just twenty-four. He was a summer baby.'

The counsellor nodded, barely looking up from the triangle shape she was doodling idly on her pad. 'Okay. What about more recently?'

Leo didn't look at his wife. 'You mean his d — '

'His disappearance?' Marnie jumped in again. 'It was four years ago. He was in New Zealand on a . . . ' Her voice cracked. 'He was . . . they were.' She paused, pulling her sleeve down over her thumb and dabbing her eye. Brisk, capable Marnie reappeared. 'They were camping. Three of them. There was a landslide. Freak accident type thing. One of his friends got out. The other, well, they found his body.'

Ruth tilted her head to one side. 'And Olly?'

'Olly disappeared.'

There was a moment of quiet. Leo frowned. Surely Ruth knew the story already? A quick web search would have shown her the news stories about Marnie and Leo's never ending search for their son. Or maybe not. He was thinking like a journalist, not a counsellor. He was thinking like a man who preferred to watch and wait and plan, rather than lay himself open to shock. He remembered the last time he'd been for counselling. They certainly hadn't been bothered about preparation then. Thirty-five minutes in the corner of an office overstuffed with files, a leaflet to read, and a general suggestion that sometimes things were complicated and he was kicked back out onto the street to do whatever he would.

In this office, the counsellor crossed her hands on her lap. The silence continued. Leo swallowed. What was supposed to happen now? Was one of them supposed to fill the extending silence with feelings and words? Leo couldn't. He had lots of words, but he didn't have the right ones. He didn't have the words that would bring Olly back. He knew exactly what he wanted to say and it was wrong. Completely, entirely wrong.

Ruth nodded towards Marnie. 'That must be difficult for you.'

'Not knowing where he is. Something must have happened, to stop him getting in touch, but I don't know what.'

'And you don't know if he's alive or — '

'He's alive.' Leo glanced down. Marnie's hands were open, resting on her lap. Her voice was calm. 'He's alive. He's out there. We just don't know where.'

The counsellor nodded. 'And Leo, how do you feel about this?'

He could feel his wife staring at him. He paused. 'Well, it's hard.'

'Not knowing?'

46

Leo nodded his assent. It wasn't true but he'd tried to have this talk with Marnie a hundred times before. The truth couldn't help him here.

The counsellor's pen retraced the triangle shape on her pad. 'Well, this is really interesting. I think we've uncovered some really useful emotions today.'

Useful emotions? Leo's face was set like stone, and his wife was staring into space. He didn't feel able to comfort or touch her. He wasn't even sure if he felt sympathy for her, or anger, and whatever he actually felt about Olly remained on hold. Parked somewhere in the back of his brain until such time as he might be allowed to bring his version of the truth into the light. Nothing about the way Leo was feeling felt useful.

'Let's talk about how you've been getting on with the exercises I gave you then.' Ruth nodded in Leo's direction, waiting for him to start. He didn't respond. 'If you remember, I asked you to write down the things that you found most attractive about the other.'

Leo closed his eyes. He hadn't done it. He'd meant to, really and truly, but he'd not quite got around to it. 'Sorry. I haven't had chance.'

'Okay. And what about you?'

Marnie pulled a crumpled sheet of paper from her bag. 'Do you want me to read them out?'

Ruth nodded.

Marnie sighed deeply. She unfolded the paper, and read it out in a flat monotone. 'Leo is intelligent. He knows about things like music and culture and politics. He's a good father to Grace.'

To Grace, Leo noted. Not to Olly.

'He's generous with money. Leo always buys the first round.' For a second there was the slightest hint of a laugh in her voice, and then it was gone. She folded the paper and stared straight ahead.

'Okay. Thank you Marnie.' Ruth turned her attention to Leo. 'Do you want to respond to what you've heard from Marnie?'

Leo wasn't sure what he was expected to say. He felt that a lot during these sessions. He shrugged. 'Thank you.' It wasn't much though, was it, to sum up twenty-five years together. He stood his round and read the Sunday papers.

'So next time, Leo, maybe you could prepare the same for Marnie?'

Leo nodded.

'And what about making time for each other? How's that going?'

He heard Marnie sigh.

'I've been away for work a bit recently.' Leo didn't meet the counsellor's eye. 'I'll do better this week.'

And that was the session. He followed his wife out to the street. 'Do you want a lift home?'

She shook her head. 'I need to go to Boots.'

They stood for a moment. Marnie stepped forward and put her hand against his arm. 'This is helping, isn't it?'

He knew how much she wanted that to be true. He wanted the same. 'I'm sure it is. These things take time.'

She nodded, kissed his cheek and walked away.

9

Louise hit refresh on her email, and then picked up her phone and switched the screen on and off again. She hadn't got in touch. The medium, Patrice, she hadn't got in touch. It wasn't good enough. Louise had waited quietly for something to happen since the night Kyle died. She kept herself to herself and she'd kept breathing. Now she had the chance to make a change. It was time to do something.

She switched off her laptop and pulled her coat around her shoulders. She would get the 11.40 into town and go to the theatre. Patrice Leigh might be there. She must do rehearsals or sound checks or something, mustn't she? And if not, she'd make them tell her where the medium was staying. That was a perfectly reasonable thing to ask. She'd met the woman already after all, and she'd promised to get in touch, so it wasn't stalking to go and try to find her.

The girl on the box office desk at the theatre didn't see it that way. She was not at liberty to give out Miss Leigh's personal details, apparently. She was prevented from so doing by data protection, she said. It was more than her job was worth, she said. Louise felt something rising in her chest, something different from the dull absence of feeling that had been her companion since it happened. This was something new: something hot and red and pulsing and

49

potentially useful. Louise saw her own hand clench into a fist, and then she watched the fist slam down on the desk in front of her. She heard her own voice rising, getting louder and shriller and more certain, explaining that she knew Miss Leigh, and was waiting for a call from her, but had simply misplaced her contact details. She heard herself say that, no, she did not want to leave a message; she simply wanted to know where Miss Leigh was staying. And then she watched as the girl smiled, more nervously now and with a hint less polish, and said she would get someone to come and talk to Louise.

The someone who came was big and podgy, and bulging out of his cheap shiny suit. His badge said that he was Elton and that Elton was the duty manager. Louise listened as the girl explained her situation. Elton shrugged. 'We can't give out contact details. Sorry.'

The lovely, powerful anger had ebbed away as fast as it had arrived. Louise nodded. She'd lost another tiny battle.

Elton moved around the desk and walked alongside Louise towards the door, never quite touching her but somehow managing to make it quite clear that she was being escorted off the premises. He wasn't unkind about it. 'To be honest I don't even know where she's staying.'

Louise didn't respond.

Elton held the heavy door open for her. 'Mostly they stay at the Grand though. It's the only half-decent place round here.'

'Is that where she is?'

Elton shrugged. 'Like I said, I dunno.'

Louise charged out of the theatre. She was being stupid. Of course Patrice Leigh would stay at the Grand. The Grand was a bit fancy. Louise had only been there twice in her life: once for the evening do when her mum's friend's daughter got married to the bloke that managed the Bradford and Bingley; and once for a recruitment day thing when the new shopping centre on the edge of town opened. She'd had to leave halfway through the morning because Kyle's nursery had phoned to say he'd been sick. She hadn't got the job.

Louise marched the long way through the town centre, down a side alley and along the road that ran parallel to the high street. She didn't go along the high street anymore, because that meant going past the turning for the bus station. Louise didn't go to the bus station anymore either. She got off one stop early, or walked that bit further to catch the bus at the next stop along. They'd cleaned up all round where it happened. Louise knew that. She knew the pools of crimson blood seeping across the pavement and staining everything in their path deep, unforgiving red were only in her imagination, but she saw them nonetheless.

The Grand was on the far side of town, just before the bridge across the valley to the posh houses on the other side. It looked down over gardens and then the sea. Louise walked up the steps and pushed through the revolving doors. The spin made her think of Kyle as a six-year-old going round and round and round in a revolving door for ages until she jumped in and picked him up and hauled him out. She couldn't even remember where that door was. She just remembered Kyle going around and around and around.

As soon as she was inside Louise regretted coming. The interior was a statement of respectability. There was piano music playing in the background, and the only other noise was a gentle hubbub of chit-chat. The reception desk was to one side of the entrance. On the other, there was a large lounge where hotel guests could sit and talk and have a snack or a drink. It wasn't busy but everybody who was there looked as though they belonged. Louise pictured herself from their point of view. Her leggings were too thin and had gone baggy at the knees. The coat she had pulled tight around herself was missing two buttons and was going thin on the hip where her handbag rubbed against it when she walked. Her hair needed washing, and pulling it back into a ponytail did nothing to disguise the fact. She wanted to run away, back to the flat where nobody would look at her. But she couldn't. She hadn't come here only for herself. She'd come here for Kyle. Wherever he was, he might be scared. He probably needed to talk to her as much as she needed to hear from him. He was only a baby in so many ways, a big lanky overgrown baby. He still needed his mum.

She approached the reception desk and tried her best to keep the fear out of her voice. 'I'm looking for Patrice Leigh.'

'And you are?'

'Louise Swift.'

The woman disappeared into a back room for a moment, before returning with a determined set to her face. 'I'm sorry Miss Swift. I'm not sure who you mean.'

'Patrice Leigh. She's staying here.' Wasn't she? The guy at the theatre had said. Or had he? He'd said he didn't know, but she must be here. She had to be here. It was the only place she could be.

'I'm afraid I can't confirm that.'

Louise waited for the anger to come back. She was growing fond of the anger. It made her feel powerful again, and she could watch angry Louise do her thing without having to get too involved herself. 'I know she's here. I need to see her.'

The woman shook her head. 'I'm afraid that's not possible.'

'But — '

'But nothing. Now if that's everything.'

The woman turned away from Louise and focused on the computer screen on the desk. She had been dismissed. She had lost. Again. Louise turned away from the desk and walked straight into the chest of the stranger standing behind her.

She stumbled backwards. 'Sorry.'

The man held up his hand in a gesture of mutual apology. He was tall, and maybe ten years older than Louise. He had black hair with flecks of grey, cropped short to disguise the hint of a bald patch. Leather jacket, jeans, t-shirt. He was frowning. 'Do I know you?'

Louise plunged her gaze back to the floor and

shook her head. 'No.'

'I do.' He stared at her. 'You were at the theatre last week. You were at Patrice Leigh's show.'

Louise looked at the man. 'You were too?'

He nodded.

Louise shouldn't want to talk to him. She didn't, generally, want to talk to people. She'd been to that one group counselling session after Kyle died. Therapy hadn't helped, but this wasn't therapy. She didn't think anyone here was going to talk to her about stages and processes like getting over her baby was just something on this week's list of To Dos. 'You lost someone?'

The man's expression changed. Confusion. Realisation. And then he nodded. 'My son.'

Louise felt the ground move, not in a swirly dramatic way. She felt it as definitely as she'd felt the leather of the stranger's jacket against her face when she'd walked into him; as definitely as she'd known Kyle would be home soon the night that he never came back. Something shifted underneath her. 'Me too.' She realised she was staring into the stranger's eyes and he was staring right back. 'Kyle. He was seventeen.'

The man didn't tilt his head in sympathy. He didn't say that that must have been awful. He didn't tell her that he understood. 'Olly. Nineteen.'

Two more years. Louise waited for the pang of jealousy. It didn't come. Two more years wasn't enough. Two more years was nothing. No amount of time would be enough. The only way it was right for a parent to be separated from their child, was when the parent died, elderly and confused and incontinent, at an age where the children, aging themselves, would shed a quiet tear and then reflect that in many ways it was a blessing. Nothing else was all right.

The man stepped back. 'Er, so . . . sorry. What are you doing here?'

Louise felt her shoulders tense. 'I was looking for Patrice Leigh.'

'What for?'

Louise was confused. 'To talk to Kyle. What else?'

The man nodded. 'Right. So you're getting a private reading?'

'I'm trying.'

'But you've not got an appointment or anything.'

Louise shook her head. 'It was silly.' She took a step away. 'I should probably go.'

'Wait.'

She stopped and let the man catch up with her.

'Would you like a cup of tea or something before you go?'

Louise looked behind him into the lounge. It wasn't her sort of place, but the plush upholstered chairs looked inviting and she found that she was tired. She nodded.

When it came, the tea was served in old fashioned pots, with a tea strainer and an extra pot of hot water, all in matching crockery. Louise let Leo pour the tea. He put the tea in first, holding the strainer against the spout of the pot. He caught her eye. 'I have no idea if I'm doing this right. I'm more a teabag-straight-into-the-mug person.'

Louise heard herself laugh. It was an unfamiliar sound, tinkly and grating. Another wave of exhaustion swept over her. She didn't want to talk. She didn't have the words. She leaned back in her seat. 'Tell me about Olly.'

The man lifted his cup halfway to his lips and the rested it down again. 'Well, Olly's dead.'

★ ★ ★

Across the table the woman frowned. 'Well, yeah, but — '

Leo shook his head. 'Sorry. You don't understand. My wife . . . ' What could he say? He could say that his wife clung to the hopeless, fairy-tale belief that somehow Olly was still out there. But that would leave him as the bad guy again. The guy who'd flown halfway around the world after the accident promising to find their son and bring him home. The guy who'd failed. It had been a stupid promise. He knew that. It had been a promise made in haste, and panic and love, but he was still the father who, according to Marnie, had abandoned their little boy out there somewhere alone and confused. He looked at the woman opposite. He didn't want to be that father. 'It's just that I don't really get to say out loud that he's gone. My wife . . . she doesn't really like to talk about it.'

The woman nodded. 'People don't. We don't have to.'

'I want to.'

56

'Okay. So what was he like then?'

Leo paused. It was four years since Olly died and during that four years Leo had become accustomed to thinking of his son as an event, an incident that coloured the lives of everything around it. Olly was his wife's mission to find her lost son on the other side of the world. Olly was the reason Grace had 'her troubles' as a teenager. Olly was the thing they skirted around with the therapist but never managed to discuss without ending up in a row that had nothing to do with who Olly actually was. Olly had ceased to be the boy that Leo knew well, or the young man who was emerging before his eyes. Leo swallowed a mouthful of too-hot tea, and stared at his shoes. 'Olly was funny.' It was true. He'd almost forgotten it, but right from his first steps and words, Olly had been a born comedian.

'And sporty. He played cricket. He talked about going professional.' The sportiness had been equally unexpected for both Leo and Marnie. They were both artsy, bookish sorts of people who had taken all their youthful exercise on dance floors and back seats of buses. Grace was the same, but Olly loved football, and cricket, and athletics. He joined every sports club that would have him at school. He'd run eight hundred metres for the county, and missed out on a national schools' team place for cricket by a hair's breadth. It had been a constant fascination to Leo — how someone who was genetically completely part of him and Marnie, could develop into their own unique, entirely different, person. It had made him wonder at Olly's glorious Ollyness, but also at what ingredients had come together to make Leo the man that he was.

'When he was little, he was scared of his dummy.'

Across the table the woman sipped her tea. 'Scared of it, how?'

Leo smiled at the memory. 'Well, we'd put his dummy in to get him to sleep and that was fine, but then if he woke up with it in, he'd spit it out like it was on fire and then kind of stare at it as if he was thinking, '*What's that? How did that get there?*' and then he'd scream until you took it away. Of course then he didn't have his dummy in, so he wouldn't go back to sleep.'

The woman shook her head. 'When Kyle was born, I read a thing that said dummies were really bad for them, so I decided I was never ever going to use one.'

'How long did that last?'

She stared into her tea. 'I did all right. The first month or so he slept so well. I remember thinking that the whole baby thing was a piece of cake, but then about six weeks he just stopped sleeping.'

'So the no-dummy thing lasted about six and a half weeks?'

She nodded. 'My mum bought them. I knew I should argue with her, but then the screaming stopped for more than thirty seconds and I just thought she was a miracle worker.'

'Did his dad help?' Leo heard himself ask the question. Why did he want to know? It was the sort of thing he remembered doing in his pulling days. You never asked outright if a woman had a boyfriend. That was too obvious. You asked casually what her boyfriend thought about x or y, and waited for the response.

The woman shook her head. 'His dad couldn't get shot of me quick enough when I found out I was pregnant.'

'I'm sorry.'

'Don't be. Just me and Kyle was fine.' She took another sip of tea, draining her cup. 'It was better than fine.'

Leo's cup was empty too. He held the pot out towards his companion. 'Another cup?'

She shook her head. 'I should get off.'

Leo didn't want her to go. He shouldn't need her to stay. He had Marnie to share memories with, and a counsellor who would probably rend her clothing if she thought it would get Leo talking honestly about anything, but he didn't talk to those people. He seemed to be able to talk to this one. 'Come on. Help me finish the pot.'

She shrugged. 'I guess. I don't really have anywhere else to be.'

Leo poured second cups for both of them. 'We haven't actually introduced ourselves.'

'Sorry. I'm Louise.'

'Leo.' He reached towards her and they shook hands. Her fingers were slim and bony against his palm, but her nails were long and smooth. They looked slightly at odds with her unloved clothes and tiny body. He realised he was staring. He dropped her hand. Then he remembered why she was here. 'You were looking for Patrice Leigh?'

Louise nodded.

'But you don't have an appointment?'

'No.'

Leo hesitated. 'I sort of know her.'

He watched Louise's face change. Suddenly she was alert, engaged with the here and now. 'You could introduce me?'

Leo paused. It wasn't very professional. He could hardly march into his meeting with Patrice, dragging Louise along behind him, and demand she contact the dead son of some woman he'd picked up in the foyer. And then there was everything else. To Patrice he was just a biographer. He had no grounds for demanding favours. He shrugged. 'I don't know her very well.'

'But you could ask her?'

'Okay.'

He handed over a pen and watched as Louise scribbled her contact details on the back page of his notebook.

'You promise you'll ask?'

Leo nodded. He glanced at the time on his phone. 'I ought to go. I have a meeting.'

Louise stood up. Leo moved forward to shake hands, or hug her, or kiss her cheek, but she stuffed her hands into the pockets of her oversized coat, closing herself off. Leo stepped back. 'I'll let you know then.'

She nodded and stomped her way out of the hotel. Leo waited a second before heading to the lift and pressing the button for Patrice's floor.

He'd got a basic picture of Patrice's early life now, but he still needed to fill in some more detail, specific incidents and anecdotes, anything at all that would tell him who she'd been.

10

Patrice lay on her bed and closed her eyes. She'd looked at the clock. It was after one. She knew she was dressed. She'd seen the tray on the table in her room that implied she'd eaten lunch. She must, she also supposed, have done a show last night, but she didn't remember it. She didn't remember the show. She didn't remember coming back to the hotel. She didn't remember getting up, or showering, or eating, and yet she appeared to have done all of those things. Her fingertips tingled slightly on her left hand. She pulled her arms across her body and rubbed her hands together. She didn't wonder what was happening to her. She knew. She'd seen it before.

She'd always thought dementia was something that came on gradually — a misplaced pair of spectacles one day, finding yourself in the shops with no recollection of what you'd come for the next, but with Georgios it hadn't been like that at all. They'd been on tour. Back then Georgios came to almost every show, even after he'd hired Barney as an assistant he'd never really trusted anyone else to get things just so. He'd been into everything, constantly looking at ticket sales, scheduling interviews, checking lighting and sound. Patrice had no doubt that theatre managers across the country hated his interference, but Georgios had insisted — things had to be right for his golden girl.

Until.

Until the night she'd knocked on his hotel room door because he was late coming to get her for a show, and found the great irrepressible hulk of a man, sitting on his bed staring at a smart patent shoe. He was stroking the laces with his fingers, unable to remember how to fasten them.

And that had been that. A few weeks later his adored wife, Thea, had died suddenly, and the Georgios Patrice had relied on had disappeared into the shell of his body. So Patrice knew what was happening. She knew what the gaps in her memory meant. She just needed to hold on for the shows and the book. That was the goal. That would be her legacy. That would mean that she'd taken this life he'd created for her and run with it as far as she could go. Patrice closed her eyes.

She knew, because she'd written it in her diary in insistent red letters, that that man Leo was coming this afternoon. And he would ask all his questions and she would fight with herself to remember the right answers. But Leo wasn't here yet. For a few blessed minutes she could let her mind go wherever it chose. She could choose not to fight this particular battle, and save her energy for the bigger war. He'd asked her a lot about her early psychic experiences. She'd told him the story that she always told. It was rehearsed and often repeated. Her brain didn't want to revisit that story. Her brain was going somewhere else.

11

'Is this where we come for the fortunes, love?'

'Of course it is. Just look at her.'

'I were only asking.'

'Well, there was no need. It's quite obvious.'

The discussion gave Pat a moment to take a look at her customers, her very first customers as Gypsy Patience. They were two women, both over fifty, both wearing rayon dresses, wool coats and hats for their day out at the seaside. Pat had a picture in her mind of them harrumphing happily along the prom, enjoying being scandalised by the mini-skirts around them.

'So you're Gypsy Nadia then?' One of the women tore herself away from the argument and stared at Patience. Pat gripped her hands together to hide the shaking and met her customer's eye.

'No. I'm Gypsy Patience. Nadia is my aunt.' She smiled, in what she hoped was a reassuring fashion. 'All the women in our family share the gift.'

Well, it was what Mr Stefanini had told her to say. He reckoned there were too many regulars for her to pretend to be Nadia, but he didn't fancy forking out for a new sign just yet either.

'That's often the way love.' Looking again, Pat began to see the differences between the woman.

One was taller, more elegant, the other shorter, fatter, less well spoken. Pat nodded and gestured for the women to sit. There was a script for the next bit and she'd learnt it by heart reciting it to herself last night in the bath, until the water turned milky and her mother banged on the door.

'Pray silence for a moment while I draw aside the veil and allow my gift to come forth.'

The women nodded appreciatively at the spiel. It was quite proper to have a bit of smoke and mirror with your fortune.

'Now, before I share my glimpses of the world beyond, the oracle demands its payment.' At this, Pat stretched out her hand towards the women and stared in what she intended to be an insistent, yet mystical, fashion. She felt daft, but Mr Stefanini had been clear. No cash; no messing about with the crystal ball.

The taller, slimmer woman pulled two coins from the recesses of her winter coat and handed them over. Pat whisked the cloth away from her hand-me-down crystal ball and peered.

'Gaze with me into the depths of time,' she intoned.

The women focused their attention on the ball and Pat risked another look at her customers. One with wedding ring. One without. Different builds but similar faces. Sisters maybe?

Pat swallowed, unsure how to start. *Just make sure you sound like you know what's what* — that was Mr Stefanini's last piece of advice, so she decided to jump straight in. She circled a hand over the ball and breathed in deeply.

'I see that family ties are important to you.'

'To which of us, dear?' the taller one interrupted.

'To both of you,' Pat improvised. 'I see a bond that has lasted from the cradle and will persist.' She caught a curt nod from the shorter women, and so continued. 'I see that bond getting tighter, even closer than before.'

'You see, Esme,' the shorter one butted in. 'That's me coming to the new flats just down from you and Harold. I told you.'

The taller one, Esme, didn't reply, but Pat glimpsed a fleeting purse of the lips. Maybe time to change track. She turned to face the shorter one, the one without the wedding ring. She seemed like an easier target.

'I see love on the horizon, not too far away, and getting closer every day.'

The woman reddened. 'Well, I don't know about that . . .'

'I see what I see,' replied Pat, trying to remember the phrase; it felt like it might be a useful one in this job. 'I don't control the visions, but love is what I see.'

The pink colour lingered on the unmarried one's cheeks. 'Well, I'll go to the foot of our stair. Love, ay?'

One happy customer. Pat turned her attention back to the married sister. The differences between the two stood out more and more. Just a little more make-up here, more carefully applied. Clothes just fractionally newer, not made to last from another year. So, already married, comfortably off, too old for children?

What then? The purse of the lips at the mention of her sister moving nearer sprang to mind. Pat gazed back into her ball.

'Oh! This is interesting! A vision for you, I think, but I'm not sure I understand.' She looked to Esme's face. 'I see a bird in a cage, but the door is being flung open and the bird is flying free.' Pat lowered her voice. 'It's quite beautiful.'

'Well, that don't make any sense.' The fatter, poorer sister shook her head. 'Esme don't keep birds, and why'd you want to let one fly away anyway?'

'Quiet, Nan.' Esme stood and leaned forward to squeeze Pat's hand. 'Thank you, my dear.'

The two women bustled out, Nan still muttering about birds and cages, unaware of her sister's small smile. Pat pulled the cloth over the crystal ball and leaned back in her seat. Her shaking hands had calmed. Her nerves had gone away. Telling fortunes, she realised, was easy.

At eight o'clock, Pat changed out of her gypsy fortuneteller garb and back into her school uniform. She walked out of the arcade and ran through the drizzle for the open-topped bus around the seafront. A group of older teenagers ran up behind her onto the same bus.

Pat took a seat on the lower deck and watched the group bowl up the stairs. Two minutes later, half of them came back down muttering about cold, and damp, and hair frizz.

'You're Pat.'

The woman leaning over the seat in front of her looked like a tall Lulu, all big eyes and bouffant strawberry blonde hair. Pat nodded.

'You work in Stefanini's café, upstairs in the arcade.'

Pat nodded again.

'You don't recognise me, do you?' Pat peered more closely at the creature in front of her. 'Come on. Two bacon baps, red sauce, one cup of tea and a big glass of water.' The woman parroted the order.

'Hester?' Hester worked in the cash office, and was a plain cardiganed eighteen-year-old. The woman in front of her looked five years older, and belonged in a magazine. 'You look so different.'

'Well, I'm hardly going to dress like that on an evening, am I?'

'No.' Actually, Pat had uniform for school, costume for work, and best clothes for Sunday. The idea of putting on a whole new character just for evening was new. It was interesting.

A hand ran across Pat's hair. 'You could do something amazing with this.' Hester crinkled her nose. 'I could do it for you, back comb it all up like Jackie Kennedy.'

Pat touched her hair, which was neatly pulled back into her schoolgirl ponytail. 'Maybe.'

'Oh, you've got to. You'd look amazing. Charlie!' Hester called across the bus. 'Wouldn't she look amazing?'

A man, a boy, a man turned his head towards them from across the aisle. His eyes skimmed across Pat's face without interest, but he rose and squeezed into the seat next to Hester.

'This is Charlie. Charlie's in a band.' Hester squealed this information.

Charlie shrugged. 'I'm a roadie.'

'And his band are here all summer. We're going to see them next week.' Another squeal. 'You should come.'

Pat opened her mouth to excuse herself — school, homework, work, her parents — so many reasons, she knew, she wouldn't be going to see Charlie's band.

'Charlie, tell her she should come.'

'Yeah, if she wants.' Another shrug, but this time his eyes locked, for a moment, with hers. Bright blue eyes, looking out at the world like a baby, when every glance is a universe of new discoveries. Pat swallowed and lowered her face.

'Say you'll come. I'll do your hair and I can lend you something to wear. You will come, won't you?'

Pat glanced back towards Charlie. His dark mop of hair was now flopping over his eyes, and he was looking away, apparently bored with the conversation.

'Promise me you'll come.'

Pat nodded.

12

Charlie. Somewhere at the back of everything there was always Charlie. Charlie and Patience and a whole other life.

A sharp rapping noise forced Patrice's eyes open. She stopped for a moment, taking in the room. The bed, where she was lying fully dressed on top of the duvet. Her clothes: her shapeless, draping old lady clothes. The numbness in her fingertips and aching in the heel of her hand. And then the rapping noise again.

The door. That man with all his questions. Patrice swung her legs off the bed and sat for a moment, smoothing down her hair with the palms of her hand. She shouldn't be annoyed with him coming. This whole thing had been her idea. She needed to tell her story before it ebbed away from her entirely. She crossed the room and opened the door.

Charlie.

She blinked her eyes closed and then open again. The black hair, the curve of the nose, but of course it wasn't Charlie. This was the man. The journalist, Leo. Patrice arranged her smile. 'I thought we might talk downstairs today.' The room was stifling her. It was suddenly full of ghosts.

She followed Leo to the lift. This was good. She was in her hotel. She was doing a residency at the local theatre. She was Patrice Leigh.

Everything was under control.

'So I think it would be good if you told me a bit more about your family life?'

That question again. She supposed he was looking for colour for the story. Some conflict with her God-fearing mother and father. That wasn't the story she was here to tell. 'What sort of things?'

Leo shrugged. 'I don't know. What sort of atmosphere was it growing up? What type of house did you live in? Were your parents strict? Did you go to church? Anything really.'

Her lips pursed at the word church. 'Chapel. We went to chapel.' She shook her head. 'It wasn't really a chapel. It was the big Methodist Central Hall in the middle of town, but my father always called it chapel, and he called the minister 'Parson'.'

Leo nodded. So that was more the sort of thing he was looking for. Well, she'd give him that, up to a point of course. 'Chapel every Sunday morning. Youth group every Sunday evening.' She shook her head. 'It was the 1960s. It might as well have been the forties though. I don't think the Swinging Sixties quite made it to North Yorkshire.' Of course that wasn't quite true, but there was a wall there in her mind. If she went too far, she'd be telling someone else's story. She smiled what she hoped was a broad, open, friendly smile. 'It was a very mundane childhood.'

13

1967

At home, Pat sat and chewed her steak and kidney. At either end of the table her father, Stanley, and mother, Lilian, chewed as well, each in their own individual silence. Only when plates were clean, Father mopping up his gravy with a thick rectangle of buttered bread, Mother tutting, did the conversation resume.

'Only one more week of school for Pat.' Lilian addressed her husband as if Pat wasn't in the room.

Father nodded, turning to his daughter. 'And will you keep working for Mr Stefanini over the summer?'

Pat nodded.

Her mother shook her head. 'I don't like to think of her in that place. All the gambling. I'm sure some of them are drinkers.'

A pause. 'She's only in the café.'

Pat didn't disagree. Her father continued, 'It'll teach her the value of money.'

'I suppose you're right.' The tone suggested that Lilian supposed nothing of the sort.

Pat stood up and started to gather the plates, before her mother shooed her away. 'I'll do that.'

Lilian left the room and Pat took her chance. Divide and conquer.

'I was wondering if I might go out in the

72

evening on Saturday.'

Her father peered. 'Where to?'

'It's a concert.' His brow furrowed. 'Like a recital. Hester who works in the cash office asked me to go. She was trying to be friendly.' Pat added this hoping to imply that refusing such a kindness might be impolite.

'In the cash office?' His eyes sharpened. 'And how old is this Hester?'

Pat twirled her dessert spoon in her fingers. 'Not sure. Eighteen, I think.' The tone was casual, off-hand almost.

Stanley shook his head. 'No, dear. I'm sorry. You know we prefer you to socialise with girls and boys your own age.'

'It's just girls.' And Charlie. Beautiful Charlie. 'And I'm nearly seventeen.' Her tone was sullen now, but she knew she'd lost.

'Not until October.'

'There's eighteen-year-olds at youth group.'

'That's not the same. Anyway, it's Chapel anniversary on Saturday. Your mother put your name down to help with the teas.'

Lilian returned, smiling brightly and clutching a tray laden with crumble and a jug of yellow custard. They ate, again in silence. As they finished the hot sweet crumble, Pat's father pushed his chair back from the table. 'Well, I just need to sort out a few things at work.'

He looked down as he spoke, looking neither at his wife nor daughter. Stanley was a pharmacist. He'd qualified back in the thirties, all ready to strike out into the world, start a career, start a family. Somehow that hadn't

73

happened until after the war was done. His work was important though, and often meant he had to go out in the evenings. People don't just get poorly in the daytime, he always said.

As Stanley shut the front door behind him, Lilian surveyed the dirty pots on the table. 'It won't hurt for these to wait a few minutes.'

She rose from the table, walked, carefully, to the kitchen and retrieved a half-empty sherry bottle from the shelf. She poured herself a neat little glass and smiled at Pat, who hovered in the doorway. 'Don't tell the parson!'

Pat chorused the familiar phrase with her mother, and watched her drain the glass. Lilian closed her eyes briefly, and when she opened them her gaze flicked from bottle to glass, glass to bottle, before moving back to her daughter. The bright happy voice returned, 'Do you have homework to get on with?'

Pat nodded. 'Revision.'

'Well, hop to it then.' Pat ran up the stairs, into her room and closed the door.

14

'Miss Leigh! Patrice! Are you all right?' He put his hand on her shoulder and shook gently.

'What are you doing?'

Leo stepped back. 'Are you all right? You seemed to sort of drift away.' She'd been right here, talking about her parents, and Leo had felt himself leaning towards her, drinking in the history behind the words. And then she'd gone. He'd had her and then she'd gone. He watched Patrice turn her head from side to side before focusing on him.

'I'm fine.' Her face softened into her normal serene expression. 'Interference from the other side.'

Leo sat down again. Somehow the idea of her being psychic had been pushed to the back of his mind. 'So you were having a psychic experience?'

'I prefer to talk about spirits rather than experiences, but yes. Somebody was trying to contact me in spirit.'

'Who?'

'A young man.'

'Is he still here?' Leo looked around.

'No. He's gone now. Sometimes the spirits feel the presence of someone with the gift and just push through. Unless I'm actually with the loved one they're trying to contact, they generally drift away again.'

'So he wasn't trying to contact me?' Leo's

voice was jovial, pointedly unconcerned.

'I don't think so.' Patrice's eyes narrowed a fraction. 'Were you hoping to hear from someone?'

Leo shook his head.

15

'I'm glad you popped round. It does you good to get out of the house.'

Louise didn't argue.

'I'll put the kettle on, shall I?'

Louise nodded. It would give her mum something to do. 'Can I use your computer for a minute?'

'If you like. What's wrong with yours?'

'Nothing.' That was true. There was nothing wrong with her computer, and if she balanced it on the kitchen windowsill she could just about connect it to the Wi-Fi from the flat diagonally opposite, but her own internet had stopped working, along with the phone and the Sky, weeks ago. Her mum's computer was an old-fashioned desktop thing on a specially purchased desk that now took up half the back bedroom. The bed was squashed awkwardly into one corner, just like it had been when Louise had last lived here and everything had been moved to make space for Kyle's cot. Louise switched the aging computer on and waited for it to crank and whirr into life. This was the sort of wait that used to annoy her. Now it was a welcome release — another tiny portion of time accounted for.

She could hear her mother clattering and moving around in the kitchen. Eventually the computer was ready to let her get online and she searched and clicked her way to Patrice Leigh's website. The prices for a private phone reading started at four hundred quid. The cost for a face-to-face reading was even more. Maybe she could sell her laptop, but it had cost her less than four hundred quid when it was new and that was a long time ago. Maybe she could sell something else. She couldn't. She didn't have anything. She already had a nice pile of red bills and letters telling her that her rent was about to go up because she was no longer entitled to Housing Benefit on a two-bed flat. She'd have to go on the rob to find four hundred pounds.

'What are you looking at, pet?'

Louise clicked the close button. 'Nothing.'

Her mum pursed her lips as she handed over a mug of tea, brewed builder-strong and laced with sugar. Louise had stopped taking sugar when she made tea at home years ago, but to her mum she was still the schoolgirl who liked everything sickly sweet. Would Louise have been like that with Kyle, she wondered.

'It didn't look like nothing.'

Louise didn't want to tell her mum about Patrice. She knew what she'd say. She'd say it was nonsense. Or she'd say that Louise needed to move on. But she wanted to tell someone. She wanted someone to agree that this was the only way. 'What do you think about psychics?'

Her mum sat on the end of the bed and sipped. 'Like mind readers and that?'

Louise shook her head. 'Like talking to . . . ' She waved her free hand. 'You know, to people who've died.'

'Like Kyle?'

She shrugged. 'Well, like anyone. What do you think about it?'

Her mum sighed. 'I think that if people who've passed away want us to know they're still with us, they'd find a way without some daft scouser having to ponce about on stage for it all to work.'

Louise didn't reply. Her mum was wrong though, because Kyle hadn't found a way, had he? And Louise was his mum. If he couldn't find a way, she had to help him, didn't she? Helping Kyle was what she did. She took another mouthful of her tea. The sweetness hit the back of her throat and she almost gagged. Almost. It was another feeling that was just out of reach somewhere beyond the cloud of grief she was wrapping tighter and tighter around herself.

Louise set her mug down on the computer table. 'I'd better go.'

Her mother protested, as she always did. Louise could stay for tea. There was a nice bit of pork in the freezer. Chops. Louise liked chops, didn't she?

Louise left the protests and the concern behind and set off slowly across the estate. Her mum had one of the big flats in the tower blocks. Louise's own was smaller and twenty minutes' walk away. It would have been five on the bus, but the walk filled more time and cost less money. It was a win-win.

She couldn't afford to see Patrice, but it was what she needed. It was what Kyle needed her to do.

Her phone trilled in her pocket. *Unknown*

number. She answered the call. Leo. Leo had called right when she was thinking that she needed another way to get to Patrice. It was a sign.

'Did you ask her about the reading?'

He paused. 'They're quite expensive.'

'I haven't got any money.'

'No. I wasn't actually phoning about that.' Another silence. Louise didn't fill it. 'I wondered if you wanted to come for a drink sometime.'

'Why?' It was the first question that came into her head. Why did he want to take her for a drink? He didn't have anything to tell her about Patrice.

He laughed. 'Because I don't really know anyone around here. Because you seemed nice. It's just a drink.'

'Okay.' They arranged to meet the next evening, at the pub opposite the theatre. Louise wanted to say no. She didn't go out and have drinks anymore, but Leo contacting her right when she was about to give up had to mean something. It had to mean that he was her way of getting to Patrice Leigh, and Patrice Leigh was her way of getting to Kyle. She could manage one drink, if it meant she would be closer to her beautiful boy.

16

Leo was in bed, eyes wide open and fixed on the ceiling above him. He didn't remember falling asleep or waking up, but supposed he must have done because the light drifting around the edges of the curtains told him it was morning. Marnie was on her side, back to Leo, knees curled up in front of her, like an animal rolled into a defensive ball against a predator.

Usually Leo would roll over, try to press his body against hers and wait for some response beyond the shrug she gave to shake herself free of him. Today he didn't bother. He stayed in his half of the bed, and left her to hers. Normally he'd get up soon after she'd shaken him away, go downstairs, make coffee and open his laptop in the kitchen to type up his notes and ideas from the previous day's interview, before driving to the coast again to meet Patrice. Then he'd drive home and they would spend the evening in silence. That was unfair. They weren't quite reduced to silence yet. They would spend the evening in politeness. Both of them were trying not to make anything worse. Both of them were civil. It was worse than silence.

He felt his wife's body shift at the other side of the bed. A glow of light told him that she'd switched her phone on. 'It's nearly eight.'

Leo nodded. 'I know.'

'Did you oversleep?'

'Not really.'

She rolled over to face him. 'Leo, I — '

They both spoke at once. 'Marnie.'

She swallowed. 'You go first.'

'I might have to stay in Blackpool tonight.'

'How come?'

'I thought I might go to her show again.' The lie came surprisingly easily. It was a good lie, he told himself. A white lie. There was nothing to lie about in him spending time with Louise. It wasn't anything seedy, or untoward. He wasn't having an affair. He was lying to save Marnie the worry that he might stray. That was all.

He felt her fingertips graze his forearm. 'Are you sure about this, Leo?'

He took a breath. She wasn't talking about Louise. She couldn't read his mind. 'About what?'

'You know what. You haven't told her who you are, have you?'

Leo didn't reply.

'It just seems a bit underhand.'

'I'm getting to know her.' He knew she didn't approve of his approach. She'd read the leaflet about mediators and letters more times that he had.

'Okay.' Marnie withdrew her hand.

'What were you going to say?'

She shook her head. 'Nothing.'

'What?'

'I was just going to say that we could do something tonight. Maybe go out somewhere, but it doesn't matter.'

'Another night though. Tomorrow.' Leo swung

his legs out of bed. Another night would be fine. Everything was under control. He knew what he was doing with Patrice. He knew what he was doing with Louise, and tomorrow he would take his wife out and everything would start to drift back towards a place where he might feel he belonged.

17

Patrice stared at the laptop screen in front of her. She really shouldn't be having to do this, not personally, not at this stage of her career, but she couldn't leave it to Barney. Had she used to do this herself? She couldn't imagine Georgios bent in front of a typewriter, churning out postal readings, but she didn't remember doing it herself. Georgios probably paid some girl. There was always some girl he had around, freshly scrubbed and ready to take a memo or fetch and carry.

Patrice skimmed through the text. *You can often come across as being in control of the situation, but inside you know that that's not always the case. You prefer not to share those anxieties beyond your very closest friends, and even there you sometimes wonder if those people really understand you.* Patrice blew the breath out between her teeth. It was odd how the utterly generic could be made specific just by telling somebody it was personal to them. The readings were fine. The email ones Barney would send out later, the postal ones would be printed and someone, probably Barney again, would add her signature to the bottom. Another slice of comfort and understanding offered out into an unsympathetic world. That was why she did this after all. Patrice Leigh, selflessly using her gift to help the lonely and the grief-stricken. That was the story. That was who she was.

Patrice was jolted back into the room by a knock at the door. She checked her watch. Was it time for Leo to come already? Maybe it was. Maybe Barney had told her. She slammed the laptop closed, and called out, 'Just a minute.'

She hurried into the bathroom and checked her appearance in the mirror, pausing for a second to pop her glasses on. She only really needed them for watching television, but she wore them all the time that she was performing. It was another thing Georgios had taught her — in this line of work it didn't do to be too glamourous. People were much more likely to trust someone down-to-earth. The glasses were part of being Patrice Leigh, and the interviews with Leo were part of that performance.

She swung the door open. 'Leo, come in. Shall I call for some tea or coffee?'

He accepted the offer of coffee, and started getting out his notepad and recorder while she rang room service.

'So what are we discussing today?'

Leo swallowed. 'Maybe a bit more about your early life?'

Patrice kept the displeasure off her face. There'd been an awful lot about her early life. That wasn't where she wanted to focus. That wasn't where she needed to be. She needed to be in Patrice's life, in the bits she knew, in the bits she could remember, in the bits where being Patrice was all there was. 'Again?'

He paused. 'Well, maybe a different track. Your teens maybe, rather than childhood.' He was staring down at his pad. 'Were there any particular important relationships in your teens?'

Patrice reinterpreted the question. 'Well, that is really when I started my full relationship with the spirit world.'

'Right. Of course. But in this world?'

The knock from room service gave Patrice a minute to think. Something wasn't right. He was too interested in some things and not interested enough in others. Or was he? Was this just how biographies worked? Finding the person behind the stories? Patrice understood people. That was her job. She didn't understand Leo.

She waited as the waiter set the tray down on the table and made his way out of the room, and then she pushed the strainer on the cafetiere down as slowly as she dared. There was probably no mystery to Leo. He was just doing his job; it was her own professional powers that were waning. She forced herself to think as she poured. There was so much she couldn't say. In past interviews, she'd got away with skimming over that period in broad pre-prepared brush-strokes, but this was different. This wasn't an odd paragraph; this was a whole book. She sat back in her seat and sipped her coffee. She could do this. She had the skills. She knew the story. She knew who she was. 'Well, I suppose Georgios was the most important new person that I met around that age.'

Leo nodded. 'How was he important?'

Patrice smiled. She fancied that her eyes might even have twinkled a little. 'Well, I'd been going to spiritualist services with my grandmother and started sharing, just from time to time, words from the spirits who made contact with me. You have to understand that this wasn't really a big thing. My grandmother was doing the same thing, and everyone else at the church was very open to the next plane. I didn't think . . . ' She paused, and shook her head modestly. 'I *don't* think I'm anything special, but Georgios thought differently.'

She took another drink. How did they meet? Had she told this story before? 'I'd never thought about using my gift professionally.'

'But you do now?'

Patrice nodded. 'Georgios realised that I could help more people this way.'

It was one way of putting it. Georgios had realised that she might have a marketable skill, and he'd also realised that she was in no position to turn down his proposal. No. That was unfair. He'd recognised that she wouldn't want to.

'And that's what you wanted?'

'Sorry?'

'To help more people?'

The trace of cynicism in Leo's voice wasn't lost on Patrice, but she chose to ignore it. 'Of course. It's what I live for.'

'So what's it like?'

'What?'

He opened his mouth and closed it again. 'Well, being able to talk to dead people, I guess.'

Patrice smiled again. This was safer territory. 'Well, I call it a gift, which I know sounds like a cliche, but it really is. It's an absolute privilege.'

'But what it's actually like?'

This was well-rehearsed ground for Patrice. Again it was all about sounding specific without ever actually being specific. 'Well, it varies. Sometimes it's as clear as talking to you now, but some spirits are confused. The next plane is different from ours. Time doesn't work in the same way, so people who died as old men can appear as strapping young lads. People get terribly frustrated when it sounds like I'm being vague, but they're sitting there asking someone living in eternal peace where they put the paperwork for their pension payout. Those just aren't things that occupy our friends on the spirit plane.'

Leo nodded. 'Sure.'

He flicked a page in his notebook. 'What about specific experiences? You must have had some difficult clients when you first started out?'

Patrice shook her head. 'Generally people are very grateful for the comfort I'm able to offer.'

'Everyone?'

Patrice sat back and listened to herself talk about grief and how it affected people in different ways. She heard herself say that she always treated mistrust and anger with understanding and recognised that some clients needed time to absorb what they'd been told. She sounded note perfect. She sounded like her old self, but she wasn't. There was something else going on behind the thin dividing walls inside her mind. She was relieved when Leo said he'd got enough for the day and she could finally take off her spectacles and close her eyes for a moment or two before she had to go out on stage and be Patrice all over again.

18

1967

Four more days of school came and went. Four more after-school shifts as Gypsy Patience. Four more family teatimes. Four more after-dinner sherries to keep hidden from the parson. Then Saturday. Her first full day as Gypsy Patience. Already, Pat was feeling like she had the easiest job in the world. She promised people love or independence or, occasionally, babies and everyone was happy. It surprised her that that was all her customers wanted. She would have thought they'd want money, but promising people wealth didn't quite seem to cut the mustard. They nodded, smiled, giggled even, but you didn't get the glow, the slight moistness in the eye.

It was twelve o'clock but the morning hadn't been busy. Grey skies and greyer seas had discouraged all but the most determined day tripper. A single male punter interrupted the boredom. Pat assessed him. Middle-aged, maybe forty or forty-five, well-dressed but dirty, stinking of alcohol in the middle of the day.

She smiled and ran through her spiel about drawing back the veil and needing to be paid. The man obliged with a crisp note peeled off a roll. Pat gaped at the amount. 'Keep the change, pet.'

The man slurred the words and winked at her as he said them.

Pat secreted the note inside her costume and started the main act. More and more, she found she was thinking of this whole thing as a performance, a theatrical pretence. She pulled the cloth away from the crystal ball and predicted a life overflowing with love and joy for her customer.

'And the rest, love?' The man grinned at her across the table.

Pat peered again into the ball, after a quick look at the clock purposefully placed behind the customers' chairs. 'The vision grows weak,' she intoned. 'I have seen all there is to see.'

'Not that. The rest. I want my extras.' The man stood and walked around the table, so his crotch was level with Pat's face. Then he started to undo his trousers.

Pat pushed her chair backwards. 'What are you doing?'

'Don't tease, pet. I know what I paid you for, fair and square. Was more than I used to give Nadia, on account of how you're not all wrinkled up like she was.'

The man pulled his half-hard penis out of his pants and rubbed his hand up the length. Pat's chair was pushed as far back as it would go, leaving her trapped between the wall and the approaching cock.

'Come on. Just a quick blowy. I'll come on your face if you prefer.' Everything about his tone was reasonable, as if he fully expected Pat to respond with a cheery 'All righty then!'

90

Closer up the cock repulsed her, purple and veined, dark wiry hairs curling around the base. And the stench of the man. Booze and piss filling Pat's nostrils. She tried to turn her head, thought of putting her hands out to push him away, but she was pinned by fear and disgust.

'What are you doing?' Hester's voice broke Pat's paralysis. She used her customer's moment of distraction to push past him and grab the crystal ball. She held it high on her shoulder like a shot put, unsure what to do next.

Hester took control. 'Get out! Get out you dirty pervert!'

The man fumbled with his trousers as Hester chased him, waddling, into the street. She yelled again at his back, 'Pervert! She's still at school, you know!'

'Finished yesterday,' Pat muttered.

'Oh my God! That was brilliant. We saw him off.' Hester strode back into the room.

Pat was still standing, crystal ball aloft, feet clamped to the spot. Hester's face softened. 'I think you can put that down now, pet.' She reached across and lifted the ball from Pat's hand. 'What were you going to do with it anyway? Whack him over the head?'

'Maybe. I don't know.'

'I wouldn't. You know Stefanini takes breakages out of your pay.'

Pat found herself giggling at the ridiculousness of the whole thing. As she laughed, her body started to relax and her muscles untensed.

'That's better.' Hester smiled. 'You going to be all right?'

'Yeah.' Pat sat down. 'He said Nadia used to . . . '

'You didn't know?'

Pat shook her head.

'Oh my God! I can't believe Stefanini didn't warn you.'

'He knew?'

'Of course.' Hester sat down across the table from Pat. 'I mean, he wasn't like her pimp or anything. I think he just turned a blind eye.'

'Well, I'm not going to . . . I don't have to . . . Do I?'

'Course you don't. You probably do need a plan for next time though.' Hester paused. 'Biting down on it usually puts them off.'

Pat paled.

'I'm joking! You should come up with something though. Anyroad, I came to see if you wanted to get lunch. We need to talk about your hair for tonight.'

Tonight. The concert. The chapel anniversary. The absolute refusal of permission to attend.

'You are still coming, aren't you?'

'I want to.' Pat was surprised how true that was. She did want to go. She wanted to dance. She wanted to be the sort of girl that knew people like Hester. She wanted the world to be big.

'Then what's the problem? Is it parents?'

Pat didn't reply.

'You can tell me. I saved you from the stinky willy man.' Pat smiled a little. 'And I'm great at getting round parent problems. Tell me. We'll make a plan together.'

19

Louise stared at her reflection in the mirrored door of the bathroom cabinet and then at the bag of make-up balanced on the cistern. She used to wear make-up all the time; not at the chip shop — it was too hot and too sweaty — but the rest of the time. Make-up had been her armour. She'd had her full face on for every single midwife or scan appointment when she was pregnant. It had been her insulation against the waiting rooms full of happy couples ten years older than her. It had been her way of showing the world that she was okay. She'd always put her face on to take Kyle to school or to go to the shops. Recently she'd stopped. You painted your face to show off to people looking at you. Louise couldn't bear the idea of anyone looking at her at all.

But tonight was different. Tonight she had a job to do. She had to impress Leo so that he'd like her and then he'd persuade Patrice to talk to Kyle for her. It was simple. She screwed the cap off her tube of foundation and scraped away a beige crust so she could squeeze a blob onto a sponge, which she rubbed across her forehead and down her cheek, before repeating the action on the other side. Then she took her eyeliner pencil and drew around her eyes, smooth, controlled black lines at first, and then big thick circles of blackness. Finally, lipstick. She picked out a deep purple colour that she remembered used to be the one she'd wear for girls' nights out with Suzi. She daubed it across her mouth, and considered her reflection. From the mirror a dead-eyed clown stared back at her. Louise heard herself laughing.

She dropped the lipstick onto the floor and walked the twelve paces to the door of Kyle's room. She didn't go in. Being in his room, wrapping herself in his clothes, touching his things — none of it was enough. If she couldn't hold herself together and do what she had to do to get the chance to talk to him again, she didn't deserve even that small comfort.

Louise went back to the bathroom, washed her face and started again. She rubbed foundation into her skin and watched the lines and freckles fade a little. She smoothed the cream over her lips until they all but disappeared, and then drew them back in with a dark cherry red. Last of all she dug a mascara tube out of the old pencil case that served as a make-up bag. It was dry and crusted up. Louise remembered seeing her mother drop her mascara into a pan of hot water for a minute to, in her words, 'Perk it up again.' It seemed worth a try. In the kitchen, she watched the water bubble and jump around the sleek black plastic tube. She was boiling her mascara so she could talk to her baby again.

* * *

An hour later, she arrived at the pub. She was late. She'd done her make-up once more and

94

then changed her clothes twice. It was the kind of thing she remembered doing as a teenager before a date with Wesley. Then, her indecision and anxiety to look just right had been part of her excitement and infatuation. Tonight it was her working out who she could allow herself to be.

Leo was already at the bar, watching the barmaid draw a wonky shamrock on the top of his pint. He lifted his head as Louise stopped beside him. 'I'll get you a drink.'

Louise ordered an Archers and lemonade, which she hadn't had for years. It was what she used to drink with Wes, and she remembered thinking it sounded like the most glamorous and grown-up thing in the world. They sat in a booth at the back of the pub, around the corner from one another, not so close as to invite intimacy, but not so distant as to shoo it away.

'I'm married.' Leo blurted the words into the silence between them.

Louise was confused. Of course he was married. He was wearing a ring. 'Okay.'

'I mean, I didn't want you to think . . . ' His voice trailed away. 'I didn't want you to get the wrong impression about . . . ' He stared at his pint again and then gestured towards the bar. 'About all this. It's not a date.'

'No.' Louise didn't go on dates. It wasn't fair on Kyle to bring men into his life that might not stick around. He'd had enough of that with his dad already.

'All right.'

'So what is this?'

'What?'

'If it's not a date.'

Leo shrugged. 'I'm not sure.'

Louise took a sip of her drink. It was sweeter and stickier than she remembered. 'Friends, maybe?'

Leo nodded. 'Friends.'

They clinked glasses. 'So what's your wife like?'

Leo grinned. 'She was stunning when I met her. She had all this dyed blonde hair, and make-up like you wouldn't believe. She was a sort of New Romantic.'

'A what?'

'Like, you know, Boy George or Spandau Ballet.'

Louise pulled a face.

'Don't laugh. It was cutting edge at the time. At least I thought it was. She blew me away.'

'Love at first sight?'

Leo smiled. 'Not for her. She fancied one of my mates. It was years before we got together. What about you?'

'What about me?'

'Are you single, with anyone?'

'I'm single.'

'So your son's dad?'

Louise took another sip of drink. 'Wes. He was a barman. Worked in here for a bit actually. Everyone fancied Wes.'

'But you got him?'

'Hardly. When I got pregnant I realised that my exclusive, together-for ever relationship with Wes was really much more of a timeshare sort of arrangement.'

'He had another woman?'

'He had several. From their point of view, I was the other woman I suppose.' She shrugged. 'That was okay. I got Kyle out of it.'

'Do you ever talk to Kyle?'

Louise was glad she'd sorted out her foundation because she could feel her cheeks turning pink. She'd told her mum she'd stopped doing that, but Leo was different. Leo had been through it. 'All the time. Do you? With Olly I mean?'

Leo shook his head. 'I can't. Marnie doesn't like it.'

'Why not?'

'Honestly?'

She nodded.

She listened as Leo explained that his wife had never accepted that Olly was dead. So far as she was concerned their beautiful boy was still out there somewhere waiting to be found. 'That's why she doesn't like me talking about him being gone.'

But, maybe Marnie was right. Louise felt hope spring for a second in her guts before reality crowded in and squashed it down. If Olly was still alive, why not Kyle? Because she'd seen Kyle's body. She'd been to the mortuary and seen him lying on a metal table. She'd watched as he'd disappeared behind the curtain to be consumed by the flames. Hope was not Louise's friend. 'Maybe your wife's right?'

Leo shook his head. 'I wish she was. Of course I wish she was. I know when people go missing, the family always say they just want to know. People think that knowing someone is dead must be better than the uncertainty, don't they?'

Louise nodded.

'I don't think that.'

'Neither do I.' Louise gulped down the last of her glass of sickly sweet liquid. 'I think people think that if you know for certain you stop being in limbo.'

She pointed at Leo's rapidly emptying glass. 'Same again?'

He slid out of the booth. 'I'll get them.'

Louise made a half-hearted attempt to object, but didn't try too hard. She'd chosen to walk into town rather than spend the bus fare. Reliance on the kindness of strangers might be something she needed to get used to.

The second drink slid down faster than the first. Louise heard more about Olly, and Leo's daughter as well.

'I would have loved Kyle to have a little brother or sister. He'd have been amazing with a baby.' She gulped from her glass. 'He'd have made an amazing dad too.' The litany of things Kyle would never do was unending in Louise's head. His classmates would be applying for university, or in jobs, or signing on. Even that piqued her jealousy. Kyle would never sign on. He would never experience the end-of-fortnight anguish of knowing that your money had long since run out. Anguish was simply another thing that reminded you you were alive.

By the age Kyle should have been now, Louise was seven months pregnant. That meant that if you added the time before he was born onto the time after he went, Louise had spent more of her life without Kyle than with him. She had held her perfect baby in her arms and promised him that she would be there for him for ever. She'd lied.

Louise drained her second drink and let Leo buy her a third. It was time to focus. She needed to remember why she was here. 'So how do you know Patrice Leigh?'

He stared at the table. 'Through work.'

That surprised Louise. 'I assumed she'd read for you.'

Leo shook his head. 'No. I'm a journalist. I'm writing a thing about her.'

'What sort of thing?'

'A kind of biography.'

Louise's stomach clenched. He didn't really know her at all, did he? He was just a journalist snooping around for a story. 'Do you really know her?'

He went quiet for slightly too long. 'I don't think anyone really knows her.' He lifted his eyes to Louise's face. 'Sorry. Yeah. It's her autobiography. I'm interviewing her at the moment. Couple of hours every day. It's kind of intense.'

'So you're like a ghostwriter? Is that what it's called?'

Leo pulled a face. 'I hate that word.'

'Why?'

He took a sip of his pint. 'I don't know. It's like you just disappear. You're not the writer. You're not the subject. You're a ghost. Insubstantial. As though you might wake up one morning and realise that there's nothing left of you at all.'

'I feel like that.'

'What?'

Louise didn't normally talk about herself like this. The Archers and the fact that he was, essentially, a stranger were loosening her tongue. 'Like I might just float away into nothingness. It's not a bad thing though. I think it would be a relief.'

'Don't say that.'

'Why not?'

He shrugged. 'I don't know. Sorry. You can say what you like.'

Louise finished her drink. Was that three or four? She wasn't sure. The evening had slid past her. She remembered that happening on nights out when she was young. She used to look at the time at eight o'clock, and twenty past, and quarter to nine, and then she'd look again just a few moments later and it would be midnight, and the night would be racing through her fingers. This was the first time the minutes had slipped past her uncounted since the night it happened. The thought jolted an iron weight into her guts. Kyle was gone. She was without him, and she ought to feel every single leaden second of her loss. She was here for a reason as well. 'Did you ask if she'd do a reading for me?'

She watched Leo's face for a reaction, but none came. He sipped his pint in silence. 'They're expensive.'

'Too much.'

Leo sighed. 'I'll ask again. I might be able to persuade her it'll help with the book.'

That was all she could expect, wasn't it? It

wasn't enough. She needed Kyle close to her again. Soon. 'I just need to know he's all right.'

Leo didn't reply. He never really thought of Olly as still being out there somewhere, living out an afterlife among the clouds and angels and puppy dogs of eternity. There was, he supposed, a vague sense of Ollyness that he carried with him. A notion that his son lived on in Leo's heart and memories. A sense of something missing, overlaying and mingling with all the things he'd always known were missing. He didn't know what to say to Louise, who was obviously imagining her son as a person who might talk back to her. 'What was he like?'

'He was a good boy. People didn't see it, but he was. Every single parents' evening they'd bang on about his behaviour, but it was never more than a bit of cheekiness, a bit of lateness, a bit of scruffiness. When I asked about his marks, they'd always say, 'Oh, his marks are fine,' like that was a surprise.'

Leo could picture the sort of boy Louise was talking about. A lot of front, but the sort of front that was all about making sure his mates never noticed that he was actually working quite hard under the surface. 'What did he want to do?'

She smiled. Something caught in Leo's throat. He was in a bar, with a woman, talking and smiling and sharing confidences. It was for work. She'd come to talk about Patrice. That was all.

'He loved sport. He'd have loved to be professional, but I don't know. He was starting to think about university. Maybe coaching or being a PE teacher.'

101

'Same as Olly.'

'You said he played cricket?'

Leo nodded. That had been Marnie's influence. Even though neither of them was sporty, the basic class divide was still there. Leo had been brought up in a household where you were devil red or sky blue. United or City. Cricket was what posh boys played. Round Leo's way it got a look in for about a week in the summer, usually played with a football and a rounder's bat.

'Kyle played football. He was obsessed. When he was little he used to try to get me to let him sleep in his United strip.'

'Which player?'

'Ronaldo.'

Of course. He saw her look at her watch.

'Do you need to get going?'

She shrugged. 'I probably should.'

It was nearly eleven. 'One more?'

'I need to get the last bus.'

'You could get a cab.'

He saw her hesitate.

'My treat.'

'Okay.'

He bought another round, aware that it was probably a horrible mistake. One drink was friendly. Two was sociable. Three was borderline. Four or five was something else. Four or five was drinking to get drunk. Four or five was drinking in the hope of getting to the point where your brain would take the brakes off and stop thinking and deciding and compromising, just for an hour or two. He put her drink down in front of her,

102

and watched her take a long, gulping swallow. At least they were both on the same page.

'So what do you do?'

She frowned. 'What do you mean?'

'Do you work, or . . . '

She leaned back in her seat. 'I don't know what I do. I'm a mum.'

He watched her face. She'd been smiling, and then frowning, and even laughing, her way through the evening, but now all that went. There was no expression left at all. It was as if she'd stopped. 'You're still a mum.'

He said it with a certainty he didn't feel. He wasn't sure that he was still Olly's dad. He wasn't sure what he was — a husband? A son? He was still a father, but Olly's dad? That didn't feel like an idea that meant anything anymore, but Marnie, he was sure, was still Olly's mum. And Louise was the same. She knew that Kyle had gone, but she hadn't given up. She hadn't accepted that she simply had to let him go. In its own way, that was glorious.

'I never really wanted to do anything else.' She took another gulping mouthful of her drink. 'Maybe I just didn't have time to think of anything else, but as soon as I found out I was pregnant it was like everything inside me fell into place. It was like my whole body just went, 'Oh, this is what I was supposed to do.' '

'You might still have other kids.'

'I don't want other kids. I had Kyle.'

'Sorry.' That had been a stupid thing to say. He remembered his sister-in-law, about three months after Olly went, clutching Marnie's hand

and whispering that at least they still had Grace, as if one child were interchangeable for another. 'I'm really sorry.'

'It's okay. Lots of other people have said the same, but what do they expect me to do? Meet some new guy, settle down, get married, have two-point-four perfect children, and let that be my real life. Like Kyle was just a rehearsal that didn't work out, but it's okay because I'll do it better next time?'

Her knuckles were white as she gripped the glass in front of her. Leo leaned forward and put his hand against hers. Very slowly he felt her grip loosen and he eased her hand from the glass until it was clasped in his own. They both stared at their intertwined fingers on the table between them.

'I'm staying at the Grand.' It wasn't an invitation, just a statement of the fact, but as soon as it was out of his mouth Leo knew it was what he'd been building up to all night. He was living in limbo, not doing or saying anything that really mattered. He needed to do something, and stupid something would still count. 'I can find you a cab, but if you don't want to be on your own, that would be okay too.'

She didn't lift her gaze from their hands. 'You're asking me to come back to your hotel room?'

'Only if you want to.'

She paused. It might not have been going to be a long pause but it was long enough for Leo to drift out of his body and see himself. A middle-aged man. A marriage on the skids. A younger woman. A much younger, emotionally vulnerable woman. 'Sorry.'

'What?' She looked confused.

'I'm sorry. That was . . . ' He couldn't finish the thought. 'I should call you that cab.'

She nodded. 'And you'll ask her about the reading?'

'Sure.'

20

Patrice watched Leo set up his recorder and pull out his notebook. The process of the interviews was routine now. Before this started she'd almost been looking forward to telling her story, but it had become a chore. Somehow the walls inside her head were breaking down. She had an image in her mind of a tiny Patrice running around the place patching holes, and shoring up weak spots for fear that the dam would break and someone else entirely would burst out of the cage. 'So what do you want to talk about today? I could tell you about some of my shows, some of the people I've read for.'

Leo shook his head. 'I'd like to fill in some gaps on your early life if that's all right.'

Patrice didn't let the smile slip from her face. 'Of course.'

'I was wondering about your romantic life.'

This again. She probably ought to put her foot down. Georgios would have. 'I really think the book should focus on my bond with the departed.'

His gaze moved to her face. She watched him suck the air into his mouth, hard and sharp like he'd been slapped around the face. Had she said the wrong thing? That was all right. She could manage that. Sometimes a reading took a turn that wasn't expected. She was Patrice Leigh. She could smooth it over. 'I mean, that's what people will be expecting.'

He nodded. 'But a bit of background . . . I just thought.'

The words were muttered into his chest, like a child who'd been caught out and forced to say sorry against their will, but he wasn't backing down. It was like gauging a punter in a cold read — you never laboured a suggestion that wasn't getting traction. 'Well, just a little background then.'

Unfortunately, her romantic life amounted to not much at all after . . . well, after that first summer. She put on a smile. 'Not much to tell there, I'm afraid.'

Leo nodded. 'I did read . . . ' He clicked through his notes 'There were a few comments I read that suggested that Georgios and yourself . . . '

Patrice let out a genuine laugh. 'He was forty years older than me. And very happily married.'

'I thought his wife died.'

She paused. Had she said that? She had. Of course — the story of his beloved wife bringing herself and Georgios together. This was getting harder. She could feel her brain fusing the stories she told with the things she actually remembered. She had to fight it for a little while longer. She smiled at Leo and nodded. 'But Thea stayed very much in his heart. Our relationship was professional. We were friends, but nothing like that.'

The words came out easily once she'd got back to the script, and the spirit of them was wholly true. True for Patrice and true for Pat. Georgios had created the woman she was. He'd

107

been more of a father to Patrice than her own father had ever managed.

'Okay. Well, there must have been someone?'

Patrice shook her head.

Leo swallowed. 'A teenage crush? A rejected proposal? The one that got away?

'Really, no.' Patrice was back in the groove now. She could tell these stories all day. 'Georgios used to say I was married to my work. When I was younger, and maybe not so in control of my gift, he used to say I lived half my life on the other plane.' She chuckled at the imagined foible. 'Hardly conducive to settling down as someone's wife.'

'And no one ever tempted you?'

'Never.' Which was also true. Nothing would have tempted Patrice to give up her life for a nice home and a nice car and a nice baby with a nice man. Patience had been tempted once. Never again.

21

1967

Pat stabbed her fork into her boiled ham and watched the rest of the inhabitants of the young persons' table chewing. Next to her Eileen Hemmings tapped a painted nail against her knife. The table shifted slightly as Ronnie Mays tried to play footsie with Eileen and made contact with the table leg instead. Denise Smith tutted loudly.

The others were changing though. Pat looked around the table with Gypsy Patience's eye, taking in the details. Eileen's painted nails, Ronald's slightly longer hair, a general minute hitching of hemlines.

'How's it all hanging here?' Their youth club leader, universally known as Fred, came over to the table.

The group nodded and mumbled their satisfaction.

'So we're all cool?'

Mute nods.

'A-okay.' He paused and hovered before returning to his own seat. Another one with a need to fit in. Not one of us, but not quite one of them either. Fred was sitting at the table with Pat's parents, the Sunday school superintendent, universally known as Miss Howarth, and the minister and his wife, Reverend and Mrs Wells.

The great and good. Pat felt her tummy flip. She'd been forbidden from going to the concert, but she'd promised Hester. A glimpse of Eileen's pink nail decided her. People were moving on.

The hall, full of people, finished their ham and they munched and gossiped their way, politely and Christianly, through trifle. Then it was time for cups of tea. The ladies rose and Pat excused herself to help. She stuck her head around the kitchen door. Her mother, who had left the hall with the minister's wife, wasn't there. Miss Howarth was organising cups and saucers like an overzealous sergeant major. Pat approached her. 'Can I help with that?'

Miss Howarth pointed at a stack of saucers. 'Nice neat rows please.'

Pat arranged the saucers on the counter and then made her excuses again. Catching the eye of one of the ladies, she gestured towards the toilet at the end of the corridor. Out of the kitchen, she changed direction and headed back into the hall. 'Make sure lots of people see you,' Hester had advised. She stopped by three or four tables, exchanging niceties, asking about elderly church-goers' ailments and absent children. She saw her father stand. Her wave across the hall was met with a curt nod and he abruptly sat down again.

A quarter to nine. Time to move. Back out of the hall and into the corridor. Quickly to the back door, hand onto the handle.

'Where are you going, dear?'

Pat turned and saw her mother coming out of the vestry. She let her instinct answer. 'Just looking for you.'

'No need to check on me, dear. I'm quite all right.'

'Good.'

'Yes.' Her mother smiled gaily. 'I'll be going back in then.' She glanced towards the main hall.

'So will I.' Neither of them moved. 'I might just . . . first.' Pat darted into the toilets and locked her cubicle. She waited, listening for her mother's footsteps moving away. Then out of the cubicle and straight through the door, running past the bins and onto the street. Hester was waiting, as promised, in the bus shelter at the end of the road.

'I didn't think you were going to come.'

'I've got to be back by half past ten.'

Hester pulled a face. 'Come on then.'

She grabbed Pat's hand and they ran together through the streets, up to the top of town. Hester came to a dead stop outside Woolworths. Pat bowled into her back.

'Let's see you then.' Hester looked Pat up and down. 'Coat off.' Pat obliged. 'Jumper.' Pat stood in the street in her brown skirt and plain white blouse. 'Right.' Hester tugged, determinedly, at Pat's waistband, rolling the material over itself until her skirt rose from knee length to mid-thigh. 'Take your hair down.' Pat pulled her hair out of its neat plait and let it fall over her shoulders. Hester frowned. 'I told you we should have met at my house.'

'There wasn't time.'

'You'll do. We'll just have to tell people we had to break you out of the nunnery. Come on.'

Hester led the way along a side road and

111

stopped outside an open door. 'So, how old are you?'

'Nearly seventeen.'

'For God's sake.'

'Eighteen?'

'Good, but it's not a question. You don't look it though. What money did you bring?'

Pat pulled her coin purse from her skirt pocket. Hester snatched it from her. 'I'd better have this. I can get drinks for both of us.'

All Pat's money was in the purse, money for new clothes, money for bus fares, far more money that she meant to spend tonight. She nodded and followed Hester up the stairs where the elder girl paid them both in and a Brylcreemed man sat at a wobbly folding table stamped their hands.

Inside was hot and smoky and louder than anywhere Pat had ever been before. You couldn't walk without being shoved and squeezed between bodies. At one end of the room was a small bar, customers three deep waiting to get served. In front of the bar were a few mismatched tables but most of the room was dedicated to standing, jumping and dancing space focused towards the stage that bookended the non-bar end of the club. On the stage, three mop-headed boys were singing and playing.

'We missed the start.'

Hester looked at Pat and pointed to her ear.

'We missed the start.' She yelled it this time.

A glance to the stage was all Hester offered in response, before shrugging dismissively. 'Support act.'

Pat nodded like she was equally uninterested. Support act? Course.

Hester pushed towards the bar. Pat hesitated before following, arriving in time to see Hester expertly push to the front of the queuing throng and reappear clutching two glasses.

'Babycham?'

Pat's ears were getting used to the conversation being shouted directly into her ear. She accepted the glass.

'You've probably never even been drunk before, have you?'

The soft tone didn't entirely hide the hint of challenge in Hester's voice.

Pat gave a shrug. Not committing, playing for time.

'My auntie's one of those Methodists like you. She doesn't even have drink in the house.'

Pat nodded, letting the noise leave it unclear whether she was agreeing about Hester's aunt or agreeing about her own home. Hester raised her glass. 'Bottoms up!'

The first sip sent tickles across Pat's tongue, but the bubbles and sweetness weren't unpleasant, a million miles from the harsh unhappy smell of drink she associated with home. She pushed the thought aside, and took a longer look around the room. The crowd was filled with people not much older than her, presumably all living in her home town, but inhabiting the world on the other side of the looking glass.

The boys on the stage seemed to be reaching some sort of crescendo, and Pat allowed Hester to pull her closer to the stage, where she was buffeted and unbalanced by the bodies around her. The band released their final chord with a volley of thank-you-thank-you-very-much, and shuffled from the stage. Most of the jumpers and the dancers vacated the floor in favour of the bar or the lavs, leaving Hester and Pat at the centre of the thinned-out crowd.

'There's Charlie.' Hester's voice screeched, falsely loud after the music. Grabbing Pat's drink-free hand she powered them both across the floor to where Charlie was leaning on a wall talking to an older man. Hester bowled up to the pair, oblivious to the flash of irritation that crossed their faces at the interruption.

'Charlie! We came!' Charlie nodded. Hester continued. 'And you know what you promised?' She turned back to Pat. 'Charlie's going to introduce us to the band. Charlie, you remember Pat?'

He turned his head towards her. The corners of his brilliant blue eyes crinkled slightly upwards for a second before his studied indifference returned, but Pat saw it, and instinctively, involuntarily, her face returned the smile.

'Hello again.'

'Hello.'

'Come on.' The older man slapped Charlie's shoulder. 'Work to do.'

Charlie broke eye contact to nod at his colleague. 'Give us a minute.'

The older man headed through a door to his left, muttering impatiently under his breath. Charlie turned back to Pat. 'So you're here to see The Revival?'

Pat nodded, unsure what the revival might be, but determined to please.

'Cool. They're okay. Kind of old school Mersey-inspired but rockier, if you know what I mean.'

She didn't, but she nodded again.

'They're amazing.' Hester snaked her arm around Pat's elbow and yelled into the space between Pat and Charlie. 'And the lead singer is incredible. You're not going to believe it, Patti.'

Pat registered surprise at the variation on her name, but maybe it suited this Pat. The Pat that went out to clubs and listened to bands who were kind of Mersey-inspired but rockier. The Pat who rolled her skirt up into a mini. The Pat who smiled at boys.

'I've got to go.' Charlie gestured towards the door. He leaned towards Pat, making it clear that his question was for her alone. 'You'll be around afterwards?'

She wanted to nod, but Patiences don't become Pattis in a single night. 'I might have to go early.'

The happy twinkle in his eye flickered off. 'Please yourself.'

A knot formed in Pat's stomach, and she ran the conversation through her head. Had he wanted to see her again? Had she ruined it?

Hester dragged her away from the corner and back onto the dancefloor, pushing her way to the front. 'I want the band to be able to see us,' she yelled, turning to Pat. 'You like Charlie, don't you?'

Pat shrugged, suddenly uncertain of how to

115

respond. The shrug seemed to satisfy Hester. 'Don't be shy. Anyone would notice you making eyes at him.'

'Do you think he likes me?' The question came out before she had a chance to repress it.

'Well, of course he does.' Pat felt warmth spreading through her body and her lips forming into an uncensored smile. Hester continued, 'Blokes like anyone. They're not fussy.'

The Revival came on stage. To Pat's initial gaze they could have been the same three boys who'd left a few minutes earlier, but there were differences if you looked for them. The hair was slightly longer, slightly less groomed. The shirts were patterned rather than plain, worn with two buttons undone — a look Pat's father would call louche, and her mother would call half-undressed. The bass player wore a long moustache that covered his top lip and framed his mouth. These boys thought they were part of today's scene, and playing a seaside club in a nowhere town wasn't dissuading them.

As soon as the beat pounded out of the drum, the crowd were transported to another place. Next to her, Pat could hear Hester screaming along with the rest of the front row, arms flung forward towards the tiny stage, mouth open wide, throwing adoration towards the band. Behind her the crowd jumped and yelled as one, and Pat found herself spectating, watching the audience watch the band, one step removed from living it directly.

22

'Miss Leigh! Miss Leigh!' A hand shook her shoulder.

Her eyes found Leo's face, bent close towards her, eyes wide, a tiny bit of spittle at the corner of his lip. 'What?'

'You spaced out again. You were humming to yourself.'

Patrice smiled. 'The Revival.'

'What?'

'The band.'

'What?'

Patrice rubbed her fingers along the fabric of the sofa next to her leg. She remembered The Revival. She remembered the sweaty throng of bodies moving as one. She remembered the touch of his fingers against her skin; the heat of his body; the joy in his eye. She focused on Leo. 'You're so like him.'

'Who?'

'Charlie.'

Leo sat down in the chair at the end of the tiny coffee table. 'Who's Charlie?'

Patrice arranged her hands on her lap. She was in her hotel room. This was the journalist who was working on her book. She had a show later, and before that a meeting with Barney to run through her diary. She was Patrice Leigh, and she existed fully in the here and now. She looked at Leo's face. He didn't even look that much like him. His hair was shorter, and starting to recede. His eyes were brown, like her own, rather than the sparkling baby-blue of the boy of her memory. She just needed to hold on a little while longer. She'd finish the season of shows. They'd complete the book, and then whatever it was that was coming for her could come and it could do its worst. She would accept the inevitable. Just not yet.

'Who was Charlie?'

'Nobody, dear. I'm sorry.'

'But I need to . . . ' There was an intensity in his expression that Patrice hadn't recognised before. She waited and watched him swallow it down. 'I mean for the book.'

'He was nobody.' That wasn't going to satisfy him. She shook her head. 'Just a rather insistent spirit. I apologise.'

'A spirit?'

She folded her hands on her lap. 'Long departed.'

'Right.' Leo put his notepad down on the table. 'Actually there was something else I wanted to ask you.'

'Mmmm?'

'I've got this friend . . . '

Patrice felt her shoulders tense. People always had a friend. A friend on the other side. A friend on this side who'd lost someone. Sometimes it wasn't even a friend; sometimes the educated ones, the tough ones, the ones like Leo, just didn't want to admit that they were taking someone like Patrice seriously. She forced a smile. This was her job. It was her choice.

'This friend, she lost someone. She asked me to ask you if you could do . . . ' He shrugged. 'Do a session with her.'

'A session?'

Leo nodded.

'You mean a private reading?'

'Yes. I wouldn't normally ask. It's just that she's struggling a bit I think for money.'

Patrice shook her head. 'I'm sorry. I'm very busy at the moment, with the shows, and the book. If you ask Barney I'm sure he could sort out some tickets for the theatre though. Someone might come through then.'

She checked the clock. 'If you wait, he should be here soon.'

Leo nodded again.

Patrice excused herself to go to the bathroom. She leaned on the hand basin and stared at her reflection. She was in there, somewhere behind the eyes, she was waiting. Patrice had taken this body on loan. Patience wanted it back.

She caught sight of a movement, a flicker of something at the edge of the mirror. She turned, but of course there was nobody there. She moved back to the mirror, and then she saw him.

Patrice smiled. 'Oh, there you are.'

23

1967

A hand on her arm pulled her back into herself. She turned. Charlie's eyes met hers. He held up one hand to beckon her to follow him. She did.

She followed him past the bar, through a door, up a flight of stairs and then through a final door out onto a ledge, just wide enough for two people to stand. 'Where are we?'

'Fire escape.' He pointed behind Pat to a metal ladder that led down from the ledge. 'Is it okay? I just wanted some quiet.'

Pat nodded as she looked around. The view wasn't much, mainly just the roofs of other buildings, but it was quiet, apart from the constant background sweep of the sea, and the air was fresh and cool and welcome after the smoky fug of the room downstairs.

'Why haven't I met you before?'

Pat shrugged.

'We've been here nearly three weeks, and Hester turned up on the first night. I thought I'd met all her friends.'

'I don't really come out very much to . . . ' She wasn't quite sure how to end the thought. 'To things like this.'

'And what kind of thing is this?'

'You know? Exciting. Young. Fun.'

'So where do you go, that isn't fun?' His eyes

120

never left her face, like bright blue searchlights.

'School.'

His eyes narrowed.

'How old are you?'

Pat remembered Hester's lesson. 'Eighteen.'

'Right.' He grinned. 'What else do you do?'

'Work.'

'You work with Hester, don't you? At the arcade?'

She nodded. 'I used to be in the café.'

'Used to be?'

Pat let out a little giggle. 'Now I tell fortunes.'

'What?'

'I tell fortunes.'

'Really?'

'Well, that's what I get paid for.'

'Fair enough.' He held out his hand towards her. 'Tell mine.'

She paused. 'I don't do palms. I've got a crystal ball.'

'All right. Let me do yours then.'

'Don't be silly.'

'I hope you're not doubting my gift.'

She shook her head and, very slowly, lifted her palm between them. He placed one hand under hers so she was resting it against his skin. With his other hand he traced a fingertip along her lifeline.

'I see a long and happy life.' He raised his head to meet her eyes, his fingertip still resting in her palm. 'How am I doing?'

'Good. A long and happy life is good. You can't tell people they're going to die young. Not before they've paid, anyway.'

He laughed. 'Okay. Now the line of head and the line of heart.' His fingertips traced two lines across her hand.

'I think they're the other way around.'

'I thought you didn't do palms?'

'Sorry.'

'So the line of head. That tells me that you're clever and you think before you act.'

'Mmmm.'

'And the line of heart. Oh, this is interesting. It's very specific. It says that you're going to meet a man and he's going to read your palm.'

Pat giggled. 'Does it?'

'It does.'

'What else does it say?'

'It says you should kiss him.' He paused. 'I mean if you want to.'

Pat silently nodded her head, still gazing down at his fingers in her palm. She watched those fingers move from her hand and come up to her chin, where they gently tilted her face towards his. She closed her eyes and waited for his lips to meet hers. They were soft and cool from the night air. She raised her head a fraction further, leaning into the kiss, experiencing it, living it, feeling it, just for one moment feeling like the star of the show, not a spectator taking it in from the sidelines.

24

Leo's phone buzzed on the arm of the chair beside him. *One New Message.* It was from Marnie, checking what time he'd be back, reminding him that Grace was coming home for the weekend, wanting to know if he'd be able to collect her from the station, wondering whether they should get takeaway for dinner. Marnie. Grace. Collecting people from the station. Picking up dinner. That was his life. That was his real life.

Last night hadn't been real. That was the only way to think about it. He hadn't cheated. He hadn't slept with Louise. He hadn't even kissed her, and that was what cheating was, wasn't it? And him and Marnie were having problems. Louise was just a friend. And if she was more than a friend, she still wasn't the problem. She was the symptom of a problem. That was all.

A sharp rap at the door brought his attention back into the room. He got up to let Barney in.

'Where's Patrice?'

'In the bathroom.' Leo paused. She'd been in there a while.

He took a proper look at Patrice's manager for the first time. He was slightly shorter than Leo and much slimmer, with light ginger hair on top of a slightly too pink face. He was wearing a light grey suit, with shirt and tie. He had the ubiquitous look of a middle manager. He stood awkwardly just inside the doorway. 'Is the book going well?'

Leo nodded. 'Fine. Early days, but fine.'

'Good. Good.' Barney glanced around the room. 'Is there still tea in the pot?'

Leo shrugged. 'It'll be cold.'

Barney smiled, suddenly energised by the appearance of a task. 'I'll have some more brought up.'

Leo watched him ring down to reception.

'Why don't you just use the kettle?'

'Miss Leigh does not like the steam in her room.'

'Fair enough.' Leo was curious. Patrice gave so little away. 'How did you end up working for her?'

'Well, I was Mr Stefanini's assistant for a long time. I worked with Miss Leigh a lot.'

'Doing what?'

Barney looked Leo straight in the eye. 'This and that. Booking rooms. Going on the tours with her after Georgios stopped travelling so much. Some research.'

'Research?'

Barney stopped. If anything his cheeks flushed even pinker. 'Miss Leigh sometimes gives talks on local history. Ghost stories and the like. She often debunks those tales with no basis you know.'

'Right.' Leo glanced at the bathroom door. 'She's been in there quite a long time.'

124

25

She couldn't stay here in his arms. There was somewhere she had to be. Pat knew that. Of course. Back to chapel. Back to meet her parents. That was it.

She glanced at her watch as she ran down the stairs from the club. Twenty past ten already. She ran down the street untwisting her waistband as she went. Her lips stretched into an irrepressible smile. Her cheeks were tinted pink, and it wasn't from the running or the cold.

Charlie.

She stopped outside the car park gate and forced herself to breathe, trying to ease the pinkness from her face. Was it best to leave her hair down to hide more of her cheeks, or would people remember that she'd had it tied back earlier in the evening?

She dragged her fingers hurriedly across her head and secured her nice safe ponytail back in place. She removed her coat, so as not to draw attention to the fact that she was coming from outside, and pushed on the gate.

A noise on the other side of the car park made her pause. There were voices. Two men arguing. She hadn't noticed them before, tucked right up in the corner where the brickwork of the church flared outwards.

'You treat me like something dirty.'

'No.' The second voice was quieter, feigning calm. Pat froze. The second voice was familiar.

'I'm sick of it.' Pat jumped backwards against the fence and dropped her eyes to the ground as the first man stormed across the car park, through the gate and charged across the road in front of her. She looked up at his profile as he walked away on the other side of the street. He was in his thirties, she estimated, but still good looking, slim, with light hair. His clothes reminded Pat of the poster she had seen for *The Graduate*. He made her think of a blond Dustin Hoffman.

She turned back towards the car park in time to see her father walk slowly into the church. She waited a moment before she followed.

26

The banging noise was horrible. Where on earth was it coming from? The door. The noise was coming from the door. The door at chapel? The door at the club? The door at home?

Something was hard and cold against her cheek. She opened her eyes and lifted her head. She was on the floor. Not fallen, she didn't think. Nothing felt sore or broken. She must have just lain down, or sat down and then slumped somehow maybe. She pulled herself to sitting.

The banging started again. 'Miss Leigh! Patrice! Are you all right?'

She had to answer. She'd keep it simple. 'Fine.'

'Are you sure?'

'I'm fine.'

It was happening more often. She was losing control. She still had two more weeks shows to do. She wasn't sure she could keep it at bay that long. She put her hand on the lid of the toilet to haul herself to her feet. She remembered watching this happen to Georgios. She remembered the first time he hadn't recognised her. She remembered telling herself that that must mean he was close to the end. She remembered being wrong.

Two more weeks. Two more weeks and then Patience could have this body for whatever she wanted. She could take Patrice's sixty-seven-year-old bones out to see bands playing. She could go and buy candyfloss at the seaside. She could lie back and let her imagination take her and Charlie skipping along the foreshore whenever she wished. Just two more weeks.

She stood up and went through to the room. Barney and Leo were both hovering by the bathroom door, anxiety drawn on their faces. Barney she could understand. His business card said '*Manager to the Stars*' but she knew full well she was his only act, and really he was still her assistant. She'd been managing her own career since she was eighteen. Georgios had held her hand and provided advice and contacts and care in return for his fifteen per cent. He'd helped her decide who she needed to be. Barney didn't offer anything a semi-competent secretary couldn't do. Leo's anxiety was interesting though. Think like it's a reading, she told herself. Why was Leo so worried about her? She didn't think he was that desperate for the money for writing this book, and frankly if she keeled over he'd probably still get to write it, and it would probably sell a lot more copies. So it wasn't his career that was flashing in front of his eyes. What was it then? She looked directly at him. 'What's wrong with you?'

'Nothing. I was just concerned. You were quite a long time.'

Patrice raised an eyebrow. 'I'm not sure it's really the done thing to comment on how long a lady takes about her toilette.'

'No. Sorry.'

'Good.' This was fine. She was doing fine, and actually their conversation from the morning was still clear in her head. 'Did you ask Barney about the tickets?'

He shook his head.

'Barney, sort out some show tickets for Leo's friend, would you? On us.'

Barney scowled. 'It'll have to be midweek.'

Leo caught Patrice's eye. 'That'll be fine. Thank you.'

She said goodbye to Leo and then ran through her diary for the week with Barney. She'd lied before. She had plenty of time to fit in a private reading, but she needed to prioritise. When there were only a certain number of hours in the here and now available to her she knew she had to spend them wisely. When Barney left she took off her shoes and lay down on the bed. She could sleep for a while. Maybe if she let Patience have her dream hours she'd allow Patrice the waking ones for just a little bit longer.

27

1967

'So, how much is a fortune?' Charlie poked his head through the layers of velvet and beading that covered the entrance to Gypsy Patience's booth.

'Don't be daft.' Pat's words slipped out unguardedly and she checked herself, thinking that Mr Stefanini would have her tanned for turning away a customer.

Charlie was still in the doorway. He stared down at his feet and Pat, suddenly, noticed how much younger he looked than his twenty-one years. He glanced up at her.

'Can I come in?'

She nodded and he stepped over the threshold. Leaning against the table with his hands pushed deep into his pockets, he peered at her through his hair.

'Was boring after you went on Saturday.'

Pat smiled and caught herself staring at his lips. The lips that had kissed her, and that she, so very hungrily, had kissed back.

'What time do you finish?'

'Five.' He took a look at the clock. It was a quarter to.

'Do you want to . . . ' He never finished the sentence, letting the words get muffled and sucked away into his chest.

Pat nodded anyway. Yes. Yes. Yes. Whatever he was offering, she knew she wanted to.

They walked along the seafront in the unpopular direction, away from the crowds of day trippers and families. After a few metres, they turned away from the sea and began to walk slowly upwards through the public gardens towards the town centre.

'We could . . . ' Charlie gestured towards a bench, and Pat nodded. They sat alongside each other, close but not quite touching. There was just a fraction of an inch between them and Pat felt as if the air in that tiny space was taut and rigid and pressing against her leg.

She tried to imagine the right thing to say. What would Gypsy Patience say? What does Charlie want? What does he need? He was staring out towards the sea.

'So . . . ' she started, but stumbled.

He turned his head towards her and they both smiled, quickly, instinctively.

'So,' he repeated. 'I had fun on Saturday.'

'Me too.'

'Why did you have to rush off?'

'Parents.' She blurted it out without thinking about what she was saying, forgetting to worry about what he thought. 'They're quite old-fashioned. They don't like me going to things like that, or hanging around with older girls.'

'Or boys?'

A laugh, genuine and rueful, not tinny and strained. 'Definitely not boys.'

They fell back into silence for a moment.

'What about boyfriends?'

131

'Boyfriends?' Pat didn't know what else to say.

He nodded. 'If you wanted to . . . '

'Yeah.'

He unleashed another magic smile. The knot in Pat's stomach disappeared in a second and she grinned unguardedly back at him.

'What time do you have to be home?'

'I normally get the bus straight after work.'

He laughed. 'So you're already late? That's not going to get me into your parents' good graces.'

'No!' She almost shouted the word.

'What?'

'I mean, I'm sure they'd like you.'

'No. You're not.' He cut through the lie easily, good naturedly.

'It's not you. It's just . . . '

'Boys generally.'

'It's not even just boys. I've not let Hester come to my house either.'

'So I'm not allowed at your house?'

'I didn't say that.'

'It's okay.' He stared back out towards the sea. 'So long as I can see you?'

She nodded. 'I can work something out.'

28

There was another knocking. Patrice thought of the landlady hammering on the door at Charlie's boarding house, her mother rapping to tell her to get up for school, nervous punters tapping on the wall of her booth for their fortune. She opened her eyes. The hotel. The tour. Patrice Leigh. The knocking continued.

She lifted her body from the bed and shuffled across the room. She wasn't happy with the shuffling. Patrice Leigh was vibrant and confident. She took a deep breath before she opened the door. One of the endless number of girls with ponytails who seemed to be forever around the hotel held an envelope towards her.

'A letter for you, Miss Leigh.'

'Delivered here?'

'Forwarded on. Your manager said to bring it up.'

Patrice accepted the envelope. Handwritten, but not a hand she recognised. She tore it open and flipped the letter inside over to check the signature. *Anthony.* For a second she thought she didn't know an Anthony, but only for a second. She'd only actually met him in passing of course, but he'd always been there. Denied and disavowed, until after her mother's death at least, but always there. She'd heard from him once before, ten years earlier. She'd had somebody decline his invitation then.

She sat, uncomfortably, on the edge of the seat and scanned the closely written lines. He had some possessions, personal items that had belonged to her father apparently, that he was keen to pass on to her. Patrice closed her eyes and tried to picture the Brylcreemed young man from the past. He was younger than her parents. She knew that, but he must surely be in his seventies, probably eighties by now. An elderly man trying to make things right before the end. She set the letter down on the table. This was the sort of thing she needed to avoid. Distractions from another world trying to confuse her. Patrice had her own affairs to get in order; let Anthony Abbot deal with his own ghosts.

29

They were sitting on a bench on the pier. Leo had bought her a chip butty with lots of red sauce. She was hungry. It was three o'clock in the afternoon, but she hadn't had breakfast or lunch. 'I forget to eat since he died.'

Leo stared out at the grey sea. 'No appetite?'

Louise licked ketchup off her fingers and shook her head. 'I just don't think of it. Time doesn't work quite the same somehow.'

Leo didn't question her. She liked that. She liked just being able to say how things were and not be questioned on it. He pulled a crumpled envelope from his jacket pocket.

'I've got something for you.'

She balanced her butty on the paper on her lap and opened the envelope. Inside was a complements slip *From the office of Barnaby Henson on behalf of Miss Patrice Leigh* and two tickets to Patrice's show in a few days' time.

'It was the best I could do.'

She turned the tickets around in her hand. 'I've been to her show before. Kyle didn't come.'

Leo pulled a chip from the pile on her lap and ate it, before leaning in and wrapping his fingers around hers. 'Maybe it's worth another try. Come on. They're free tickets.'

Louise nodded. Two free tickets. 'I don't have anyone to bring.' She paused. 'Do you want to come?'

He was the only person she could ask. Her

mum would think it was silly, or worse she'd put too much onto it and there'd be long talks about how Louise felt about everything, and how she'd cope if Kyle didn't come through. There'd be printouts from the internet from people who said that they'd found peace through using a psychic and other printouts from people who said it was all a con. There'd be discussion and analysis and questions would be asked that she would be expected to have answers for. Louise couldn't do any of that. Leo wouldn't ask her to.

He picked the ticket from her hand. 'It's Wednesday.'

She nodded.

'I'm not sure.'

'Of course. You've probably got stuff with your family.' Leo's living family weren't something they really talked about. To Louise he was the dad of Olly, like she was the mum of Kyle. His other separate life was just that: separate. It wasn't something Louise needed to think about. Her part of Leo was the part that was here. Their part was something else.

He was quiet for a moment. 'We go to marriage counselling on a Wednesday.'

'Right. I went to counselling once. After Kyle. It was stupid.'

'Yeah.'

'Why do you go then?'

'Marnie wanted to.'

'Is it helping?'

'No.'

Louise thought for a moment. 'Then don't go. Come with me.'

Leo turned towards her. 'This isn't an affair, is it?'

Louise shook her head. 'It's just what we need at the moment.'

'Okay.'

'Okay, you'll come?'

'Okay. I'll come.'

She stuffed the tickets into her bag and went back to eating her butty. 'Kyle never liked chips.'

'All kids like chips.'

'Kyle doesn't. He never did. Right from when he was weaning — he'd eat carrot sticks, and broccoli, and peas.' She paused. 'Well, he didn't really eat peas; he just sort of chased them round his plate, but he liked them. But he'd never eat chips. If I put one on his tray, he'd just chuck it on the floor.' She winced at a memory. 'Do you have any idea how gross it is to stand on a cold chip in bare feet?'

Leo laughed. 'That's something they never tell you.'

'What?'

'Well, there's all the antenatal classes and health visitor visits, and none of them ever tell you that having kids is mainly just a catalogue of stuff you're going to end up standing in.'

'Or cleaning up.'

'Or sifting through in the hope of finding some lost valuable.'

Louise chewed the last mouthful of her chips. 'I only went to one antenatal class.'

'We went to three, I think. There were four, but one was just for the mums maybe.'

'I went to one. Wes had done a bunk as soon

137

as I told him I was pregnant, so my mum came. She rolled her eyes through the whole thing and then announced that there was nothing she couldn't have told me without having to get two buses to the community centre, so we didn't go again.'

'You didn't want to go back on your own?'

Louise shook her head. She remembered that first class. The two groups of parents eyeing each other from opposite sides of the room. The young ones, like her, wearing low-rise jeans, tucked under their bumps, with spotty faced boyfriends or hard-faced mums in tow. And then, at the other side of the room, the yummy mummies-to-be. The ones who'd planned their pregnancies and already read a thousand books, and come along with their perfect partners, who had names like Martin and James and pockets full of jotted-down questions for the teacher. Then she remembered the health visitor telling her that the teenage mums who didn't have a clue coped much better with their new babies that those list-making, perfectly prepared women. The teenagers were used to living out of control, used to being without a plan, comfortable going with the unpredictable flow of their baby's needs.

'Was Wes ever involved in Kyle?'

Louise hesitated. 'Why do you ask?'

Leo shrugged. 'I can't imagine not having had Olly.' He paused. 'Or Grace.'

'He came round a few times. First time was when Kyle was just a couple of months old. He brought a book that must have been meant for a seven-year-old, peered into the cot for about four seconds, and then asked if I wanted to go out to a club.'

'What?'

'I think he was properly confused when I told him I couldn't because of the baby.'

'And that was it?'

Louise shook her head. 'No. He was better than some dads, I suppose. He'd send fifty quid at Christmas most years, and he'd come round if he was in town visiting other mates. I think Kyle only asked about him once.' She could remember the day. Wesley had been over and she'd let him take Kyle to kick a ball around on the grass between the blocks. She'd gone with them and sat on the wall with a mug of tea to keep an eye on things. After about half an hour Wes had lost interest and announced he had somewhere to be and Kyle had come and sat next to her. 'Wesley said he was my dad.'

Louise wasn't sure if she was more surprised that Wes had told Kyle that, or more surprised that her clever little boy had never noticed before. 'Is that like Grandpa was your dad?'

'That's right.'

'You said that mummies and daddies mix bits of themselves together to make a baby.'

'That's right.' Louise remembered her rudimentary 'how babies are made' talk with Kyle that had come about when his reception class teacher left at Easter to go on maternity leave.

'Is that why I'm brown like Wesley and not pinky like you? Is that the bit of him that got mixed in?'

She'd stroked her son's perfect brown arm, as

she had done so many times before. 'Yes.'

Kyle had run off onto the grass and picked up the ball, apparently entirely satisfied with his mum's explanation of sex, paternity and race.

'Louise!'

Her attention jolted back to the bench on the seafront, and Leo sitting beside her. 'Louise! You were miles away.'

She smiled. 'Sorry. Sometimes the memories feel real. You know?'

'I know.' He nodded and stared at the ocean. 'So you must have been pretty young when you had Kyle?'

'Seventeen.'

Leo was silent for a second. 'And you never thought about . . . '

A flash of outrage surged through Louise. 'No. I'd never . . . '

'No. I meant like adoption, not . . . not that.'

Louise tried to swallow the anger away, but it wouldn't go. 'It still sounds like you're saying I didn't really want him.'

'No. No. Not at all. I just wondered. It's just, with being so young. You couldn't blame you — well, not you. You couldn't blame anyone if they couldn't manage. That might not mean they didn't want to manage.'

Louise folded her arms. She knew what he was trying to say. It wasn't like it hadn't been mentioned at the time. She'd refused to listen then as well. 'I did want him. I'd never have given him up.'

'No. Of course not.'

'Why'd you ask that anyway?'

140

'No reason.' He turned towards her. 'Forget I said it. Please.'

She nodded.

'So before I put my foot in it, you were telling me about Wes?'

She looked away. 'He started coming round again after Kyle went. He wanted us to get it on again.'

'Did you?'

She shook her head. 'I know it's hard to believe from someone who had a baby when she was seventeen, but I'm pretty old-fashioned about sex.'

'How?'

'I just don't really do one-night stands. Sex is never just sex, is it?' She looked into his face. 'Maybe it is for men.'

'Don't ask me.'

'You're a man.'

'I'm a married man.'

'So?'

'So I'm a married man who goes to relationship counselling. Everything I do means something at the moment.'

'Have you got a hotel room for tonight?'

He nodded.

'Take me back there.'

He didn't answer for a second. Louise watched the ocean. His lack of response should make her feel something. She should be embarrassed or nervous. She just watched the ocean.

★ ★ ★

Leo thought about his answer. It would be so easy, and it would be him finally doing something decisive. Something that wasn't nodding along with the counsellor, or coming up with excuses to spend nights in Blackpool rather than driving home. It would make everything simple, wouldn't it, if he could walk in to the kitchen, sit down opposite Marnie and tell her he slept with someone else. Then she'd react; she'd make decisions. He could let himself get swept along in the flood.

He tried to picture how it would go. What would Marnie say? What would she do? He didn't know. Marnie, in her clubbing days, would have hacked his little gentleman off with a kitchen knife. Marnie, the young wife, would have done the same, but then fried it up in olive oil and served it with rocket leaves and parmesan shavings. But Marnie now? He tried to see her face. He tried to visualise her rage, but it wasn't there. There was a hole in his imagination where his wife ought to be.

Louise was still sitting, silently, at his side.

'I'm married.'

'I know.'

'Sorry.'

She shrugged. 'Not your fault.'

'I'd probably better go.'

'Okay.'

He stood, fastening his jacket in front of him. 'I'll see you for the show though.'

She nodded.

He was going to leave. He was going to step out of the bubble that was holding them here together. 'Drink before?'

'Same place?'

He nodded again. So now he was going to leave. He took a step. He stopped. He turned and walked back to her. He leaned forward, waiting for her to raise her head in response and kissed her hard on the mouth. He felt her lips open slightly under the pressure of his own. He felt her fingers against his stubbled jaw. He stepped back again. 'Wednesday then?'

She nodded.

He walked away. The bubble around them morphed and stretched to take him in.

30

Patrice pulled a notebook towards her. It was perfectly simple, she'd decided. She was simply going to have to get used to living in two worlds. She could do that. She knew she could do that. She'd been doing it all her life. The important thing was to keep them separate. The letter from Anthony was still lying on the table. She scooped it up and stuffed it in a drawer. Out of sight, out of mind. Then, she took a pencil and drew a line down the middle of the page. At the top of the two columns she'd created she wrote headings: *Real* and *Not Real*.

She quickly jotted down a list of those things that were actually happening in the here and now, the things she needed to hold onto:

Barney

The Theatre Shows

Leo and the autobiography

This Hotel — *it's called The Grand and you're staying here*

Work — *research, preparation.*

And then she paused. Georgios' voice rang in her ears. 'Tell them what they want to hear,' he'd told her. She paused and added the advice to her list.

She let the pencil hover over the *Not Real* column. It wasn't the right heading, but she knew what she meant. It was those things she had to hold back, the things she'd never let her audience see.

Charlie.
Mother, Father, Anthony.
Hester and the arcade.
Him.
Him.

Her pen traced a line beneath the final item on her list. He was what it was all about, wasn't he? He was the thing Patience would never forgive her for. For everything that Patrice had gained, he was the price she'd made Patience pay.

31

1967

Charlie walked Pat towards her home. They stopped, as had become habitual over their single month of chastely passionate romance, at the end of the street. Charlie's arms snaked instinctively around her waist and Pat lifted her head towards his kiss. They stayed there, clinched and exploratory, feeling the heat from each other's bodies and the chill from the cooling night air. Her tongue was pushing into his mouth, drinking him in, trying to pull him closer with every breath.

His hands responded, finding the narrow sliver of skin above her skirt, revealed by the raising of her arms around his neck. His fingertips on her skin raised her temperature as surely as the push of a button. For a second her body tensed, but her senses overrode her shyness and she welcomed his hand sliding further under her blouse.

Eventually he pulled away. 'Sorry.'

She shook her head. 'What for?'

'I don't want to rush . . . '

'You're not.'

They were still for a moment. Charlie swallowed.

'Are you coming over tomorrow?'

'Course.'

'To my room?'

'Yeah.'

'Just us.'

She paused. Hester and another girl had come and listened to music with them one night, but for the most part it had only ever been her and Charlie. She didn't see why he needed to check that right now.

'Of course.'

'Do you want to . . . ' He stopped.

Pat realised what he was working up to. It was insane. She knew about that sort of girl who did that. Pat was not that sort of girl. She was the sort of girl who went to chapel and did her schoolwork and came straight home after work. She looked at Charlie.

'We don't have to . . . ' He looked scared, as if he'd pushed too far and knew it.

'No!'

'That's fine. I shouldn't have — '

'No! I mean, yes.' Pat took a breath and extended her fingertips across the space that had grown between them until her hand was resting on his cheek. 'Yes. I do want to, y'know.'

'Right.' They gazed at the floor for a moment until they both cracked in unison, flinging their arms around each other and kissing. But this kiss was different. This was a grown-up kiss. They weren't children playing at this anymore. It was real, and it was theirs.

★ ★ ★

At home, Pat let herself in through the kitchen door. There was a light on in the dining room, but the door was closed. She could picture her

147

father with papers from work or chapel spread across the cleared dining table, adding up columns of figures and reading out the totals to her mother to enter in the ledger. She walked quietly along the hallway towards the sitting room. Not quietly enough.

'Stanley!'

Her mother's voice sounded thin and strained. Pat stopped outside the door.

'No. It's me.'

The voice brightened. 'Patience! Come and talk to your mother.'

Pat pushed the dining room door open. Her mother was sitting at the dining table with her bottle of sherry and a single glass in front of her. Her hands were folded neatly on her lap, her face composed.

'Darling. Where have you been?'

Pat hovered in the doorway. 'I was at Denise's. I told you when we were clearing the breakfast things.'

The habitually bright smile snapped into position on Lilian's face.

'Of course you did.' She looked around the room, as if surprised by her surroundings. 'Your father's gone to . . . '

Her voice tailed away and she gave an indecisive wave of the hand.

'To work?' Pat questioned.

'Yes. To work. That'll be it.' The smile was immoveable now. Lilian leaned forward and patted the stiff backed dining chair beside her. 'Come and sit by your mother.'

Pat slid into the seat.

'What shall we do this evening then, dear?' Lilian ran a hand lightly over Pat's hair, smoothing a few loose strands against her head.

'Such pretty hair . . . ' she muttered, almost to herself. 'We could do one of those jigsaws from the cupboard. Do you remember all the jigsaws we used to do when you were little?'

Pat nodded. She did remember, the quiet, companionable hours spent hunting for corners and straight edges, and doing battle with tricky expanses of plain blue sky. 'Daddy doesn't like it when we take up the table though.'

'No. No.' Lilian shook her head and the smile slipped for the tiniest fraction of a second. 'We should get one of those boards. Mrs Hassock at Ladies Group has a board that she puts down for jigsaws. We'll go to the big department store tomorrow and have a look.'

'All right.'

'So what shall we do this evening instead? Shall we go through and put the television on?'

Pat forced herself not to turn her head towards the clock. 'It's quite late.'

'What time is it dear?' Her mother looked confused for a moment, her eyes flicking back to the bottle.

'Nearly eleven.' Pat remembered her strict curfew. It was twenty past. 'I'm quite tired.'

'From being at Denise's?'

'Yes.'

'What did you do at Denise's?'

'Not much.' Pat looked at her mother's face. She couldn't be suspicious, and she didn't know Denise's parents well enough to have talked to

149

them. 'I showed her the new song she missed at choir last week. We listened to some records.'

'Your father and I used to listen to records. The band music from America. And we'd go to the films. He took me to all the films.' Her mother had drifted to another place.

'I might go to bed.'

'Right.'

Pat stood up and moved towards the glass and bottle. 'Shall I clear these away?'

Her mother's shoulders tensed slightly. 'It's all right dear. I can do it.' The smile reappeared. 'You get off to bed. I might just wait a minute longer for your father. I've got things to tidy and . . . ' She waved the hand across the table. There was nothing out of place, except for the sherry.

Pat stood and walked towards the door. She paused, but couldn't work out the right thing to say. 'Night night, then.'

32

Talking to Louise had felt good. In the past, he'd sat with two different counsellors in two different faceless offices, and he'd never got it. He'd never got the point of talking about feelings, but now Leo was starting to think he could see it. It was about truth. There was something powerful about simply saying the truth out loud. He was used to telling other people's stories, finding their version of what was real. Now it was his turn.

He didn't hesitate at the entrance to the hotel. He hit the call button for the lift quickly and confidently. About this, at least, Marnie had been right. He couldn't do this by watching and waiting. Leo strode along Patrice's corridor and rapped on the door.

'Just a minute.'

He waited in the hallway until the door opened. As always, Patrice was perfectly turned out. Hair tidy; clothes pressed and clean. Everything just so. 'Leo! Come in.' She smiled. 'Of course, we have another interview.'

Leo shook his head. 'No.'

She stopped, resting her hand on the side table for a moment. 'No. Of course not. My mistake.' She glanced around the room and then scurried to the bed, scooping a notebook into the drawer of the bedside cabinet. 'What can I do for you then?'

Now he'd made his decision it would be easy to blurt everything out. Leo forced himself to take a breath. He sat down. 'I need to talk to you.'

She took the seat diagonally opposite him. 'About your son?'

'No.' Not about Olly. 'What about my son?'

'I just assumed.' She smiled again. 'Shall I order us some tea?'

'No. There's something I need to talk to you about.'

She raised an expectant eyebrow. 'A problem with the book?'

He shook his head. 'No. It's personal.'

She didn't reply. He supposed there wasn't much she could say. He was the one who had words he needed to get out. They were there fully formed in his head, but suddenly there was a blockage between his thoughts and his mouth. He remembered the release of telling Louise that Olly had died and her accepting that. The truth. Another breath. This was it. 'You're my mother.'

'Sorry?'

'I think you're my mother.' The second time sounded calmer, more certain, even to Leo's own ears. He scanned Patrice's face for a reaction, but she turned her head away, gazing towards the window.

'I'm sorry. Is this a joke?'

Leo's stomach clenched. Of course it wasn't a joke. He'd looked. He'd searched. He'd found her. He knew he'd found her. 'No.'

She shifted in her seat so that she was properly facing him. 'Then I'm sorry.' She tilted her head to one side. 'So very sorry. But you're mistaken.'

'No. I was born in 1968. In York.' He stopped himself. It wasn't that she'd just forgotten exactly where and when she'd given her baby away. Filling in the details wasn't going to prompt an awkward laugh and a flurry of apologies that the whole darn thing had momentarily slipped her mind.

He was wrong.

But he couldn't be wrong. 'Patience. You're Patience Bickersleigh?'

Patrice's face remained impassive. 'I'm afraid not. Patrice Leigh.'

'It's not a stage name?'

'No.' For a second he thought he heard the word catch slightly in her throat, but she swallowed it away. 'It's just who I am.'

There was nothing else to say. The euphoria of realising he needed to tell her the truth had evaporated, leaving him empty. 'I'm disturbing you. I'll go. I'm sorry.'

'Not at all. An honest misunderstanding, I'm sure.'

Leo nodded mutely and marched out of the room.

★   ★   ★

Patrice didn't say anything. She didn't call out to him. The Patience inside her mind was screaming, but Patrice stayed quiet. Where would this come on her two lists? It was happening in the here and now. She was certain of that. She could recognise when she'd drifted

153

away into the other life; it felt so very much more real. So this was just an echo of something from Patience's world, but that wasn't real. That was how the lists worked. She kept everything separate and then everything stayed under control.

Patrice counted the heartbeats as she waited for the door to slam shut behind him. One, two, three, slam. And then she opened her mouth wide and let Patience cry out into the empty room. The wail she'd expected didn't come. This was more visceral and more absolute than mere noise could encompass. She gulped and retched on Patience's loss. He'd been here. She could have let Patience take over and reach towards him. Patience would have done that — touched him, held him, drunk him in — but it wasn't Patience's time. Not yet.

Looking back, she'd seen it, hadn't she? The black hair, the shape of his jaw. She'd seen her beautiful Charlie in him and she'd pretended it was all another silly dream.

33

1967

'Where are you going?' Mrs Pickering, the landlady of Charlie's boarding house, stopped Pat as she made her way up the stairs.

'I'm visiting Mildred.' Mildred was a woman from Essex of indeterminate age who seemed to have permanent residence of the room above Charlie. Mrs Pickering wouldn't believe her but Pat didn't care. She bowled through the door to Charlie's room at a quarter past seven.

'You're early.' Charlie grinned.

'I couldn't wait.' She undid the buttons of her duffel coat as she talked and, once unbundled, flung her arms around his neck, met immediately by the warmth of his body as he squeezed her against him.

They kissed. A happy, uncomplicated kiss. Pat was becoming someone new, someone Charlie knew instinctively but who would be barely recognisable outside this room.

The kiss continued. His hand moved to the buttons at the front of her blouse, and slowly he began to undress her. She responded, reaching for his jumper and allowing him to break the kiss so they could pull it, together, over his head.

'Shall we?' She moved her gaze toward the bed, surprised to hear herself be so forward.

'You're sure?'

She nodded. 'Are you?'

He laughed. 'Oh yes.'

She took his hand and they moved together to the bed, lying down on top of the floral counterpane. She shivered.

'Are you cold?'

'A bit.'

'We could get in.' Somehow getting in the bed felt like a bigger step than moving from kissing to lying down. She would actually be in bed with another person, a person who would be undressing her and touching her and making love to her.

'All right.'

They stood up and each grabbed a corner of the counterpane, blanket and sheet below. They tugged in unison, loosening the bedclothes from the mattress. Pat pushed off her shoes with her toes and jumped under the covers. Charlie paused, watching her pull the blanket over her unbuttoned top.

'What are you waiting for?'

'Nothing. Just looking at you.'

Embarrassment coloured her cheeks. 'Why?'

'You're really pretty.'

'Come on then.'

He jumped into the bed beside her. His arms reached towards her. She lifted her head and placed it against his shoulder, raising her chin to him for a kiss.

They proceeded slowly, tentatively, removing clothing one piece at a time, never rushing, never stopping until they were both naked. The whole body rush of skin against skin unlocked something, something glimpsed in earlier kisses but never realised. Pat felt him hard against her thigh. She pulled her body away.

'What's wrong?'

'Nothing.' She lifted the covers and peered downwards. 'Can I?'

'What?' He followed her gaze. 'Right. Yeah. Sure.'

She let her fingertips drift down his stomach to the tip of it. 'What do I . . . ?'

'Erm . . . ' He giggled, embarrassment suddenly apparent on his face. 'Just put your hand round it.'

She wrapped her slim fingers around the shaft. The skin was soft and smooth, the hardness new and unfamiliar.

'What now?'

'You sort of move up and . . . '

She moved gently, slowly at first. 'Like that or quicker?'

'Yeah. Like that . . . or quicker . . . ' He gasped out the words. 'Whichever.'

She carried on, listening as his breathing came faster and shallower. Suddenly he pushed her away.

'What? Did I? Was that wrong?'

'No. No. I just don't want to . . . ' His words drifted away. 'Not yet.'

'Oh? Oh! Right.'

He lay back on the bed for a moment panting for breath, before pulling himself up on one elbow and grinning. 'Your turn?'

'What?'

His fingers mirrored hers earlier down his

chest, skimming down the side of one breast, across her tummy and pausing just above the soft black curls between her thighs. 'So what feels good?'

'I don't really know. I've never . . . '

'Really?'

'No! Ladies don't do that.'

He moved his face in close to her ear and whispered. 'Really?'

'Well, sometimes when I'm in the bath . . . '

'All right. So what feels good?'

She buried her face into his chest and hooked one leg over his. 'Just sort of stroke and . . . '

His hand moved over the small mound of hair towards the soft slit between her thighs. 'You're wet.'

'Mmmm . . . '

He pushed his fingers further and found her opening. The tip of one finger pushed a little deeper, moving inwards.

'Is that okay?'

'Yeah . . . ' The word came out as a breath.

'Okay.' He continued, pushing his finger deeper inside her. Then it was two fingers, and she was gasping against his chest, wrapping her leg tighter around his body and digging her fingers into his back. And then they were rolling together, and he was pulling his fingers away, replacing them with his penis, and sinking deep and hard inside her. Eyes wide open, they gazed at each other in wonder and disbelief, and then he was moving above her, allowing instinct to take over, getting faster and harder in response to her gasps beneath him. And then they were coming, her first, hot, wet and ready, and then him seconds later, moaning with pleasure as he came deep inside her body.

They lay back on the bed, both panting for breath. He laughed.

'What's funny?'

'Nothing. Just happy. Are you okay?'

She responded with a small giggle and a nod.

'Good.'

He shook his head as he stared upwards at the peeling ceiling. 'I thought first times were supposed to be awful.'

'That was your first time?'

A pause. 'Yeah.'

'I wish you'd said. I thought you must have had loads of girls.'

'What made you think that?' He rolled onto his side to face her, and she mirrored the movement.

'I don't know. You're cool. You're with a band. You're older too.'

'Ah.' He eyes flicked sideways for a second.

'What?'

'I should tell you something.'

'Go on.'

'I'm not twenty-one.'

'Yes. You are.'

'I'm eighteen.'

'But Hester said. You've always been twenty-one.'

'I told the tour manager I was twenty-one because he wanted someone with experience.'

'You lied?' She sounded genuinely shocked.

'You tell people you can see the future for a living.'

'That's different.'

'How?'

'Well, no one really believes that.'

'Hester does.' They were disagreeing but not really arguing.

'She doesn't.'

'She does. She keeps telling people her friend can tell their fortune.'

'But she knows I used to be in the café. She knows I only got the job because Nadia did a bunk.'

'I'm just telling you what she says.'

'Well, it's still different.'

'Sorry. I just lied to get the job. I didn't expect to . . .'

'What?'

'What?'

'You didn't expect to what?'

'You know. Meet someone special.'

She grinned at the idea of being special to anyone. To someone. To Charlie.

'So you're not angry?'

She shook her head.

'Good. Now you have to tell me something.'

'Like what?'

'Like anything. Something secret. It's only fair. You know mine.'

'There isn't anything.'

'I bet there is. And you can tell me anything.'

She took a breath. 'I think my mum might be a drunk.'

'Right.'

'She drinks half a bottle of sherry every night. That's a lot, isn't it?'

160

'Yeah. I think so.'

'I've never told anyone that before.'

He reached an arm around her torso. 'Well, thanks for telling me.'

'Your turn again.'

'What?'

'Your turn. Another secret.'

'All right. I haven't told my dad that I'm not going to university in October.'

'You're supposed to be going to university?'

'Cambridge.'

'You're clever. You never told me you were clever?'

'It's my dad's plan. I haven't definitely got in yet.' He kissed her quickly. 'I'm not going anyway.'

'What are you going to do?'

'I thought I'd tour some more with the band, maybe start my own band, or see if I can work in a club or at a record label or . . . '

'Or what?'

'Or maybe stay here.'

She laughed at him. 'Why would you stay here? The whole point of here is to leave.'

He kissed her nose. 'There's lots to like here.'

'Gerroff.'

'You're right though. We don't have to stay here.'

'We?'

'If you want.'

'All right.'

'Your turn again . . . '

And they carried on until after ten, when Pat glanced at the clock on the side table and jumped out of bed like she'd been shot, running around the room gathering clothes and disentangling them from the piles of Charlie's stuff wherever they lay.

'I have to go.'

He watched her getting dressed. 'Can I see you tomorrow?'

She shook her head. 'Sunday. Church.'

'Which church do you go to?'

'The Central Hall.'

He looked blank.

'The big one on Princess Street, by the department store. Why?'

He shrugged. 'No reason.'

Pat leaned over the bed to share a final kiss. 'I really have to go.'

'I know. Are you at work on Monday?'

She nodded. 'You could come meet me after and walk me home.'

'Okay.'

One more kiss and she ran out of the room and down the stairs, straight out of the big front door, not worrying about the bang as it slammed behind her. She walked quickly down the side street and stopped at the corner of the main road. Did she feel older, more worldly, more grown up? Not really. If anything she felt younger, less certain, less decided on her course in life. Suddenly she felt everything was possible. Nothing that she'd relied upon before seemed quite as definite.

She turned the corner and walked more slowly along the main street.

'Pat!'

162

The shout came from behind her. There was a gaggle of girls, so she didn't see who shouted immediately, but as the group separated out she saw Hester tottering towards her on sky-high boots.

'Pat!'

She looked quickly at her watch. Curfew at eleven. Twenty-five minutes to walk home.

'Where have you been?' Hester gabbled the words as she pulled Pat into a hug. Her breath was hot, sticky and scented with Babycham. 'I never see you anymore.'

'I've been around.' Pat felt unexpectedly shy about what she'd been doing that evening. 'Hanging out with Charlie.'

'I know that! Everyone knows that! Total lovebirds.' Hester turned back towards the group of girls. 'This is Pat. She's going out with Charlie from the band.'

'He's a roadie.'

Hester kept her arm proprietarily around Pat's shoulder. 'I introduced them.' She turned back towards Pat. 'Didn't I?'

Pat nodded.

'All down to me.'

The group of girls started to move away. 'You go. It's okay. I'll catch you up,' Hester called after their receding backs. 'So have you been with Charlie tonight?'

'Yeah. But I've got to go . . . I . . . '

Hester looked down the street. 'His boarding house is down there! You've been at his room.'

Pat nodded again. 'Listening to records.'

Hester laughed. 'I don't think so. Come on. You can tell me.'

The urge to shout from rooftops battled with the shyness and won. 'Actually, we did it tonight.'

'What?'

'You know, it!'

'Pat! I thought you were a proper good girl.' Hester put her arm back around Pat's shoulder. 'And how are you feeling? Don't worry if it wasn't that good. I'm sure you'll get better at it.'

'It was amazing.'

'Oh. Well, that's good.' There's a brittleness in her voice. 'Great. And I'm sure he won't really have minded that you're not very experienced.'

'No. Not at all.' Pat can't stop the smile at her lips.

'Great. And don't worry if things are different now. Boys are just like that. Once they've got what they want, they kind of tend to lose interest.'

Pat's smile quivered and fell away. 'Right.'

Hester patted her shoulder. 'But you've always got your girlfriends, haven't you?'

'Yeah.'

34

The theatre was full, just like the last time, but Louise was sitting nearer the front. She was toward the end of the row, with Leo next to her in the aisle seat, stretching one leg out into the gap.

'Do you think he'll come through?'

Leo shrugged.

'I think he will.' Louise rolled her tissue between her fingers. 'He must know I'm here. He's a good boy. He'll come.'

She tore a tiny piece of paper from the corner of the tissue and rolled it between her thumb and forefinger, before dropping it onto the floor. She needed to get Kyle back. She could barely admit it, even to herself, but he was fading. He was still her first thought in the morning and her last thought at night, but recently she'd found that she would wake up and realise that she'd been asleep for four or five hours, rather than lying awake communing with her son. Just that weekend she'd caught herself watching a dancing thing on TV, and realised that she was actually watching the dancing rather than simply counting down the seconds and minutes of existence. It was horrible. She didn't want to move on, but she was being swept up by the world. Her own body was fighting against her inertia, overriding her grief with its need to eat and sleep and move. This was going to be her way back to the centre of her grief.

The house lights dimmed and music started up. A ripple of whispers moved across the audience, dampening the louder chatter and giving way to a wave of quiet in its wake. Patrice Leigh came onto the stage, and just like the last time, the audience went crazy. Louise didn't clap. She sat, pulling at her tissue, and she waited. She wasn't interested in hearing about Patrice's gift. She wasn't interested in her spirit guide. She was waiting for Kyle. Eventually Patrice made a start, closing her eyes and focusing on the world beyond. The first spirit was a woman with a message for her daughter in the fourth row. Louise balled her tissue tighter in her fist and silently hated the woman in the fourth row. The second spirit was an elderly man who'd died of a heart attack. The muscles in Louise's hands started to tense and cramp. Old men who died of heart attacks had no business taking up her time. Old men dying of heart attacks was the natural order of things. Seventeen-year-olds taking a kitchen knife through the belly was not.

Leo leaned across her and unprised her fingers from the tissue, wrapping his own hand around hers. Patrice stopped communing with the spirit plane for a moment and chatted to her audience about what life was like on the other side. Time and reality were different there. Sometimes spirits who died as old men would come through as strapping teenagers, or vice versa. That was nothing for the audience to be confused or upset by. Time and age didn't have the same meaning for the spirits as they did for us.

'Oh!' Patrice put her hand out to the side of her. 'Oh. There's a spirit coming through very strongly now.' She turned towards the apparent apparition and held up her palm. 'It's okay. It's okay. I can hear you.'

She nodded at the empty air, before turning back to the audience. 'This spirit is exactly the age he was when he passed though. And I think that's right. I'm feeling someone who was a very strong presence in this world, and he's kept that same strong sense of self in the realm beyond.' Suddenly her face changed to an expression of deep sadness.

'Oh, this is awful. He's telling me that he died suddenly. He was perfectly well and then everything happened at once. That's what he's telling me. That's so sad for someone this age. He's young. Just a teenager. And he wants to talk to his mum.'

Louise heard the noise that came out of her own mouth before she realised it was her making it. It was a gasp of hope.

Patrice continued. 'It's Mark?' Then she laughed. 'Sorry. He's telling me his mum's name. It's Marnie. Sorry. Marianne.'

Louise's stomach turned to iron. It wasn't Kyle. He hadn't come. She realised that Leo's grip on her hand had tightened.

'And now he's telling me that his mum isn't here tonight, but his dad is.' She looked out into the audience. 'Does Dad recognise this?'

Leo cleared his throat. 'Yes. Here.'

A hand with a microphone appeared alongside

them. Leo spoke into the mike. 'That's my son.'

'And you're Leo?'

'Yes.'

'Leo, I've got Olly with me. That's right, isn't it?'

'Yes.'

'Leo, Olly wants to pass a message to his mum. He needs her to know that he really is on the other side. Does that make sense?'

Leo raised the microphone to his lips. 'We didn't know for sure. They never found the body.'

On the stage Patrice nodded and smiled benignly at the universe. 'Well, he's at peace. He says you shouldn't worry about his body. He says that it was buried well.' She paused. 'I'm sorry. I might have misunderstood. I'm sure he's telling me that he was buried, but you said they didn't find the body. Does that make sense?'

Next to Louise, Leo nodded. She realised that there were tears streaming down his face. He gulped before he spoke. 'There was a landslide. He was camping. The whole camp was buried.'

Patrice nodded again. 'I see. And he was a long way from home? New Zealand?'

'That's right.'

'Well, Olly wants you to know that there's no reason to worry about him, or look for him anymore. Where he is things like that don't matter anymore. He's happy. He's peaceful, and he's still keeping a close watch over you.' She paused, apparently listening to the spirit world once more. 'He wants you to give his love to Grace too. Grace — does that make sense?'

168

Louise watched as Leo nodded again. She should be relieved for him. She was supposed to be his friend. Friends didn't tear the microphone from the other friend's hand and scream, *What about me?*

'And he's fading away now.'

Another spirit quickly came through, and Patrice continued with the show. Louise listened, but hope was dwindling. Kyle wasn't coming. Olly had come. All these other people's sons and brothers and lovers had come, but not Kyle. When he'd been taken from her, he'd been ripped from the world completely. She was never going to get him back.

⋆ ⋆ ⋆

Patrice sat down on the hard plastic chair in her dressing room. On the very first night of the run, the theatre manager had promised her an armchair. She was still waiting. Georgios would never have put up with that. Barney was a wimp though, and Patrice was too tired to fight battles over chairs. And, she thought, she couldn't get too comfortable in this seat; if she wasn't too comfortable her mind wouldn't wander and maybe she'd be able to hold on a little bit longer.

Reading Leo had been a risk. There was a danger that he'd say something that made it clear that they knew one another, but she wanted to give him something. After their conversation . . . she swallowed . . . after their misunderstanding it only seemed right to offer him some comfort. It wasn't that she was desperate to make sure he stayed around. Besides, she'd already had Barney do the research after all.

There was a tentative knock at the door. 'Come in.'

She'd started to detest even Barney's knock. He managed to be uninspiring from the other side of a closed door. He slid into the room and popped a handful of pieces of paper down on the table.

'Anything interesting?'

'Couple of things.' He riffled through the sheets and pulled two pieces to the top. 'This woman was in the local paper, but we didn't know for sure if she was coming. And this is Leo's friend.'

Patrice glanced over the notes. There was very little that she didn't already know, but it was good to have things confirmed. Local newspapers were depressingly unreliable, and nothing hampered the suspension of disbelief like the dearly beloved deceased getting their own mother's name wrong because of a typo in the local rag.

Barney was hovering.

'What?'

'I wondered if you still wanted me to talk to Leo's agent.'

'What about?'

His eyebrows knitted together like a pair of small anxious caterpillars. 'You said you wanted to let him go.'

Patrice closed her eyes. Had she said that? She knew she'd talked to Leo about wanting to let Barney go. Or was she confused about that as well?'

'Did I say why?'

'No.'

The black-haired boy. Her black-haired boy. She wondered about the son Leo had lost. Was he another black-haired boy? Her grandson, perhaps. Charlie's grandson. She shook her head. 'I think I must have had a moment of cold feet about the book. Silly of me. Of course I don't want to let Leo go.'

She flicked through the remaining sheets of notepaper and rolled her eyes. 'The dog woman is here again?'

Barney nodded. 'I don't suppose you could — '

'I don't do pets.'

'Some of the others do.'

Patrice shot him a look. 'I don't care what the others do. I do not crawl around the stage on my hands and knees yapping like a toy poodle.'

'I believe the beloved Dennis was a Pekinese.'

'Not the point. What day is it?'

Barney frowned. 'Wednesday.'

'I thought I might go to church on Sunday.'

'Okay.' If Barney was surprised by the suggestion, he didn't let it show.

'Find out when the services are. Methodist preferably.'

'All right.' He glanced at his watch. 'Five minutes to curtain Miss Leigh.'

★   ★   ★

Louise didn't want to go back in. He wasn't going to come, so what was the point, but she didn't want to go home either, so she let Leo drag her back into the theatre. He hadn't said

171

much during the interval. He'd wiped away his tears before the lights came back up and simply claimed to be fine when Louise asked. She hadn't asked anymore. She couldn't find a way of putting her thoughts into words that didn't involve balling her hands into fists and beating against his chest at the utter unfairness of his son coming through and hers being utterly gone.

The houselights dimmed again, and Patrice Leigh returned to the stage. Louise felt she knew the drill by now. Spirits came through. Relatives were emotional and thankful. Patrice chatted a bit about life as a medium, and then more spirits came through and more families were overcome with gratitude. She stared at the back of the head of the woman in front of her and waited for it to be over.

Leo grabbed her hand. 'Louise!'

'What?' She glanced at him, but his eyes were fixed on the stage. She tuned back into what Patrice was saying. 'A young man. Carl? Sorry!' She laughed. 'My hearing — I'm not as young as I was. Kyle. Kyle's looking for his mum.'

Louise lifted her hand into the air. She heard Leo next to her directing the roving microphone towards her, but she didn't care. Kyle was here. He'd come. She should never have doubted him. The microphone landed in her hand.

'Stand up, dear.'

She did as she was told.

On the stage Patrice Leigh tipped her head to one side. 'I've got Kyle here. Are you Louise?'

'Yeah.'

'You're Mum. Is that right?'

Louise nodded.

'Speak up, pet.'

'Sorry. Yes. I'm his mum.'

'I know. I know. He's telling me.' Patrice paused. 'Now he's telling me it's been a few months since he passed.'

'Yes.'

'And he's telling me that he's been trying to come through, but you've not been hearing him, pet.'

Louise shook her head. 'I've tried.'

Patrice nodded, full of sympathy. 'Sometimes when we're grieving we just don't see our loved ones. They can be there, but it's like they're banging and banging on the door to be let in, and you just can't hear them.' Louise froze. Her baby had been trying to contact her all this time and she hadn't heard. She'd left him out there somewhere, alone and frightened. Louise had let her baby down.

On the stage, Patrice raised her head to address the whole audience. 'That's why it's such a privilege to be able to do this. All I really do is just pop that door open.' She turned back to Louise. 'He wants you to know that he's not in pain anymore.' Her brow furrowed. 'So I think you know that he was in pain when he died?'

Louise cleared her throat. 'He was stabbed.'

'I know. I know dear. He was stabbed, wasn't he? Not so far from here?'

'It were in town.'

'I know. He's safe now though, and there's no more pain.' Patrice put her hand to her forehead and closed her eyes, as if overwhelmed. 'I'm sorry, pet. He's fading. There are so many spirits who want to come through tonight. It's hard to keep hold of just one of them.' She shook her head. 'And he's gone.'

The room faded to darkness around Louise. Patrice's voice continued on the stage but it was as if she was whispering at the very far end of a long long tunnel. Louise dug her fingers into the arms of her seat to anchor herself. Her boy had been here. Her boy had come to talk to her. He'd been trying for so long, and she'd let him down. Something brushed her arm. She spun her head to see Leo's fingers on her skin. That wasn't right. She didn't want Leo. She wanted Kyle. 'I'm sorry.'

She barged over Leo's legs. She was up the aisle and out of the theatre in seconds, and she stopped in the street outside. The air was still warm. That was wrong. It was cold on Kyle's last night. It ought to be cold for ever. Then she knew where she was going. She marched across the street, making a van brake hard to avoid her. The driver leaned his head out of the window and yelled obscenities at her.

She strode down the high street and then turned down the hill to the bus station. She knew exactly where it had happened. Outside on the approach path, just before the first shelter. She stopped, breathed in the bus fumes and the fag smoke and lifted her head. 'I'm here! I'm here Kyle. I'm waiting.' Surely if she waited, he would come. He'd come to that woman in the theatre. She'd said he'd been trying to come through. And this was where it had happened.

This was where he'd be. Wasn't it? She waited for the sound of his voice, for the hint of his laugh on the night air. She waited. Nothing. She raised her voice to the sky. 'Kyle! I'm here. It's Mum. I'm here.'

'Are you all right, love?'

A woman in an anorak put a hand on Louise's shoulder.

'Go away!'

'What?'

'Go away! He doesn't know you. What if he won't come?'

'Are you sure you're all right?'

The stupid woman in the stupid anorak was getting in the way. What if Kyle came and saw this stranger here? Louise shoved the woman hard in the shoulders. 'I told you to go away!'

Another voice jumped into the argument. 'All right, love. Calm down.'

'She shoved me! Did you see that? I'm calling the police.'

Louise screamed. It was a deep angry wail from the pit of her stomach. Why wouldn't these people leave her alone? Why wouldn't they let her be with her child? It wasn't fair. All this noise. All this commotion. He wouldn't come now, would he? Maybe it was her fault. Maybe she wasn't strong enough to find him on her own. That Patrice woman could do it though. She'd found Kyle when nobody else could. A hand came down on her shoulder. 'Miss! Miss!'

She turned to see a uniformed man, tall and wide, head shaved clean. 'Miss! I need you to calm down.'

All these people, hassling her, getting in the way. None of them understood what she needed. She reached forward and pressed her hands against his shoulders to get him away. And then another uniform appeared and then a third. Louise screamed and kicked as they dragged her to the waiting police car. She'd let Kyle down, but she wouldn't let him down again. He'd found her. She'd had him back for the briefest moment. She needed to do it again.

35

The Methodist Central Hall was a rather uninspiring building somehow built into the shopping centre in the middle of town. Patrice went in to the door next to the discount shoe shop and up the stairs. She took a seat at the back. She told herself that different was good. She hadn't come here to commune with the past. She wasn't actually sure why she'd come here at all. It didn't seem like something that Patrice would do.

When Barney had given her the times and directions, though, she'd been picturing a different central hall in another seaside town. She'd been remembering the black, leather-covered, swing-down seats and the massive central pulpit set in front of the pipes of the organ. She'd been remembering the section at the front to the right where the young people sat, gradually progressing back through the rows as they got older, from the toddlers at the front to the teens three or four rows behind. She'd been remembering different ministers — Reverend Wells of course, but who was the one before him? She couldn't remember. For a second, she wondered what the rest of that little youth group were doing now? Retired probably, with families, two cars on the drive, aging parents in homes to be visited and fretted over. She didn't know. She hadn't kept in touch.

Patrice took another look around. This wasn't at all the sort of place she'd expected, and she shouldn't be letting her mind wander down memory lane. But then why had she come if not to remember? Maybe she could sneak out before the service started, but before she had a chance to decide, the preacher, a big-bosomed redhead, who delivered her comments in a thick Scouse accent, was waddling to the front. The children were allowed to play in the aisle, and the words to the hymns and prayers were projected on a screen at the front of the hall. Everything had changed.

36

1967

'Pat!'

Her mother was standing outside the bedroom door.

'Pat!'

'Yeah?'

'You've got to get up. It's time to get ready for church.'

She heard her mother muttering about teenagers as she headed off down the stairs, and pulled herself out of bed. She dressed quickly. She wasn't actually tired, and hadn't been asleep for hours. Her regular clothes felt more and more like a costume, only feeling part of her as Charlie peeled them away from her body.

Church was what it always was. Before the service, Pat smiled politely at her parents' friends and then went to sit with the rest of the young people's group, three rows back, behind the Sunday school children but in front of the grown-ups.

Eileen came and sat beside her at the end of the pew. The fingernails that had been vivid pink on the Saturday evening of chapel anniversary were now scrubbed Sunday clean. Eileen was turning in her seat, watching people come in at the back of the church.

'Wow.'

'What?'

'Look at him! He's delicious. Who is he?'

Pat turned her head and followed Eileen's stare. Charlie was standing at the back of the church, clutching a notice sheet and hymnbook. He scanned the room, settled his gaze on Pat for a second and smiled before slipping into one of the hard-backed seats behind the final row of swing-down chairs.

'Did you see him look at me?' Eileen was still twisted in her seat, straining to get a better look at the stranger. 'He looks like Davy Jones.'

'No. He doesn't.'

'He does. He's beautiful. I've always wanted an older man. How old do you think he is? Twenty? Twenty-five?'

'Eighteen.'

Eileen turned back towards Pat, who checked herself.

'Eighteen-ish, I mean. I didn't really get a proper look at him.' The lie came out so easily, reminding Pat how separate her two lives were becoming.

'No. Definitely older.' Eileen was salivating at the prospect of her older prey. 'How are we going to get talking to him?'

'I don't think you should talk to him.' Pat's tone was sullen.

'Why not?'

Why not indeed? 'Well, what about Ronnie? I thought you had a thing going with him.'

'He's just a kid.'

'He's older than you.'

'You know what I mean. That guy is dreamy.'

Eileen's further thoughts on Charlie's attractions were curtailed by the organ slowly grinding into life and sounding out the notes of the introit. The ladies, and it was predominantly ladies, of the choir stood and began to sing as the preacher was led to the pulpit by the steward on duty. It was an oddity of the start of the church service that had always confused Pat. It remained unclear to her why preachers were deemed to need accompanying on the way to the pulpit to commence worship. Was the pulpit considered particularly hard to find? Were preachers considered to be nervous types who might take fright and attempt escape if not carefully supervised?

These were the kinds of thoughts that increasingly filled Pat's head during services. Today though her thoughts were all leading in one direction. Charlie. Charlie here. What was Charlie doing here?

She got through the service, standing up, sitting down, singing, responding along with the rest of the congregation during intercessionary prayers, mumbling 'Amen' as appropriate, but not really paying attention, not particularly aware of the presence of the Almighty.

After the service, people filed slowly, chattily towards the hall for cups of tea and custard creams. From the front of the church, Pat could see Charlie, still in his seat at the back, but there were pews and pensioners between them. Too many dawdling bodies blocked the way for Pat to race up the aisle, pull him into a corner and demand to know what he was doing.

But Eileen was more determined. She grabbed Pat by the sleeve and pulled her into the aisle.

'What are you doing?'

'He might get away.'

As Eileen dragged her through the sluggish congregation, Pat kept her eyes fixed on Charlie. He was now leaning on a pillar a few feet away from his seat, watching the churchgoers file past him. Pat saw her father before Charlie did, and pushed hard into Eileen, urging her to move faster.

⋆ ⋆ ⋆

Stanley Bickersleigh approached the young man standing at the back of the church. He didn't look like the usual sort of visitor, holidaymakers who still considered chapel part of their unalterable weekly routine, even when getting away from it all at the seaside. He also didn't look like the usual sort of young people Stanley saw at church services. He looked more like the sort of young person Stanley had read about in the local paper, hanging around on the seafront, playing at the arcades, causing, Stanley suspected, some form of unspecified trouble and nuisance.

'Are you a visitor to the area?'

The young man turned his head in response to the question. 'Yeah.'

'Very good. Visiting from?'

'London.'

'Ah. Our great capital. And what brings you to North Yorkshire?'

The young man turned his full attention

182

towards Stanley for a moment. 'I'm working, just for the summer, before university.'

'Excellent. Really excellent to see a young person taking responsibility, learning the value of money.' Stanley extended his hand. 'I'm Stanley. Stanley Bickersleigh.'

'Bickersleigh?' The young man took Stanley's handshake.

'Yes. Why? Do you know people of that name?'

The young man hesitated. 'No. No. I don't think so.'

'Right. And you are?'

'Sorry. I'm Charlie. Charles.'

'Charles. Excellent. Excellent.' The conversation lulled, Stanley wishing that he'd left it to one of the women to greet the stranger. It had to be done, extending the welcome of Christian fellowship and all that, but still. Women were much better with the chit-chat. Looking around the church for inspiration he saw Pat and the Swintons' daughter heading towards them. 'Pat! Pat dear!'

He summoned her over, ignoring the horror in her face. Obviously, he wouldn't normally thrust his daughter at a strange young man, but the Swinton girl was there as well, and the chapel collection wasn't going to count itself.

'Pat, come and meet Charles. He's here over the summer before he goes to university.'

★   ★   ★

Pat's face didn't shift from the frozen expression she'd adopted to mask her panic. 'Really?'

183

Her father turned back towards Charlie. 'And this is Pat. She's my daughter. I'm sure you'll be happier talking to some younger people rather than an old duffer like me.'

Charlie made a vague gesture of his hand as if to imply that Stanley wasn't a duffer at all, but Mr Bickersleigh was already striding away. An important man with important things to be getting on with.

'And I'm Eileen.' Pat was shoved in the side as Eileen pushed herself towards Charlie. 'It's fantastic to have some new blood around here. Normally everyone's so boring.'

Eileen was talking too loud, trying to hold his attention.

'Right. Yeah.' He turned back towards Pat, a smile dancing across his familiar blue eyes. 'So are you at college or anything?'

Pat shook her head and played along. 'I just finished school. My mum and dad want me to go and do secretarial after the summer.'

'Right. And what do you want?'

'I'm not sure.'

'Well, I'm going to get a job and earn some money, so I can move away from this place.' Eileen pushed herself back into the conversation. 'Right, Charlie?'

He shrugged. 'I don't know. There's plenty to like here.'

Eileen was not easily discouraged. 'Well, I could show you around, and that, you know. I've lived here all my life.'

'What about you, Pat? Have you always lived around here?'

Pat nodded.

'So maybe you could show me round?'

'I'm not sure my parents would like that.'

Charlie paused. 'Well, maybe both of you then?'

Pat let the thought run through her head. That might actually work. 'Maybe.'

The church around them was emptying. Charlie looked around. 'Are we supposed to go somewhere?'

Eileen looped her arm through his. 'There's tea in the hall. I'll take you.'

Extricating his arm, Charlie smiled. 'Lead the way.'

Behind Eileen, Charlie leaned towards his lover and traced his hand down her back. She jumped away, glaring at him before looking behind them. There was no one there. She grabbed his hand and pulled it to her lips, planting a kiss on the end of his index finger, before dropping the hand away. It took only a second, and only Charlie would ever know anything of it.

In the hall, Eileen led them towards the group of teens leaning on the stage blocks piled up against one wall. The noise around them allowed Pat to whisper one question. 'What are you doing here?'

'I came to see you.'

'Why?'

Charlie didn't get a chance to answer because Eileen was busying herself introducing her trophy to the group. Pat heard bits and pieces as Eileen paraded him around the group. 'This is Charlie . . . '

'He's here for the summer . . . '

'I'm going to show him around.'

Charlie interrupted that one. 'And Pat.'

That wasn't the only interruption. Ronnie Mays butted in too. 'You might not have time to be showing him around, Eileen.'

Eileen's eyes lit up. 'Might I not?'

'No.'

'All right.' Eileen sat herself down next to Ronnie, her new toy, having served his purpose, discarded in favour of the old.

Charlie moved back towards Pat at the edge of the group.

'So why are you here?' She only dared lift her voice to a whisper.

'Well, we have to sneak around because of your parents.'

'And your boss.'

'Well, yes.'

'And your landlady.'

'Yes, but mainly your parents.'

She nodded.

'I just thought that if they met me here and I made a good impression then they might eventually let me take you out officially.'

Pat shook her head. 'I doubt it.'

'Why ever not? I'm charming.'

Pat giggled. 'Who told you that?'

'Well, Eileen likes me.'

'I think she's over it.'

They were interrupted again by Pat's mother. Lilian approached in a haze of perfume, masking the faint odour of something else, something unspoken underneath the floral scent.

186

'Pat, it's time to go.'

Pat dropped her eyes. 'Yes, Mother.'

Lilian stalked away with barely a glance at Charlie. Pat raised her head in an apologetic shrug and tried to psychically communicate her desperate wish to see him again as soon as was possible. Charlie nodded.

Pat scurried after her mother, out into the car park, where her father was already starting the engine on the family Morris Oxford. Pat climbed into the back seat and watched her mother remove her hat and gloves in the front of the car.

'Who was that young man?'

Pat hesitated for a second. 'I'm not sure. Dad introduced me to him.'

'Really?' Lilian only needed the single word to make her surprise clear.

'What's that?' Stanley's attention was on driving, but he glanced at his wife.

'The young man that Patience was talking to?'

Pat watched them from the back seat, her head flicking from left to right.

'Charles. Yes. He seems a good sort. Well spoken. Hardworking.' Stanley nodded to himself, confident, as always, of his own conclusions.

Pat smiled.

Stanley rapped his fingers on the steering wheel. 'I might have to go into work this afternoon.'

Lilian's lips pursed. 'On a Sunday?' Her hand rested on the Bible on her lap.

'Well, we're going to be tied up with stocktake this week. Need to get a head start.' He flicked his eyes towards the back seat in his mirror.

'You're coming to help with stocktake, aren't you?'

Pat nodded. There would be no snatched hour with Charlie after work tomorrow. She'd be stuck counting liniments and bandages and checking the numbers in her father's neat little columns. They would all be right anyway. They were always all right. None of Stanley's staff had the heart to tell him if they were wrong.

37

Louise was back in her mum's spare bedroom, using her mum's ancient desktop to check her email. There was never anything interesting, but it filled time and it gave her something to do that wasn't talking or thinking. She clicked through, deleting spam and messages telling her about all the things she might like to buy, based on things she'd bought before for Christmas or birthdays. Computer games, music, clothes — all of which screamed Kyle.

The machine pinged for a new message. Katy, Kyle's girlfriend, who'd promised her she'd send her some memories of Kyle. Louise stopped and pushed her chair away from the computer. Kyle was in there. New stories about Kyle just a click away. She leaned forward and clicked.

The message loaded on her screen. Louise closed her eyes. Maybe she shouldn't read it all at once. Maybe she should ration herself. That was ridiculous. Of course she was going to read it all now. Whatever Katy had to share with her, she was going to devour it, drink it in, soak in every last detail. She opened her eyes.

The message was two lines long.

Katy was sorry she hadn't kept in touch. She hoped Louise was well. She missed Kyle, but was looking forward to starting college soon. That was all. That was everything. Louise reached for the screen, scraping her fingers across the glass as if to claw something more out of the message. Then she keeled forward onto her hands and knees on the floor. The sobbing, when it came, shook her whole body, taking her over, unlacing her from the numbness that had been keeping her safe.

'Oh my God.'

Her mother rushed in, and hauled her onto the bed, wrapping her arms around Louise and rocking her like a baby. 'It's all right. It's all right.'

The words continued over and over, drumming their way into her mind. They weren't true. It wasn't all right. Katy had let go. Louise's mum had let go. Louise wasn't going to do the same. She pulled herself out of her mother's hold. She wasn't going to sit here crying over her loss. Kyle wasn't lost. Patrice could bring him back. She'd proved that already. All Louise needed to do was get to see her again. Seeing Patrice meant seeing Leo. It meant persuading Leo to persuade Patrice to talk to Kyle. That was all she had to do.

Her mother patted her on the shoulder. 'Come on, pet. I'll make a pot of tea. A proper pot.'

Louise shook her head.

Her mother fell silent for a second. 'Well, what then?'

'I don't want anything.'

'I want to do something.'

Louise shook her head. 'I've got to go.'

She left her mother standing in the doorway, cardigan pulled around her middle. Louise knew she'd be watching as she marched off down the road.

38

'Hello.'

Leo listened to his wife's voice at the other end of the line. He'd called her as soon as he got back to his hotel after the show, and hung up twice before she answered. He'd told himself that things would feel clearer in the morning. 'Hi.'

'Oh, hi.' She was curt. Maybe this was the wrong approach. Maybe he should have waited until he got home.

'Do you believe in mediums?'

'What?'

'Clairvoyants and ghosts and talking to the other side. Do you believe in all that stuff?'

'I don't know. Why?'

Leo didn't answer straight away.

'Look. I'm about to go to bed . . . ' He could hear the irritation in her voice. She sighed down the phone. 'Sorry. Why do you want to know?'

He could picture her, leaning on the island unit in the kitchen, handset wedged against her shoulder. 'What are you wearing?'

'Leo!'

'Not like that. I was just trying to picture you.'

'My dressing gown. I just had a bath.'

'You know the woman I'm doing this book with?'

'Yes.' He could hear the caution in her tone. She thought he was pursuing Patrice for all the

191

wrong reasons. He closed his eyes. He hadn't even told her that Patrice wasn't his long-lost mummy after all. There was a lot he hadn't told the woman he thought he told everything.

'Yeah. Well, I went to her show again.'

'I know. What about it?'

'Olly came through.'

'Don't.' The word was shouted down the phone.

'I'm just trying to tell you what happened.'

'Don't you dare.' His wife lowered her voice to a hiss. 'Don't you dare try to tell me that some charlatan told you they'd talked to my son.'

'Our son.'

'Who we don't even know is — '

'Marnie . . . ' Leo could hear the cajoling tone. This is what they did. He started to try to say something about Olly. She shut it down. He placated her, and nothing more was said. 'Marnie, Olly's dead.'

'I'm going to put the phone down.'

'Marnie, don't.'

'I'm not having this conversation.'

Normally this was where Leo gave up. This was when he let the silence fall. 'She knew things about how he died. I think it was real.'

'It's bollocks. We don't believe in this sort of crap.'

'A minute ago you said you didn't know.'

'Well, I know now.' He heard her take a gulp of something. 'Look, Leo. I understand that you're in pain. I understand that you want this woman to be something special. I value that feeling.'

Leo shuddered at his life reduced to a set of

therapy sound bites.

'It doesn't mean that what she's telling you is true though.' Another gulp. 'And I need you to hear me telling you that I don't want to hear this.'

Leo let his body weight drop onto the bed, and lay flat on his back staring up at the ceiling. 'Fine.'

'Good.' He didn't answer. Let her fill the silence if she wanted. 'So you'll be home tomorrow?'

'Afternoon.'

'And you know we've got a counselling session on Friday?'

'Yeah.'

'Okay then.' She paused just for a second. Leo's thoughts swam around his brain. He should tell her about the other stuff. About Patrice not being who he'd hoped she was. About why he'd gone looking in the first place. About the desperate hope that he could find some sort of family once again.

Marnie clicked her tongue against the roof of her mouth at the other end of the line. 'So I'll see you tomorrow then.'

And the line went dead. Leo was alone again. Did he believe that Patrice had actually been talking to Olly? In his head, he could rationalise the whole thing very easily, but his head wasn't in charge anymore. In his heart, he'd heard his son confirming what Leo thought he'd already accepted, and it had given him permission to grieve. It had given him permission to say out loud, 'My son is dead.'

193

The room phone rang. Leo hesitated. Patrice didn't know he was staying, although she might have guessed — she knew he'd been at the show. He picked up the handset.

'Mr Cousins?'

'Yeah.'

'There's a Miss Swift in reception for you.'

'Who?'

He heard a mumbled conversation at the other end of the line. 'Louise Swift. She says she's a friend.'

'Right.' Louise? He could talk to Louise. Louise wouldn't doubt him or tell him not to lose hope. Louise would let what was true be true. 'Yeah. You can send her up.'

He hung up the phone. He should have gone down. Of course he should have gone down. Going to the pub was one thing. The theatre show was another. Entertaining her in his hotel room was something different. The knock came.

She looked as though she'd made a bit of an effort. The saggy leggings that she seemed to live in had been replaced with tight jeans and a low-cut top. She pulled a bottle of cheap-looking red wine from her bag. 'Them minibars cost stupid money, don't they?'

He took the wine and collected the two glasses from the bathroom.

She perched on the edge of the bed. 'You haven't asked why I'm here.'

Leo stretched out beside her. 'So why are you here?'

'Wanted to see you.'

'Why?'

194

'Because you understand. Nobody else under-stands.'

Leo sipped the wine. It was truly terrible, but he didn't care. He took a bigger gulp. 'Marnie doesn't understand.'

'Why not?'

'She won't accept that he's gone.'

'But if you tell her about last night?'

Leo shook his head. 'Already tried.'

'You said you were doing marriage counsel-ling?'

Leo nodded.

'Is it helping?'

'Not really.'

She took a sip of wine. 'So do you think it's over?'

'I can't work it out.'

She bit her bottom lip. 'I could help you decide.'

He watched her as she stood up and put her glass down on the bedside cabinet. Then she walked across the room, pulled off her shoes and climbed onto the bed. She crawled towards him, spreading her knees to straddle his legs. Eventually they were nose to nose. She was going to kiss him. Then her hand would go to his belt and start to remove his trousers. Then he would slide a hand under her top, and pull it over her head. And she would lean back and unclip her bra while he pulled his own shirt off, before wriggling out of his jeans and helping her do the same. Then he'd roll her over, so she was beneath him, and she'd wrap her legs around his torso. And they wouldn't speak. Somehow he knew that. They'd kiss, and they'd each bury their face in the other's neck, and they'd close their eyes and just let whatever was going to happen happen.

There was a moment, right now, where he could laugh, shake his head, and they could pretend it had all been a daft joke — just two friends mucking around. He didn't really think he fancied her. He was sure she wouldn't normally be attracted to him. But she understood. She understood the need to share something that wasn't sympathy or understanding or cloying compassion. Leo tilted his head slightly to one side, leaned towards her lips, and accepted the oblivion.

39

Patrice sat opposite Leo across a table in the hotel restaurant. She'd had Barney ask the manager if they could sit in there once the lunchtime bustle had died down. After their last meeting she thought it would be better if he didn't come to her room anymore. She'd had time to think now. Nice calm thoughts. Whoever Leo was she'd made a decision nearly fifty years ago, and she'd known there was no turning back. Nothing had changed.

'About what you said last week . . . ' She tried to keep her voice light, but she could hear the edge in it.

He didn't look up, keeping his eyes fixed on the notes in front of him. 'Apparently I was mistaken.'

'I'm sorry.'

'It's not your fault.' He clicked the button on his sound recorder. 'We should get on.'

Patrice felt a flutter of disappointment and squashed it away into her gut. Patience could weep and wail inside Patrice's head all she liked. She wasn't in control yet. 'So what's the subject for today?'

'I wanted to focus a bit more on your work.' He cleared his throat. 'On your gift.'

She nodded. She could talk about that. It was a story she'd learned by heart.

'So your grandmother identified this gift, and

now you're a huge success doing big shows and private readings. We need to talk about the journey from there to here.'

Patrice let her habitual warm smile settle on her face. 'What sort of things, pet?'

'Well, how did you start doing readings for people?'

Patrice folded her hands on her lap. 'Well, I was still very young. My grandmother started taking me to Spiritualist Church meetings. I didn't really understand what was going on but I think she wanted me to see my gift as something quite normal; something that could be useful and something that other people experienced as well.' She paused. 'I do believe, you know, that we all have the ability to communicate with the other side. It's like anything — playing the piano, or speaking a foreign language — some people have a natural affinity for it and others have to work harder, but we're all capable of learning if we're open to the experience.'

She stopped. What had she been talking about? She glanced around the room. The hotel restaurant. Leo sitting across the table with his notepad and infernal recorder. Everything was as it should be. She'd simply lost her train of thought. That was normal. That could happen to anyone. It was getting harder to tell, though, what was a normal everyday instance of some detail slipping her mind, and what was Patience stripping away Patrice and taking back the body and mind that were rightfully hers. She chuckled. 'I'm sorry. I got off track.'

Leo shrugged. Patrice peered at him. He was

198

quiet today. She'd put that down to the fallout from their conversation, but maybe there was something else. 'Are you all right?'

'What?'

'You seem a bit preoccupied.'

He froze in front of her for a second. 'Olly.'

'Olly?' Of course. 'Your son.'

He nodded. 'Him coming through last night. It was unexpected.'

Patrice could have kicked herself in the shin. What had Georgios spent all those years teaching her? The punters are never interested in you. They think they're the star. They think they're the main character. She'd cast Leo as a supporting player in her own struggle against the coming tidal wave of memory and loss, but he didn't know that. He was living his own story. He was just another punter at the end of the day. 'It can be a very emotional experience, but I got a great sense of contentment from him. He was definitely at peace.'

Leo coughed. 'I don't think he was ever at peace. He was restless, you know, right from when he was a toddler. He never kept still. You'd tell him to get a toy from the box and five minutes later the whole box would be strewn across the floor. He'd have played with everything for thirty seconds and then moved on. He was always moving on. He was in New Zealand when he died.'

Well, a Google news search had told her that. Patrice nodded sympathetically. 'I know. He sounds like a wonderful young man.' She wanted to ask more — what was Olly like? She knew he was nineteen when he died — just a year older than Charlie when she'd lost him. Had he looked like Charlie? The pictures on the news reports had been from his trip and had shown a tanned young man half-hidden under baseball cap and sunglasses. Patience was screaming inside her head to know more, but Patrice knew she couldn't ask. She wouldn't ask. Firstly, she was supposed to have spoken to him, and secondly she couldn't be too curious. She wasn't his nan. She'd been definite about that.

Leo rubbed the back of his thumb along his cheekbone, catching a stray tear that had slipped from his eye. 'I was kind of a sceptic when we met, you know?'

Patrice laughed. 'I'm a sceptic myself. I can't stand some of the charlatans who prey on people in this business.' A bell rang in her head. That was the story. 'That was how I got started doing readings.'

Leo screwed his eyes tight shut and then opened them again. 'Yes. How you got started.' He picked his pen up from the table and tapped the end against his pad. 'Go on.'

'Well, I was at the Spiritualist Church with my grandmother. I was thirteen, I think. Thereabouts anyway. I'd been going with her for years and sometimes when there were open meetings I would share visions I'd had, but I'd never been up at the front or anything like that. Anyway, at this service the speaker was quite a well-known clairvoyant at that time. He'd come from Leeds or Manchester. It was quite a coup to have him come speak at our little meeting above the library. And there was a lady at our church, who'd lost her son. She came every week hoping for a message, and this man up on the stage claimed to have her son there, and I remember thinking that was odd because I couldn't see anyone, and normally when spirits came through I'd be able to see them standing there next to the speaker. But I thought, what do I know? He was the famous medium after all. And he starts talking about this woman's son, and I realise that there's a young man I don't know sitting next to me. And I don't remember him coming in, but partway through the man on the stage talking, this lad leans towards me and whispers, 'Why is he making all this up?' Well, I don't know who the lad is, but when I turn back to answer he's not there, and I look over to where this poor grieving mother is, and he's sitting right next to her. That's when I realise. He's her son. The man on the stage is just making stuff up and she's lapping it up, but he's not actually talking to her son. I was . . . ' Patrice paused, and let her voice break slightly. 'I was shocked. I'd been going to those meetings for years and I thought that everyone was there for the same reasons, and then this man comes in who's playing the great I Am and telling whatever story he fancies.'

'So what did you do?'

Patrice shook her head. She always did at this point. Her character here was unassuming, not seeking praise or fortune. She'd played this scene a hundred times at different meetings, with different interviewers, and the telling had barely changed since the very first time, sitting in

Georgios' office at the bowling alley where they'd spent a whole day working out who Patrice Leigh should be. 'I'm ashamed. At first I didn't do anything . . . ' That was important. They were building a human being, not a Hollywood movie. Flaws were important; flaws made you believable. 'I could see the lad sat next to his mam, desperately wanting a real conversation, but I didn't say anything. I came so close to letting both of them down.' She wished, for a second, that she'd ordered tea. If she had, she'd pick up the cup now and take a tiny sip, to let Leo see the effort she was making to compose herself. 'The thing that tipped me over was the way he finished, the great medium from Leeds. He suddenly announced that he'd lost the connection, right in the middle of the conversation, and then he looked around the room, at all the people who'd been coming to those meetings for months and years, at that poor mother's friends, and said that he was sensing a lot of negative energy in the room. And then he said that her son had sensed it too, and that feeling that people weren't open to him coming through was why he'd disappeared. And then he told her that the only chance of talking to her son again was if she came for a private reading.' Patrice bit her bottom lip. 'It was outrageous. The woman's son was sitting right beside her. The man on the stage could no more have communicated with him than I can talk to aliens. He was just out to make money. He was a con artist, pure and simple. And that was when I said something. I stood up, right in front of everyone, and I pointed at that man on the stage and I shouted, '*He's lying!*' '

Patrice smiled at the image of a memory in her head. It was a nice picture — the pubescent girl challenging the great successful man on the stage. It had echoes of the emperor's new clothes to it. Georgios had always known how to spin a tale. She continued with her story. 'He went bright purple in the face; he was practically spluttering with fury at this little girl challenging him. I nearly sat straight back down again, but my grandmother was beside me, and I remember feeling her hand on my back, and she just whispered, 'Go on, Pat.'

Patrice swallowed back the pretence of a tear. 'So I walked right over to that woman in the front row and I told her exactly what I could see. I described the boy, and what he was wearing, and then I just repeated back to her what he'd told me, and by the end she was crying, and the congregation were all gathered round her holding her hands and patting her on the shoulder, and then her son, eventually, did drift away, but he waited until she'd cried all her tears and she was ready to let him move on. It was beautiful.'

'What happened to the great medium from Leeds?'

Patrice shook her head. 'I don't remember seeing him afterwards. I think he must have skulked back home. He kept working though. I remember seeing his name from time to time in different places.' She waved a hand. 'He died years ago. Of course.'

'And you've not heard from him since?'

She laughed. 'Oddly no. I don't think I was his favourite person.'

She watched as Leo shifted in his seat. 'So how do you reconcile that with the amount you charge for readings now?'

Patrice knew she was expected to bristle, but she'd been doing this for too long. 'Well, firstly I have a genuine gift. You know that.'

He didn't look up from his notes.

'And the reality is that I'm inundated with requests for help from people who've lost loved ones. If I didn't charge I simply wouldn't be able to spend the amount of time that I, do putting people back in touch with those they think they've lost.' She allowed a frown to settle briefly on her face. 'It does pain me though, how many people I'm not able to reach, both here and on the other side.'

Leo clicked his pen off and put his pad down on the table. 'It would be really helpful if I could sit in on a reading.'

Patrice frowned. Normally her private readings were just that: private. People were paying a premium to feel like they were getting one to one attention. And Georgios had always been very clear — this whole thing went wrong when she lost control of it. One-to-one in a room, she could keep control — even if she missed the mark she could pull it back, so that the person left so confused that they believed they themselves were misremembering the hair colour of their long-lost dad. On stage, she was in charge. She picked who she talked to. She decided how far the roaming microphones were allowed to roam. Doing a one-to-one with Leo in the room would upset the balance.

'I've found someone who's happy to have me sit in. Her name's Louise. I told you about her before, and you talked to her last night.'

Patrice needed to focus on the night before. She knew she'd done Leo's son, and then — yes — she'd done his friend's son. The details were hazy, but Barney would have it written down.

'To be honest, she's a bit desperate.'

'I thought you were asking because it would be useful for the book.'

Leo hesitated. That was interesting. Why would he hesitate? If he was asking for a friend, there was nothing wrong with that. A bit unprofessional maybe, but not embarrassingly so. Not just a friend then? Patrice lay the pieces of Leo out in her mind. Wearing a wedding ring. Lost his son. More than just friends with a mother who'd lost hers. She gathered the pieces together and filed them away.

'Well, it would be great for the book . . . '

Patrice held her hand up. 'It's fine. I'll do it. Arrange a time with Barney and your friend.'

She left him in the restaurant sorting out his notes, and went back to her room. Today was a good day. Today she felt like she could be Patrice for ever.

40

1967

Monday morning came around quickly. It was a normal sort of morning in the fortune-telling booth. Afternoons were always busier than mornings, but the school holidays were underway now and the season was picking up. Most of the customers were women, which was normal. She tended to get a few lads later in the afternoon, after they'd had a couple of beers, but Pat was getting more and more adept at dealing with them.

A lone woman peered her head through curtain.

'Come in. Come in.' Pat smiled at the customer. 'You have come to seek truths from beyond the veil?'

The woman looked uncertain.

Pat sighed. 'You've come to have your fortune done?'

The woman nodded.

'Then come. Sit.' Pat gestured towards the plastic chair at the customer side of the table. She rattled through her normal spiel about taking a moment to commune with the spirits beyond the veil, extracted the payment from her customer, and drew back the cloth that covered the crystal ball.

She peered, as she always did, into the ball, having taken a good look at her customer while she was occupied taking her seat and fumbling with her money. Pat always watched closely when they got their money out. If you were lucky, you would sometimes get a glimpse of a name on an envelope or a photo stuffed inside a wallet or purse. Nothing this time. The customer was young, not that much older than Pat probably, but clothes made for a woman ten or twenty years older. Pat pictured Hester's going out clothes as she looked again at her customer. A young girl in a respectable woman's clothes. A wedding ring, plain, probably not expensive, but still shiny. A newlywed perhaps? Pat smiled. Newlyweds were easy.

She swept her hand over the crystal ball. 'The mists are clearing. I see great change in your life. I see love.'

The woman nodded ever so slightly.

'But this change has already come, I think?'

Another nod.

Pat swept her hand across the ball again. 'I must venture deeper into the mists, to see what is yet to come.'

She let the silence hang for a moment, and glanced back at her customer. 'I see new life.'

The woman gulped.

Pat continued. 'A baby, perhaps?'

The woman stood hurriedly and pushed her chair away from the table. 'How did you know?'

Pat kept her face composed. 'I see what I see. This is the vision that came to me.'

The woman looked suspicious. 'It's just what you saw in that thing.' She pointed at the ball on the table.

'Of course.'

'Right.' The woman sat back down. 'So you don't know?'

'Nothing is definite in these visions. There is always some uncertainty,' Pat improvised.

'So I might not be?'

Pat felt as though the ground beneath her was shifting unexpectedly. Newlyweds were easy. You told them how in love they were, and promised them babies. The customer wasn't following the script.

'Might not be?'

'Having a baby.'

'Maybe not.'

And then she burst into tears. Pat watched her cry for a moment, uncertain what to do next. Mr Stefanini didn't like her to spend too long with each customer. *Get 'em in, get 'em told and get 'em out.* That was his philosophy, but this woman didn't look like she'd be ready to go anywhere particularly soon.

'Sometimes I see visions of things that are a long way off. It's probably one of those.'

The woman's sobs intensified. 'It's not though,' she spluttered. 'I'm late.' She looked up at Pat. 'You understand?'

Late? Yes. She understood. At the back of her mind, the very first whisperings of the beginnings of an unformed thought started to vie for her attention. She ignored them, and leaned forward to pat the hand of the woman in front of her. 'Well, I'm sure your husband will be really pleased.'

'What? It's not . . . ' The woman looked up at

Pat and then down at the band of gold on her third finger. 'Husband? Yeah. Probably.'

The mention of her husband seemed to compose the woman. She wiped her eyes on a handkerchief produced from her neat jacket pocket. 'Well, things to do. I've kept you too long.'

She excused herself as if from an unwanted conversation in the baker's shop, and walked, slightly unsteadily on her heeled court shoes, out of the booth.

'Well, you handled that right well, love.' Mr Stefanini appeared through the curtain, evidently having been eavesdropping for some time.

'Thank you.'

He lowered himself onto the plastic chair, looking for all the world like a friendly giant visiting an infant class.

'You've done right well down here all round.'

Pat nodded but didn't speak. With Mr Stefanini you knew that when he had something to deal with you were best off sitting quiet and waiting for him to say his piece.

'Takings are up, and you know I like it when takings are up. You've got me starting to fancy that that Nadia had her hand in the till for a lot longer that I knew, which I'm not best pleased about.'

Pat could imagine, and she knew it was true. Hester said everyone in the cash office knew about it.

'And the punters seem to like you.'

Pat nodded again. There hadn't been any real problem customers, apart from the pervert that

Hester had chased away, and Pat didn't think he was very likely to complain.

'So that got me to thinking. The girl we had before Nadia used to do these parties. Clairvoyant parties. Up in the café after closing. Get a whole group in and do a whole evening of fortunes and that. Bit of food. Bit of booze. Charge 'em per head.'

'Right.'

'So what do you think? There'd be a bit extra in your pay packet for doing it.'

'All right.'

'Grand. The first one's Wednesday. Eight o'clock, so you'll need to be there in all your garb by half past seven.' He stood up slowly from the too small chair and made his way out of the booth. 'If it goes well, I might even see about a new costume for you, girl.'

★   ★   ★

The weather turned suddenly around lunchtime, covering the foreshore in a deluge of heavy grey rain that extended from a sharp shower into an interminable downpour. With the seafront cleared of holidaymakers, Mr Stefanini sent Mrs Oakley down to tell Pat she could knock off. She put the closed sign up and changed out of her costume in the booth, leaving her gypsy dress and shawl hanging from the peg at the back.

She looked at the time. Half past two. Charlie would already be out and about, probably trying to persuade shopkeepers to put up posters for the band's gigs in their windows. If she went straight to her father's pharmacy, though, she might be able to sneak away early enough to surprise Charlie later.

She walked up the steps, pausing halfway to catch her breath and switch her umbrella into the other hand. Then she made her way through town to her father's shop. It was a proper chemist's shop with a long counter where her father would stand dispensing cures and wisdom to the local community. Behind his counter he was somebody. Recently he'd started adding more and more displays where the customers could help themselves to shampoos and perfumed soaps. It was the modern way, he said. A lot of the older ladies still came up to the counter every time though.

Pat placed her hand on the door. She could hear her father laughing inside. She waited for a moment, listening to the sound. She could remember him laughing with her mother when she was a very little girl. Pat pushed the door, setting the bell ringing. When she walked through she was surprised to see an empty shop, her father alone at the counter. He looked up from his ledger at the sound of the bell.

'Pat?'

'Mr Stefanini said I could go home, because of the weather.' She leaned against the open door and shook her sodden umbrella outside as she spoke.

'Right. Well, you can head off home then.'

'I thought you wanted help with the stocktake.'

'Well, not until after closing.'

211

Pat let the door shut. 'Why not? I can start in the back.'

She started to walk towards the open end of the counter.

'No.' The vehemence of her father's tone surprised her and she stopped dead still in the middle of the shop.

'What did you say?' The voice came from the store room.

'Nothing.' Stanley didn't look around as he replied. 'Look, love, you've been at work all morning. Why don't you go home, like Mr Stefanini said?'

'Who's in the back?'

'Sandra.' Sandra was one of her father's shop girls. She was only twenty-two but she'd worked at Bickersleigh's since she'd left school.

Pat was still confused. 'I could go and help her.'

'No.'

There was sound of someone moving around in the stockroom. Pat saw her father's cheeks start to colour and his fingers were tensed around his fountain pen. A man appeared through the curtain, which separated the shop from the back room. He smiled uncertainly at Pat.

'Anthony, this is Pat. My daughter.'

The man nodded.

'This is Anthony,' Stanley continued, starting to find his rhythm. 'Anthony was just helping me sort out a problem with the plumbing in the back kitchen, weren't you?'

Anthony didn't reply. Stanley carried on.

212

'Anthony rents the flat upstairs, don't you?'

This time the man nodded.

'He quite often helps out around the place.'

Pat wasn't sure what to say. She looked at the stranger. He was wearing a shirt and pressed trousers. His blond hair was Brylcreemed back. He looked familiar, but she couldn't think where from.

Stanley clapped his hands. 'Right. Well, you'd better be off then, Anthony. I can't keep you doing chores around here all day.' He laughed heartily and slapped the younger man on the back. The younger man remained rigid, not responding to Pat's father's buoyant tone.

He reached back behind the curtain and fetched out a long coat and hat. 'I'll be going then.'

He walked across the shop, without a glance at Stanley. He pulled the door and paused, with one foot holding it open, to put on his coat and hat. As he walked out, Pat saw him in profile and a flash of déjà vu hit. It was the same profile she'd seen walking away from her father once before. The man in the chapel car park. The man who, apparently, lived upstairs.

41

'Madam! Madam!'

Patrice opened an eye expecting to see her father's shop. What had happened? Had she slipped on something? Had she hit her head?

'Madam! Are you all right?' The voice again. It was a woman, so not her father, not the Brylcreemed man. One of the shop girls maybe. What on earth were their names?

She moved her head to focus on the owner of the voice. A stab of pain went through her temple.

'You're bleeding.'

Well, that explained the pain. It didn't really help with the where or the who. She went back to basics. She was lying on the floor, one shoulder wedged against a wall, her feet pressing against something else, a table leg maybe? There was carpet against her face and hands. Not her father's shop then. The floor there was cold and slick. She looked at the hand that was resting in front of her face. It was tanned and manicured and old. It was an old woman's hand.

'Madam, I'm going to get someone to help.'

'No.' That was her own voice. She didn't want help. Whatever was going on, she knew she needed to manage it for herself.

'You've hit your head. You need someone.' She heard footsteps moving away from her and then voices in the distance.

She focused again on the hand on the carpet. The carpet was familiar. She closed her eyes. Of course. The hotel. She was in her hotel room. She must have fallen and hit her head, and now she'd come round. That was all. Nothing to be alarmed about.

She pressed her hand into the floor and pushed herself up to sitting. Apart from the pain in her head, everything else seemed fine. A bit sore perhaps but nothing broken.

'They've called an ambulance.'

Patrice turned her head properly towards the voice. It was a young woman in a cleaner's uniform. 'I'm fine.'

The girl's face was pale.

Patrice tried to smile as best she could. 'I'm sorry if I gave you a fright.'

'Not at all. My nan has falls all the time. It's normal at your age.'

The smile evaporated. 'I really don't think there's any need for an ambulance.'

'Better to be safe than sorry.'

'At my great age?'

The girl shrugged.

Patrice touched a fingertip against her temple. Another spike of pain made her gasp. The finger came away sticky rather than wet. 'I think it's stopped bleeding actually.'

The girl looked uncertain. 'The manager's called them now.'

'Very well. There's no need for you to wait around though.'

'He said I had to stay with you.'

'That's really not necessary.'

She shrugged again. 'Manager said.'

'But I'm fine.'

'You're still sat on the floor.'

There didn't seem to be any way to get rid of her bodyguard short of leaping up and proving her good health, so Patrice had no choice but to attempt just that. She pulled herself to standing. 'See.'

The girl folded her arms but didn't budge.

A second later the first wave of nausea hit. And then the second. The third crashed full-force into Patrice's body and brought her breakfast rushing up. She staggered to the bathroom and bent over the toilet bowl slightly too late, sending vomit spilling over the tiled floor.

The girl sighed. Presumably she'd be the one who had to clear up. 'See. You're concussed. Vomming up. You get that with concussion.'

Patrice slid herself towards the bathroom door, away from the stink and the mess. From there she could see the patch of blood on the carpet where she'd fallen. She took a second just to be quiet. A second was all she got. Somewhere along the hall the lift pinged and there were footsteps and voices and people. An Indian woman in a dark green jumpsuit pushed the cleaner out of the way and squatted down in front of Patrice. She let the questions come. Yes, she knew her name, and what day it was, and where she was, but yes, she had blacked out and thrown up, and she did feel a little dizzy. She let the paramedic decide that she needed to be taken to hospital just in case. As they were

216

popping her into a wheelchair, Barney arrived, and she let him insist on cancelling the evening's show. It was restful, in a way, to simply let things happen around her.

They popped her in the ambulance and then, once they'd got her to the hospital, they popped her onto a bed, and a nurse just popped in to check her blood pressure and clean the cut on her temple. When the doctor came, Patrice realised her mistake.

'I'm Mai. I'm a doctor.'

Patrice nodded, focusing her attention on the young woman. East Asian descent, an accent but very good English. Hong Kong maybe?

'I will be your doctor today.'

'You said.'

The girl smiled. 'I'm Mai. I'm your doctor.'

That was three reassurances that she was a doctor in less than a minute. The girl was young. Newly qualified, Patrice decided, and not yet confident in her own position. That lack of confidence was translating into a lack of confidence from the patients, which was reinforcing the girl's own doubts. *Cross my palm with silver, dearie,* Patrice thought. *Gypsy Patience could tell your fortune in a second.* She'd tell her she foresaw great career success and huge respect from her peers. The girl would believe it, and because she believed it, it might even end up being true. Life was easier for Gypsy Patience.

Patrice realised she'd stopped paying attention. The girl was still talking. 'So you'll need to wait here till they're ready to take you for the scan.'

217

'What scan?'

The girl tipped her head sympathetically to one side. 'Have you suffered with short-term memory problems before?'

Well, how would she know? wondered Patrice. The little slips in time, the moments where she wasn't quite where she expected to be, the days when she felt like Patience was taking over more and more. She could call those short-term memory problems, she supposed. But she wouldn't today. She fixed the girl in her gaze. 'I don't have memory problems now, dear. I just wasn't paying attention to your wittering on. I assumed you'd be discharging me.'

She swung her legs off the bed and stood up, not daring to do it as tentatively as she normally did these days, in case the insufferable doctor-child took it as some further sign of infirmity. Patrice knew full well what was going to happen. There were going to be tests. They would show that Patrice was slowly but unstoppably slipping away. And after that there would be care plans, and residential homes, and a slow demise into something that Patrice had viewed with building dread since she first realised it was coming, but increasingly saw as a comfortable slide into the abyss. That was a silly thought. She had no way of knowing what it would be like. Whatever she told her clients, she had always known that people were alive and then they were dead. It was absolutely binary. Perhaps all Patrice was about to do was prove that she'd been wrong all this time. She was destined to live in a world halfway in between.

She was going to become her own ghost.

She picked her clothes up from the chair beside the bed. 'Where might I put these back on?'

The girl looked confused. 'You need to stay in your gown for the scan.'

Patrice rolled her eyes. 'I don't need a scan. I am perfectly all right. Now, are you going to leave me to get dressed?'

'I'm your doctor . . . '

Oh, thought Patrice, *that old chestnut*.

'I'm your doctor and I have to advise you that a CT scan is potentially life-saving for someone of your age.'

'Of my age?'

The girl nodded enthusiastically.

Patrice mentally revised her Gypsy Patience fortune for the girl. Now she would fail horribly at work and face certain financial ruin and the loss of her family's respect. 'Life-saving how?'

'There could be a clot or something else going on in your brain.'

Patrice shuddered. She had no wish to find out what was going on in her brain. She imagined the scan picture showing a tiny Patience crawling her way through the grey matter of Patrice's mind, quietly rewiring her synapses to erase the person she'd so carefully created and chosen to become.

'That won't be necessary.'

'But I have to advise . . . as your doctor . . . '

'And you have advised, and I've heard your advice and I'm telling you that I do not want to be scanned or prodded or observed anymore.'

The doctor was still hesitant. Patrice tried again. 'Is that clear?'

It was one of her favourite phrases. The answer was invariably yes, and by nodding, the listener inadvertently gave their approval to whatever Patrice was clearly telling them.

It worked. The girl nodded.

Patrice relaxed slightly. 'Marvellous. Now how might I get discharged from this place?'

42

From bed with another woman to the marriage counsellor's office in less than thirty-six hours. Leo's self-image reeled, unable to fix on a favoured identity. Unable to work out where he was supposed to be.

The counsellor consulted her notes and then rested her hands on her lap. 'Let's start with you, Marianne. How have things been since our last session?'

Leo waited for the usual litany of complaints and blame. He could script their counselling sessions in advance. He could predict who would score a point where, and he could predict that Marnie would invariably win.

'Well, Leo has been away a lot for work.'

One point to Marnie, but at least she believed that he was only working when he was away from home.

'But I think that's been good in some ways. It's given us both some space. I've had time to think.'

Marnie's tone was calmer, more conciliatory than he'd heard for a long time. His heart lifted and fell. Even if they could find their way back to each other, there would still be last night. He'd never cheated on Marnie, not once in over twenty-five years of marriage. Technically it was longer than that. He'd been committed heart and soul to his wife long before they even started dating. In nearly thirty years, he'd been faithful to Marianne. Until last night.

His wife shuffled her seat around so that she was facing her husband. 'I know I should probably be saying this privately at home, but you've been away so much, and I couldn't have another session of going through the motions and not really talking about us. And then you said what you said about Olly and that woman and . . . ' Her gaze was fixed on a spot on the wall somewhere behind Leo's head. 'I keep remembering when we first got together. We had so much fun. I felt like we could do anything together.'

Leo felt himself nodding. That was exactly how things had felt. Everything about Marnie has screamed of opportunity and potential, and in her slipstream he'd soaked up a little bit of the same.

'I'm not sure when it stopped being like that,' his wife continued. 'I've told myself it was when Olly went, but I don't even know.'

She turned her gaze to his face, and swallowed hard. 'But it has changed, and I don't think any of this is going to change it back. And with Olly and what that women said, and you just believed her . . . ' She was almost weeping, but not quite. 'I think we both know it's not working. We're too far apart.'

Leo closed his eyes. It was a pointless gesture. The oncoming train was going to hit him head-on whether he watched it bearing down or not.

'I think we should separate.'

Leo didn't reply. He didn't nod or shake his head. Whatever words he ought to be offering were lost to him. This was it. Olly was gone. His parents were gone. His birth mum wasn't out there waiting to scoop him up. And now Marnie was gone too. The last tether holding him in the world was cut.

The counsellor cleared her throat. 'That's quite a big statement, Marnie. Do you want to tell us a bit more about why you're feeling that way?'

He heard her shuffling her chair back to its original position. 'Not really.'

'Okay. And, Leo, do you want to respond?'

As he always had, he took his lead from Marianne, always one step ahead of him, one step more prepared for anything. 'Not really.'

'Maybe we should talk about the practicalities?' Marnie's tone had changed to something cooler and brisker. 'I'd like to stay in the house, but I'm happy to buy Leo out of his share.' She pulled a handful of papers out of her handbag. 'I can get valuations if you want, or we can just agree whatever seems fair. I'm happy for you to take whatever furniture you want, and you can keep your car obviously.' She paused, tongue stuck out to one side, as it always was when she concentrated on trying to remember what she needed to do. 'I think we should tell Grace together. I know she's all grown up now but it'll still be a shock, so I thought maybe we should go and see her. We could take her out for lunch, do it somewhere neutral.'

Leo nodded. It sounded like the whole thing

223

was very much in hand. Marnie could be relied upon to think of everything, and she'd decided to cut him adrift. 'Where will I live?'

She paused. 'I hadn't really thought. Anywhere you like, I suppose.'

A knot of anger tightened in Leo's stomach. 'What if I want to stay in the house?'

She looked surprised. 'You're hardly ever there.'

'I am.'

She raised one eyebrow. 'What colour are the walls in the spare bedroom?'

'Blue.'

'They're Sunshine Glow. I painted them three months ago.'

So that was that. Leo was a terrible husband who didn't notice what was going on in his own home. What else might he not have noticed? 'Is there someone else?'

She paused.

That was all he needed. Marnie was ahead of him, just like she always was. The knot of anger formed into a burning red ball that rose through his body. 'Well, I fucked somebody else too.'

For once Leo was going to win. He might have lost in every conversation they'd ever had. He might have lived through thirty years of knowing that he was never going to be good enough for the woman he'd fallen in love with. She might have won every tiny contest of their marriage, but now he was going to win the divorce.

The colour ran out of her cheeks. Her chin trembled. He saw her fingers tighten around the arm of the chair. She sniffed the air in through her nose and stopped any duplicitous tears from falling from her eyes. 'No, Leo. There's nobody else.'

43

She checked her reflection in the mirror. She was looking older. Professionally that was no bad thing. Georgios had known. People really didn't trust pretty. Every line on Patrice's face made her act seem less of an act and more like a kindly sharing of her gift. But it wasn't just about the professional anymore. She could imagine how Georgios would react to that. Everything was about the professional, he would have told her. This wasn't a job that she could pack up and leave at half past five. What she did wasn't about what she did at all; it was about who she was. Being Patrice Leigh was a vocation. Whatever made her more convincing in the role was for the good.

She flicked through the notes in front of her, jotted, as always, on thin tracing paper. That had been Georgios' idea, like so many things. She'd got some details from the local paper; some bits she'd picked up from chatting, as casually as possible of course, to Leo. And then she'd had Barney call the boy's old school, pretending to be a journalist writing about the 'human cost of knife culture'. When the Data Protection Act had first come into force, Patrice had been nervous about that sort of research, but she needn't have been. Someone would always talk. It was just what people did.

There was a knock at the main door to the suite. 'One minute.'

She was as prepared as she needed to be. She scooped up her notes, dropped them into the toilet bowl and held down the flush. She could have just stuffed them in a pocket or bag, but that was lazy, and shoddiness cost careers. That was what Georgios would have told her.

She opened the door and let Barney, Leo and the Louise woman in. Patrice let Barney fuss with teas and coffees while she watched the client. Young to have had a seventeen-year-old son. Slim. Potentially pretty in a poor man's Kate Moss, council estate sort of a way. The woman sat with her arms wrapped across her body, and then held the cup of tea Barney offered her tightly in front of her like a shield. She was uncomfortable. That was good. A relaxed client was nobody's friend.

'Thank you, Barney. That will be all.'

Her manager hesitated. 'Are you sure, Miss Leigh?' Since her trip to A&E, he'd been watching her like a hawk.

'Quite sure.'

He nodded and slid out of the room, closing the door behind him with a barely perceptible click, leaving Patrice alone with Louise and Leo — her client and her audience. Show time.

'Thank you for seeing me, Miss Leigh.' The woman's voice was quiet. 'I was so relieved when Kyle came through to you. I couldn't hear him before. I tried.' Then her voice broke completely. 'I really tried. You have to tell him that. Tell him I was trying to hear him. I sat for hours in his room with all his things and his clothes. Tell him that, won't you?'

Patrice paused. Some clients were too easy. You spent all that time and effort making sure you had things clear, making sure you weren't going to get slipped up, and then they walked in and did half your job for you. She leaned towards Louise and reached out a hand to her forearm. 'It's all right, dear. In the spirit world, it's not like here. There's no anger, no bitterness. Your boy has just been waiting quite calmly for you to be ready to hear him.' *Don't be too kind,* she reminded herself. *You need to keep her on the hook.* 'It's not your fault you weren't ready. I'm sure he knows that really.' That 'really' at the end might have been too much, she thought. Louise wasn't actually the person she needed to get on side here, was she? This was a performance for Leo's point of view. This was all about the book. This weeping girl was just a working example.

'Is Kyle here now?'

Patrice nodded. 'I can feel him. He's very close by.' She held up a hand to discourage further questions. 'Just give me a moment while he comes through more fully.' She turned her gaze slightly to the left of Louise's seat. 'There we go. Hello again, Kyle.'

Louise's head flicked towards the space Patrice was apparently engrossed by. 'He's right here.'

Patrice nodded. 'He's telling me about what happened to him.'

She heard Louise gasp.

'He's showing me a top, a jumper. It's grey with a number on it. Here on the front.' Patrice patted a hand to her chest and then rolled her eyes and shook her head. 'Not a jumper. One with a hood, you know.'

'His grey hoodie? He was wearing that.'

Well, of course he was wearing that, thought Patrice. That's why the police released pictures of it when they were asking for witnesses. She nodded to Louise. 'That's what he's telling me. He's . . . ' She shook her head and let a small rueful smile play across her lips. 'He's telling me to tell you he's sorry it got so dirty.'

She watched Louise gulp down a sob. 'That's like him. I don't think he knew what the washing machine was, but he was a good boy. Always said please and thank you and sorry. A good boy.'

'I know, dear.' She patted Louise's shoulder to reinforce the bond between the two of them, nice and slowly so that Leo could see her sympathy with the poor bereaved mother. 'I'm talking to him right now. He's ever so polite.'

Louise gulped and nodded again. 'Thank you. Thank you so much. Will you tell him I love him?'

'You can tell him yourself dear. He's right here.'

She sat back and watched as Louise poured out her affection for her darling lost boy. A torrent of motherly love, undimmed by time or separation.

229

44

1967

Hester came in to Pat's booth just as she was about to put the Closed sign up.

'Do my fortune.' Hester sat herself down in front of the table.

Pat laughed before she remembered Charlie reckoning that Hester was a believer. 'You know it's just a bit of fun, don't you?'

Hester leaned back on two chair legs and wrinkled her nose. 'Yeah. Course.' She swung the chair back onto firm ground. 'Do it anyway though.'

'I'm supposed to charge you. Mr Stefanini doesn't like freebies.'

Hester rolled her eyes. 'He'll be lucky.'

Pat watched her friend. What did Hester want? She was, in Pat's eyes, the girl who had everything. Teased-up hair, black-kohled eyes, apparently bottomless resources for the purchase of Babychams, her very own bedsitting room, freedom. Hester burned brighter than anyone Pat had ever known. Happily, for Pat, Hester had no worries about unduly influencing the revelations of the occult.

'I need to know when Levi the drummer's going to stop seeing that trollop.'

That trollop, Pat knew, was Stephanie Lancaster, barmaid at the Duck and Feather and

230

Hester's most recent rival for the fickle affections of Levi the drummer.

'All right.' Pat pulled back the cloth from the crystal ball. 'Let's have a look then.'

She promised Hester an imminent victory over a rival, which went down well.

'And what about Levi the drummer?'

Pat heard herself giggle. 'What about him?'

'You know. Does he . . . '

Pat was surprised to see Hester tongue-tied.

'Does he . . . Is it . . . Is it love?'

Pat stared back at the crystal. She hesitated. She promised young women love at least once every day of the week, more on Saturdays. Young women who weren't her friend. Young women who she didn't absolutely know were going to be left disappointed. Charlie had told her stories about Levi the drummer, and about June the drummer's wife, mother of the drummer's growing clan of drummer babies.

Hester had lowered her face and was gazing into the crystal ball herself. 'I can't see owt.'

'No.'

'It must be amazing to have the gift.'

Pat swallowed. 'Yeah.'

'So what do you see?'

'Erm, love. Definitely love.'

'With Levi?'

Pat felt her hands getting clammy. 'It's not clear. The visions from beyond the veil are not always easy to interpret.'

'Course, but definitely love with someone?'

Pat nodded.

'Cool. Let's get out of here then.'

Pat glanced at the clock. It was nearly seven. If Charlie had been able to slope off to come and meet her, he'd be here by now, and she'd already told her parents that Mr Stefanini had asked her to stay late. In the café, of course.

'Okay. Where do you want to go?'

'The castle.'

'What?'

'Come on.'

'I've got to get changed.'

'Why? Come like that.'

Pat gestured towards her costume. 'I look stupid.'

Hester looked her up and down. 'Yeah. You do,' she said.

Pat changed hurriedly out of her costume, aware of Hester watching her, assessing her functional underwear and pale white body.

'You could be quite pretty, with a bit of effort.'

They left the booth and walked along the foreshore. It was still light and families lingered on the beach. They walked past the lights and noises of the arcades, smelt the aroma of battered fish in the air, felt the breeze from the sea on their faces, refreshing in the July sun rather than blowing right through them as it would in the winter months.

'I'm going to get out of here.' Hester broke the silence.

'What do you mean?'

'I'm going to find me a ticket out. Maybe one of the band. Maybe Levi. I'm going to find myself someone who's going places and go with them.'

Hester was striding out, and Pat found herself having to do a little half-jog half-skip to keep up. They reached the bottom of the castle steps up the side of the cliff from the seafront to the ancient clifftop castle.

'You really want to go up there?'

'Yeah!'

Pat was already out of breath from struggling to keep pace with Hester. 'It'll be shut.'

'That's okay. We can sneak in.' Hester was already charging up the stairs, slowed only marginally by the impracticality of her heeled boots.

Pat had never snuck in anywhere in her life. She was very much a knock-on-the-front-door-and-wait-politely-for-a-response sort of a girl. 'Really?'

Hester stopped partway up the steps and turned back towards Pat. 'Yes. God, Pat, I thought you and Charlie were doing it.'

'What?'

'Well, you act like such a virgin. We're sneaking in. All right?'

'All right.'

Pat followed Hester up the remaining steps and along the path. Hester stopped short of the main castle gate and pulled on the wire fence to make a gap. She beckoned Pat over.

'Why do I have to go first?'

'Oh, for goodness sake. In case we get caught by the armed guards, of course.'

'What?' Pat heard the horror in her voice and laughed quickly, before Hester could laugh at her. She wriggled through the fence and held it

233

open while Hester followed her. Inside the castle grounds Hester led the way again, walking along the cliff top out to the furthest edge of the headland, the point where you could stand high above the town, surrounded by sea below you on three sides, the ruined castle keeping guard over the fourth.

'I love it here.'

Pat looked around. 'I haven't been here since I was a kid.'

'Really? I come here loads.'

Pat was surprised. Twelfth-century monuments didn't seem like Hester's sort of thing.

'It's the only sodding place in this town that you can be alone. My mum used to say you could see Norway from up here.'

Both girls stood in silence for a moment scanning the horizon.

'I think that might be crap though.'

'Is it Norway over there?' Pat tried to picture the atlas her father kept on the big bookshelf in the sitting room. 'I thought it was Denmark.'

Hester shrugged.

'It is pretty up here.'

'It's not pretty. It's incredible.' Hester took another step towards the edge. 'Look! Just look. There's a whole world out there, and we're right on the brink of it.'

Pat looked out at the ocean. It didn't quite look that way to her. It looked like they were on the edge of nowhere. She tried to see it through Hester's eyes.

Hester sat down. 'Girl talk.'

Pat sat down next to her.

'So you and Charlie are doing it?'

Pat nodded.

'I can't believe that. God! Do you remember the first time I took you out? We had to *Great Escape* you from your parents' clutches.'

'I know.'

'And look at you now!'

Pat paused. Look at her now indeed. With Charlie. Earning money. Planning for . . . planning for what?

Hester was still happily talking away. 'I remember my first time. Willard Jefferies. Willard. Whatever must I have been thinking? He had the tiniest little . . . ' Hester's voice drifted away and she held up her little finger to make the point.

Pat smiled.

'And I remember afterwards. I was like three days late and I went completely crazy. I thought I was going to end up being Mrs Willard with all these little Willards around my ankles.'

Pat stopped smiling. 'You weren't though?'

'No.' Hester laughed. 'You can't get pregnant the first time anyway. God, Pat! Everyone knows that.'

'Really?'

'Course not. It doesn't really go all the way in the first time, does it?'

'Right.' Pat wasn't certain she liked the idea of talking about how far it went in, but Hester seemed very certain of her facts.

'That was crazy though. I was the same as you. Had to do all the sneaking around. It was so much better after I moved out. Now I can do what I like with whoever I like.' Hester paused. 'Which is loads better.'

Pat had always been fascinated by how Hester got to live on her own. She couldn't imagine her father allowing her to leave home until she was ready to marry. 'When did you leave home?'

'Two years ago.'

Pat did the mental arithmetic. 'You were sixteen?' She couldn't keep the shock out of her tone.

'Yeah. But it's great. Best thing that ever happened to me.'

'And your parents didn't mind?'

'My mum.' Hester's face closed up. 'My dad's not really around. But it's great. It's brilliant. My mum was just a drag anyway.'

Pat didn't answer. The distance she'd grown away from her own parents in the last few weeks was becoming more and more obvious. It was getting harder to pretend that there weren't two different Pats. It was getting closer to the point when she was going to have to choose just one.

'So tell me all about you and Charlie? It's love, isn't it?'

After the fortune-telling, Pat was starting to recognise a hopelessly romantic streak in Hester. In this case, it wasn't far off the mark though. Pat didn't reply but could feel her lips tugging into a smile.

'I knew it. You love him.' Hester clapped her hands. 'So how are you going to make him love you back? You shouldn't have done it with him, you know. That's like our best weapon. If you want them to get serious, you've really got to hold that back a bit. Do it with the ones you're not so bothered about. Do it with the Willards, not the Charlies.'

'I think he does.'

'What?'

'I think he does love me.'

'Well, has he said so?'

Pat shrugged. 'Not exactly.'

'Well, it doesn't count till he says it.'

Pat wondered about that. She wasn't sure anyone had ever told her they loved her. Maybe her mother three-quarters of the way through a bottle, but certainly not her father.

'Well, I haven't told him it either.'

Hester rolled her eyes. 'But it's different for girls. If you do it with them, then they just assume you love them. Willard definitely thought I was in love with him.' She sighed. 'It took months to get rid of him. I'm better at picking now. I just go for the ones who are going to be easy to get rid of. And I'm careful too. I don't want any more three-days-late scares.' Hester laughed.

In Pat's mind, the tiny thought that had been clamouring for attention since she told the young newlywed's fortune struck another blow. She went cold despite the evening sun still shining. She sat up straighter on the grass, getting ready to stand. Very calmly, very casually, she took a breath. 'I'd better get going.'

'Why?'

Pat kept her tone light. 'Parents, you know. Better get home.'

Hester seemed to accept that explanation.

'You can stay up here though. You don't have to walk me back.'

'Okay.'

Pat was relieved that Hester let her set off alone. She walked slowly across the grass, and back past the castle keep, until she was confident she was out of view of her friend. Then she started to run. Back to the fence. Through the gap. Along the lane. Past the Coastguard cottages and the old parish church. Down the tiny winding streets of the old town until she was outside the boarding house.

She stopped, paused to catch her breath, to try and calm herself. She was being silly. She knew she was being silly. She wiped her sweaty hands down her skirt. There was probably nothing to worry about. She turned away from the building and started to walk back towards the main street to get the bus home.

'Pat!'

The voice came from an upstairs window. Charlie was leaning out, trying to catch her attention. She held her hand to her brow and looked up at him.

'What are you doing here?'

'Came to see you.'

He looked confused. 'Then why don't you come up?'

'Okay.'

She walked up the stairs slower than she'd ever done before. Charlie was leaning on his open door waiting for her. He looked at her flushed face and her crinkling bottom lip.

'What's wrong?'

She walked past him and sat down on the bed. 'I think we might have a problem,' she said.

45

She floated away from Patrice's suite, vaguely aware that Leo was following her along the hotel corridor and into the lift. He was no more than a ghost to her. Kyle was real. She'd been in the room with him. She'd talked and known, for the first time, that he was listening. 'When can we do it again?'

Leo was leaning on the wall staring at his feet.

'Leo, when can we do it again?'

He lifted his head and shrugged. 'I'm not sure. I'll have to talk to Barney. Next week maybe?'

Next week was too long. Already she was struggling to hold onto her elation. She'd been so close to her boy, but still so far away. It was like talking for a few seconds on a crackly phone line. It was better than nothing but she needed more. She needed another hit.

'I could do sooner. It's fine. If it would help with your book. We can do whenever you like. Or we could do more now.'

Leo shook his head. 'I've got to drive home now.'

Underneath the deep fill layer of Kyle that was dominating her emotions, Louise felt a tinge of relief. If Leo was going home that meant she wouldn't have to do anything with him again, not that she'd been under duress the first time, but it was done. It had served its purpose. She

240

wasn't interested in any earnest conversations about what things meant, and how they felt. She'd told him that sex was never just sex. It turned out she was wrong.

'So you'll set up a time to do it again.'

He nodded.

'Soon?'

'I'll see what I can do.'

She could see that he was distracted. Distracted didn't help her. Distracted didn't get her closer to Kyle. The lift pinged and doors slid open on the ground floor.

Leo walked out ahead of her. 'I've got to get off.'

She didn't have time for this. She didn't have time to placate him and work out what was wrong. But she had no choice. Leo talked to Patrice, and Patrice talked to Kyle. She followed him through the lobby. 'What's up?'

He shook his head.

She reached her fingers to his hand, and waited, watching his face. There was a moment of indecision before he wrapped his fingers around her own. She let him lead her to the bottom of the steps and sit down on a low wall in front of the building. She perched beside him.

'Marnie wants a divorce.'

'Why?'

Leo shrugged. 'Lots of reasons. I told her about us.'

Louise was the other woman. 'And she's divorcing you?' She felt sick at the thought. 'Because of me?'

'Not just that.' He stared into the distance.

'Not even that, I don't think. I told her after she said she wanted to split up.'

Louise shook her head. That was insane. Why make everything even worse than it had to be?

'I shouldn't have said anything. If I hadn't said anything, she might have changed her mind.'

'Is that what you want?'

Leo shrugged again. 'I don't know.' He looked at the scene around him. 'I've got to go. I've got to move my stuff out of the house.'

'Where are you moving?' Louise asked the question as blankly as she could. Nothing that could be interpreted as more than friendly concern. Nothing that could be misconstrued as an invitation.

'I'm going to stay here until the interviews for the book are finished. Marnie's rented a storage unit for my stuff.'

'That seems a bit . . . ' Louise knew what it seemed. It seemed controlling. It seemed like Leo's wife had been planning their separation for a while.

'We think it's for the best that we have a clean break.'

'We think?'

Leo nodded. 'Yeah.' He pulled himself up from the low seat and pulled his car keys from his pocket. 'So anyway, I'll be back here tonight, if you wanted to . . . ' He hesitated. 'Get a drink or something?'

Louise's stomach clenched. All she wanted to do, if she couldn't see Patrice again straight away, was sit in the flat and replay her memory of the afternoon over and over again. But she needed to talk to Kyle again, and that meant Patrice, and Patrice meant Leo. She nodded. 'Text me if you want.'

She watched him stride across the car park. Did Kyle see what she was doing to get her chance to be with him? Maybe this was better. If Leo was single, then she wasn't doing anything wrong. And her baby was still out there. That was what mattered. That was all that mattered.

46

1967

Pat perched on the railing at the edge of the beach, facing out to sea, back to the bus stops, day trippers and arcades. She watched Charlie walk from where she was sitting to the very far end of the beach, by the lifeboat station, before turning and walking back along the beach parallel with the sea. He walked straight passed her and continued towards the opposite end of the bay.

Pat moved her head to follow his progress. The evening was turning colder, and she pulled the sleeves of the jumper she'd borrowed from Charlie's room down over her hands. It was something her mother regularly reprimanded her for doing with her own clothes. Charlie was continuing his slow progress along the beach, walking carefully over the wet sand.

I'm going for a walk. I need to think. That's what he'd said. That was all he'd said. The only words that had passed his lips since she'd stood in the middle of his room and mumbled that she thought she could possibly be a little bit pregnant. She'd followed him out of the room, along the street, and down the hill to the beach. She hadn't got the feeling that she was unwelcome. In fact, he'd held her hand as they were walking. But he hadn't said a word.

She supposed she probably ought to be thinking too, but that wasn't happening. Her first thought, sat on the castle headland with Hester, was that she needed to talk to Charlie. Shock, and her brain's ability to cling to disbelief in rejection of available evidence, seemed to have rendered her empty-headed since that point. She'd told Charlie, and now she was just watching the world around her go past.

There weren't many families still on the beach. It was older people now, walking along the promenade and drifting towards the pubs further along the front. A voice from behind her drifted into Pat's attention.

'Well, you're not having it.' A woman, maybe twenty-two or three, was dragging a red-faced sticky-handed toddler along by the arm. With her free hand she was thrusting a half-eaten ice-cream cone towards the bin. The child screamed.

Pat turned her attention back to Charlie. He was at the farthest point of the beach now. He'd stopped and was looking out to sea, his hand stuffed into his pockets. Pat waited. Eventually he turned and set off back up the sand towards where she was sitting. Pat watched as he got closer and closer, trying to make out his expression, but he kept his face bent forward, looking at his feet as he walked. He glanced up only briefly to check his direction, each time slightly altering his path to bring himself back. He stopped in front of her, his head only reaching her chest as he stood on the sand looking up towards the footpath railing.

'Sorry.'

'What for?'

'Needing time.'

Pat almost laughed. 'That's okay.'

'I think . . . ' The wind blew across them and he turned his face out of the sweeping sand. 'I think it's good.'

'Really?'

'Yeah. I think it's brilliant.'

She jumped off the railing and into his arms. He pulled her tightly against his body, burying his fingers in the folds of the oversized jumper.

'Oh my God!' The words were muffled into his shoulder. He pulled back.

'What's wrong?'

'The time!' It was nearly half past eight. 'I told my dad I was working until eight.'

Charlie pointed at the road. 'There's a bus.'

He grabbed her hand. They ran to the bus stop and straight onto the open-top tourist bus that went around the headland to the north bay. He paid both their fares, and turned to Pat. 'You cold?'

'A bit.'

'Okay.' He led her to a seat downstairs and squeezed in beside her. He glanced around the bus. 'This is where we met.'

'Is it?' She looked about.

'Not this precise bus, you daft thing. But it was on the open-topped bus, wasn't it?'

Pat nodded. 'I didn't think you'd noticed me.'

Charlie grinned. ''Course I did.'

'You hardly spoke to me.'

He squirmed a little bit. 'Was trying to play it cool.'

'Right. Is that what you normally do?'

'Normally?'

She looked out of the window as she spoke, rather than meeting his eye. 'When you're chatting up girls.'

'I don't know.' She turned her face to meet his cobalt eyes. 'I've not really done that much chatting up.' He took a deep breath. 'And I guess I'm not going to be doing any more now, am I?' He didn't sound unhappy at the idea.

'Why not?'

'Well . . . ' He gestured towards her belly.

'Oh.'

Another deep breath. 'Look. I know this probably isn't really the right time or place, and I'll do it properly later if you want, and everything but . . . '

'What?'

'Pat.'

'Yeah.'

'We'll get married, won't we?'

Pat opened her mouth and closed it again.

'Pat, will you marry me?'

She nodded. Of course she would marry him.

They got off the bus and walked towards Pat's home, forgetting to rush despite the dwindling light that should have reminded them both how late it was. Their fingers entangled, and their bodies brushed against one another as they walked.

'How are we going to do it then?'

'What?'

'Are we going to tell them? Are we going to run away? What?'

Pat stopped for a moment, trying to make a plan, trying to be practical, but the practicalities wouldn't form in her mind. 'I don't know. I don't think we can run away and get married. Aren't I too young?'

'You're nearly seventeen.'

'Does that make a difference?'

Charlie shrugged. 'I don't know. I've never eloped before.'

'Let me think about it.'

He nodded.

'Come see me at work tomorrow?'

'Okay.'

They kissed briefly on the corner of the street, still out of sight of the house. Pat made her way up the driveway alone. Her home, so utterly familiar, appeared unwelcoming. For the time being though, there was no choice. She unlocked the Yale and went inside.

'Stanley!' Her mother's voice rang out from the sitting room. That was unusual. Normally on a weeknight the family sat in the dining room after dinner. The sitting room was for Sundays, visiting aunts, wakes and best.

'No. It's me.' Pat realised, just in time, that she was still wearing Charlie's jumper. She pulled it over her head and stuffed it quickly in the back of the understairs cupboard. She paused to flatten down her static-lightened hair in front of the hall mirror before going into the lounge.

The Brylcreemed man was sitting in the good high-backed chair from Grandma Bickersleigh's house.

'Hello, Pat.' He smiled warmly.

Lilian looked momentarily uncertain.

The man, Anthony she remembered, continued. 'I ran into Pat at the shop earlier in the week, didn't I?'

Pat nodded. 'Stocktake day.'

'Right. Yes.' Pat's mother gripped her tea cup, a slight tremor in her hand. 'Mr Abbot called in looking for your father, but he's gone to work.'

The man shrugged elegantly. 'We must have just missed one another. Anyway, I ought to be going. I've kept you too long.' He placed his cup neatly on the side table, and stood.

'Oh. Right.' Lilian stood with him. 'I'll fetch your coat.'

Pat's mind threw up an image of an unfamiliar coat hanging on the back of the door to the understairs cupboard, and Charlie's jumper stuffed too quickly in the same hiding place. 'I'll get it.'

She ran into the hall, retrieved the coat and slammed the cupboard shut before her mother could follow her. She watched Anthony Abbot put on his coat. She tried to look at him with Gypsy Patience's eyes, but there was nothing out of place, nothing individual about him at all. His hair was Brylcreemed neatly, not rebelliously, forgettably. His clothes were well-kept, stylish but not fashionable. Everything about him was precisely as it should be, but the overall effect was ghostlike. There was nothing for her to get hold of, no imperfections, no way of scratching at the surface. She hoped he would never want his fortune told.

He thanked her politely for fetching his coat,

and thanked her mother, equally politely, for the cup of tea. Pat watched him, as he walked down the drive and turned onto the street.

Her mother was in the kitchen, moving the empty cups from the tray to the sink. She reached for her sherry bottle.

'Don't tell the parson.'

Pat didn't join in. 'What did he want?'

'To see your father.'

'What about?'

Lilian's face closed up. 'Well, I don't really think that's any of our business now is it? Don't you have homework?'

'I've left school.'

Lilian nodded. 'Right. Yes.'

'I might go and have a bath.'

Lilian didn't say anything about the hot water. She poured another sherry instead.

Pat ran the bath warm, not too hot. Hester had told her stories about girls who'd got themselves into trouble running themselves very hot baths. That wasn't what she was looking for. She undressed and stepped into the warm, wet cocoon. She leaned back, lowering her head into the warmth and closing her eyes. In the darkness, she tried to picture the life ahead of her.

There'd be Charlie, and there'd be the baby. Her hand went to her belly and she felt herself smiling. In her mind, she saw Charlie so clearly, and she felt their child, but what else? Beyond their faces everything was grey. She couldn't picture their home. She couldn't see the teas they'd eat together, or the paint they'd use in the nursery. She tried to think about that other future, the future her parents thought she was going to be having. Secretarial college, and then what? Maybe a year or two of work before making a good marriage to an appropriate sort of a man. And then a baby, she supposed, a different baby though, not this baby, not Charlie's baby. And there'd be chapel every Sunday, and probably a Young Wives group on a Tuesday afternoon, with coffee from green cups and weak cordial for the children playing around their ankles. She could picture that life. It was the life she'd been raised for, but she couldn't see the appropriate sort of man. She couldn't imagine feeling anything when she held his baby.

She knew that people would say she was a stupid girl who'd got herself into trouble. People would talk. People would judge. People would say she had no choice, but Gypsy Patience knew that people were stupid and only ever saw what they wanted to anyway. She knew she had no choice, but that was fine. It wasn't the baby in the belly that meant she had no choice. It wasn't even the beautiful blue-eyed boy she'd met on an open-topped bus. It was just that the girl he loved was the girl she'd always hoped to be, the girl who didn't lie, didn't pretend, didn't have to be anyone other than exactly who she was. If it was a lifetime of being that girl, or a lifetime of being sensible, appropriate Pat, there had never been any choice at all.

47

He had far less stuff than he'd expected. His clothes fitted into one decent-sized suitcase and a holdall. He'd let Marnie keep most of the CDs, but taken the mp3 player, the vinyl and the record player. He'd taken the leather chair from his study that had come from his father, and a couple of boxes of books and papers, but that was really it. As Marnie had, quite rightly, pointed out, he wouldn't need much in the way of kitchen things if he was staying in a hotel and the bulk of their furniture had been chosen specifically by her to fit in the space in the marital home. The storage unit she'd rented seemed grossly oversized. As he pulled the rolling door down and snapped the padlock closed, he wondered whether Marnie had intended him to sleep in there as well.

He got back in his car and sat for a second. He was going back to Blackpool. He was going to stay at the hotel and finish the interviews with Patrice. And while he was doing that he would search the internet for a flat to rent. The realisation hit him that that flat could be anywhere. He could move back to London. He could rent a deserted farmhouse in the Welsh hills. He didn't need to be anywhere. He could simply cut his moorings and float away. Grace was grown up. Olly was gone and Marnie was not his Marianne anymore. He had no more ties.

He paused. He had one thing. He had the thing he'd been searching for to give him that elusive sense of belonging. He had a mother. Somewhere. He'd thought he'd found her, but he'd been wrong. He'd been so sure. Patience Bickersleigh had given birth and then, so far as he could tell, she'd disappeared. No marriage record. No death certificate. No trace of her online. Of course that meant nothing. It just meant that she hadn't married, hadn't died and wasn't on Facebook. It didn't even mean that. She could have married abroad, or changed her name. Her death certificate could be just one of the millions of pieces of paper out there accidentally misfiled or mislaid.

It was just that he'd been so certain. Patience Bickersleigh disappeared, and Patrice Leigh seemed to pop into existence. And just after Leo had first made that connection, Patrice's name had been mentioned in passing by his agent. Celebrities who were looking for a ghostwriter. He hadn't been supposed to want to work with Patrice. There was a boxer at the top of the list that his agent was keen on. Preliminary contact had already been made. It fit with the sort of stuff Leo had done before, but hearing Patrice's name had grabbed him. In his desperately searching head, he'd let himself think it was some sort of sign.

He could refocus on trying to find the real Patience. But not yet. His reasons for taking this job were crazy, but he still had a contract. He still needed to finish Patrice's book. So he would concentrate on work. He'd immerse himself in somebody else's life. Leo pulled his mobile from his pocket and dialled Barney to set up another reading for Louise. It genuinely was good additional colour for the story, and, anyway, he owed her.

'How about tomorrow morning?'

Leo agreed on Louise's behalf. He suspected she'd go for another reading at any time of the day or night Patrice could offer. He ended the call and swiped and clicked his way to Louise's number. He should call. That would be easiest. He'd know she'd got the message. It would be over in a few seconds. He selected Send Message instead and typed a text giving her the time for the reading.

She replied within seconds. *Thanx. Will u b there?*

He started to type. *Yes but staying in Manchester tonight.*

Leo hesitated. There was no reason to. He had to be at the reading — the whole idea was that it was helpful to the book. And there was no reason that he shouldn't be spending time with Louise anymore either. He was single man now. He deleted the last five words. *Heading back over there now. Drink later?*

★ ★ ★

The next morning he was woken by his mobile frantically beeping and vibrating on the floor at the side of Louise's bed. He scrambled to find the phone. His daughter's name popped up on the screen as he hit Answer.

'Dad?'

'Hi, sweetheart. What's up?'

'I need to see you.'

'What? Why?'

'I don't want to tell you on the phone.'

Leo stomach clenched. 'What's wrong, sweetheart?'

Her voice was strained. 'Nothing's wrong. It's good. It's good news, but I can't tell you over the phone. Please, Dad.'

'Okay. I'm busy this morning, but . . . '

'Mum's going to be here by lunchtime.'

Leo glanced at the clock. Eight thirty. The reading was at nine. He could be away soon after ten. He just about had time. 'Look. I'm working. And me and your mother aren't really talking at the moment.'

Grace paused on the end of the line. 'She said, but you need to both come.'

Leo hesitated. 'Is this about me and your mum?'

Grace moaned. 'No. It's not about you. Not everything is about you. Or Mum.' She lowered her voice. 'Please, Dad. Just be here. My halls, at half twelve.'

He didn't have much choice. 'Okay.'

He pulled his jeans and top on and went to find Louise in the kitchen. She was washing up plates from goodness knows when, standing at the sink in an oversized t-shirt over greying jogging bottoms. Everything she wore looked too big. 'There's a problem.'

She spun around to look at him, spraying bubbles from her fingers around the room.

'What? With the reading?'

Leo nodded. 'I might have to go a bit early. There's some problem with Grace.'

'But I can still go to the reading?'

Leo nodded. 'Yeah. I'm just going to ring Barney and let him know I have to get straight off.'

He leaned on the wall and flicked through the contacts on his phone. Barney answered on the second ring.

'Leo, I was about to ring you. Miss Leigh isn't feeling very well. I was wondering if we could move the reading to the afternoon.'

Leo grimaced. 'Sorry, I can't do later. Erm . . .'

Louise dropped the bowl she was washing in the sink. 'What's wrong?'

'He wants to move it to later, but I can't.'

'I could still go.' The need in her voice was palpable.

He covered the phone with his hand. 'It's supposed to be for the book.'

'I could take notes or record it or something.'

He closed his eyes for a second. Whatever he did at the moment he seemed to be letting someone down. Eventually he nodded, and relayed the suggestion to Barney. He didn't actually have to be there. He could listen to the recording and interview Louise afterwards. He finalised the timings with Barney. 'I hope Patrice feels better.'

There was a pause. 'I'm sure she's just tired.'

He hung up the phone.

'Thank you.' Louise took another step toward

him, and he found his arms wrapping around her instinctively.

'I do know how you feel, remember?'

'I know.' Louise rested her head against his shoulder. 'Why didn't you ask her to contact Olly again?'

Leo bent his face into her hair and thought about the question. 'I guess it was enough to know that he was definitely gone. I knew he was anyway, but you always wonder a little bit. I'd see a lad his age with the same hair, or a similar shirt walking down the street and I'd always look. I'd always check, just in case it was Olly. Even though I knew, someone else confirming that he's gone. For now, it's sort of enough.'

48

1967

It was a works do, mostly women, about fifteen in total, but a mix of ages. Pat had gleaned that they were mainly machinists from the knicker factory, but watching the group she could see the divides between them. There were two who kept themselves slightly separate from the others. They were quieter, more contained, less prone to shouting to their colleagues across the room. Probably they were the office girls, Pat thought.

Mr Stefanini had set her up a table in one corner of the café. The idea was that the women would come in ones and twos to have their fortune done, while in the meantime there was music and food and drink that they could buy.

The fortunes themselves were easy. Pat could hear the women talking about what they were hoping for before they came over to her little corner of the occult, and she rattled off promises of love and wealth and security as if she'd been doing it for years.

Mr Stefanini watched and nodded to himself. The girl was a natural. He looked around the room. There were possibilities here. If he moved the snooker tables, and took a few feet off the café, he'd just about have room for a five- or six-lane bowling alley. Bowling mind, not skittles. American bowling for the kids. He turned his attention back to Pat. Across the table from her a barely adolescent knicker-stitcher was smiling in awe at the great joys her life was apparently going to bring. Selling dreams, ay. It was a darn sight less investment than building a bowling alley.

The evening went smoothly. Mr Stefanini was getting ready to count his take when he saw one of the quieter older women from the group approach Pat. He'd thought they'd all gone, charging off down the front to find themselves a half of stout to end the night. Mr Stefanini sat down behind the café counter and listened.

★ ★ ★

'Excuse me, dear.'

Pat looked up. 'Sorry. Yes?'

'Do you have the gift?'

Pat paused. 'I see visions of the future.'

'Yes. Yes. But do you . . . can you . . . ?' The woman stopped. 'It doesn't matter.'

Pat was curious now. 'No. It's all right. What did you want to ask?'

'Well . . . ' She was still reluctant.

'Sit down.' Pat smiled broadly. 'Tell me.'

The woman sat opposite Pat and placed her hands neatly in her lap. She was one of the office workers Pat had identified earlier. Pat tried to think back to her fortune, but she couldn't remember the woman coming forward. 'Do you want your fortune done? You didn't come up before, did you?'

The woman shook her head. 'No. No. Well,

not exactly. I was hoping . . . ' She stopped again, and Pat noticed that she was holding back a sob.

'It's okay.' Pat leaned back in her chair, waiting to see if the stranger would continue.

When she did her voice was quieter, subdued but under control. 'It's my boy. It was last year he passed over. He was only nineteen. A good boy.' The woman's gaze was fixed somewhere over Pat's shoulder. Whatever she was looking at it wasn't in this room. She coughed slightly and gathered herself. 'Anyway, I know some people who have the gift, the sight, they can talk to people, can't they? People who've passed.'

Pat swallowed. 'Some people. Yes.'

'Can you, dear?'

Pat shook her head. 'I don't really do that.'

'Don't though? Not can't?' The need was overcoming the woman's reticence now. Her hands, placed so calmly on her lap, had balled into fists, pulling and twisting at her skirt.

'Well . . . ' Pat wasn't sure what to say. Mr Stefanini hadn't briefed her for this. What had he briefed her? *Find out what they want and promise them they can get it.* She swallowed. 'I can try.'

She was improvising now, but she had a willing accomplice to help.

'I brought something of his. That's supposed to help, isn't it?'

The woman reached for her handbag, placed carefully on the floor beside her, and pulled a man's watch out of the clasped pocket. She placed it on the table in front of Pat. 'It was a present when he was eighteen. I thought it seemed a bit much. I thought we should have waited until he was twenty-one, but his father said eighteen.'

Pat placed her hand over the watch and closed her eyes. What should she say? What did this woman want to hear? She was quiet, composed, apart from the momentary loss of control when she first mentioned her son, but she'd brought the watch with her, waited to approach Pat at the end of the evening. Whatever she was hoping for, it was a hope she'd been carrying with her.

'The sea,' the woman murmured. 'You live right by it, but you never think. They were just messing about.'

Something started into life in the corner of Pat's mind. Something from the local paper. Something her father had grumbled about. 'Stupid kids,' he'd said. She remembered. A young man swept off the Marine Road playing chicken with the spring waves. Could this be?

Pat started to sway gently in her seat. It was something she sometimes did to give herself time to think when she was doing fortunes. She hoped it gave the impression of being overcome by forces from beyond the veil. 'Water. I'm seeing water.'

She opened her eyes and saw the woman nodding. 'The sea. The sea took him.'

Pat held up a hand. 'Don't tell me. I see the waves. I have a sense of something just being swept away. Is that right?'

Another nod.

'That's good. That's what he's showing me.'

261

That felt like the right thing to say, as if he was right there next to her. But why would he show her that? The woman must already know. Pat swallowed. 'I think that's just to confirm that it is him.'

The woman's eyes had started to moisten. Pat lifted one hand and reached to pat her shoulder. 'Oh, I'm sorry. The name?'

'He was John.'

Pat giggled slightly, involuntarily. Even so, she realised that her slight awkwardness was adding a ring of authenticity to what she was saying. She could see how the woman might see her — the innocent young thing, still uncertain of her gift. 'No. I know his name. He's telling me. I meant your name.'

'I'm Margaret.'

'Margaret. Of course. He's just saying 'Tell my mother . . . ''

'What does he want you to tell me?'

Pat closed her eyes again. 'He just wants you to know that he's safe and feels well now. He doesn't want you to worry.'

The woman reached back into her bag for a handkerchief. 'I was always worrying.'

'I know. He's telling me, but there's no need anymore. He's peaceful now.'

The woman nodded.

Pat opened her eyes. 'He's drifting off now. I'm afraid we can only see glimpses of the world beyond.'

'Of course.' The woman wiped her eyes, and pulled the watch back off the table. She clasped it in her hand. 'Well, I'll be going now.'

She stood and rested her free hand on Pat's shoulder. 'Thank you, my dear. You have such a gift. I'm going to tell the people at church about you.'

Mr Stefanini moved from behind the counter, smiling broadly. 'Shall I show you out?'

The woman nodded. 'That would be kind.'

He walked Margaret towards the stairwell and listened to her talk. 'She was amazing. Did you hear?'

Mr Stefanini shook his head. It was a lie but not, he felt, a bad lie.

'She knew his name and everything.'

Mr Stefanini didn't comment. He didn't point out that the woman told Pat his name herself.

At the bottom of the stairs they stopped, while Mr Stefanini unlocked the big side door. 'You can go out this way, rather than through the arcade.'

'She is amazing. There are so many charlatans out there.'

Mr Stefanini nodded sympathetically, a thought starting to form.

'It's wonderful to meet someone with a genuine gift.'

'I did overhear one thing. You mentioned your church?'

'The Spiritualist Church? Yes.'

'Spiritualist Church?' Mr Stefanini's brain was working to keep up with his mouth now. He smiled. 'So you've tried to make contact before?'

She nodded. 'Never like this though. Do you think she would come along to a church meeting? It would be amazing.'

Mr Stefanini nodded. 'The thing is, Patience is very young, and her gift must be protected. There are so many people who would try to take advantage of her.' He allowed a thoughtful expression to settle on his face. 'I worry for her. Such a sweet nature.'

'Of course.' The woman looked horrified at the very idea of Pat's undoubted gift falling into unscrupulous hands.

'I try to take care of Pat, you see. I make sure she isn't overcommitting herself.' Mr Stefanini pulled the door open. 'Although a church visit, I'm sure that wouldn't be inappropriate.'

'Well, we meet on a Wednesday morning in the hall next to the library.'

'I'll see what we can arrange then.'

The woman filed out of the open door, asking, once again, that Mr Stefanini pass on her thanks to Pat. She seemed to be a real fan.

*   *   *

Back in her normal clothes, Pat checked her waistband for signs of tightness as she rushed home. Her tummy was still its normal size. It was only August. Her first time with Charlie had only been six weeks ago. She knew she couldn't be showing yet, but still she checked.

At home the light was shining under the door from the back room, but there was no sound from the wireless or television. Pat guessed that her mother was sitting alone in there, silently toasting the parson. She hung her coat up and paused for a moment. She felt she ought to go and say hello, but increasingly she was finding that all she really wanted to do at home was hide away in her room or in the locked bathroom, clutching her secrets tightly to her. She started up the stairs, calling out, 'I'm home.'

'Patience!'

The voice that came from the dining room was her father's, at home after all. The tone was not encouraging. Pat stopped on the stairs and waited a second. Her father stepped into the hallway.

'Patience, can we have a word?'

She smiled brightly. 'I was going to have a bath and go to bed. I'm quite tired.'

He frowned. 'Tired after the youth group barbeque?'

She nodded. That had been tonight's white lie.

'Come downstairs please.'

She followed her father into the back room, and sat in a hard dining chair at the bare table. Her mother was already there. He father hadn't sat down but was standing in front of the fireplace, his hands clasped behind his back.

'It rained this evening.'

Pat nodded. She'd been inside the booth or the café all day. She had no idea what the weather had done, but her parents didn't know that. They thought she'd been at the youth group barbeque. Pat closed her eyes for a second as she realised. Father quickly confirmed her fear.

'The barbeque was cancelled because of the weather. They're going to have it next weekend.'

Pat nodded. 'Yeah. I know. I wasn't at the barbeque.'

'Clearly.'

Pat didn't respond. Gypsy Patience wouldn't respond to that. She'd wait, let them talk a bit, work out what they wanted to hear. Pat let the silence extend, feeling like she was watching the scene from somewhere deep inside her own head.

'You understand that we expect you to come straight home from work, if you're not at youth group.'

Pat nodded but still didn't reply. What could she say? The truth. That she was pretending to talk to dead people. Where else could she have been? Normally she lied to hide the fact that she was with Charlie, whose baby she was now having, and whom she had agreed to marry. She said nothing.

'But that, I'm afraid, is not the worst of it. The worst of it is that you then lied to us.'

Pat dropped her head to avoid eye contact.

'That's right. You should be ashamed. So, I have to ask you, where were you this evening?'

Answers flew through Pat's brain. She could tell the truth. The whole truth or part of the truth. She could tell them she'd been having sex with a roadie in his boarding house room. Technically, that would be another lie, but it would have been true if they'd asked her any one of the other recent evenings she'd lied about having to work late, or going to someone's house, or getting stuck at choir practice.

Start with what they wanted to hear. 'I'm sorry. I only lied because I didn't want you to find out.' Which was obviously true. What other

266

reason was there ever to lie?

'Find out what?' Her father's expression was unchanged.

'About work.'

Lilian seemed to awake from her stupor. 'That job! I told you it wasn't appropriate.'

Stanley was distracted by the attack from an unexpected side. He hissed his wife's name, his eyes flicking back towards Pat. He was displeased by the breakdown in their united front.

'She's just in the café.'

Pat remained silent, watching her parents. Her father turned his attention back towards her.

'So you were working in the café?'

Pat nodded, which was actually not a lie. 'It was for a private party. Mr Stefanini has started doing little buffets and things for works dos and that.'

'And why did you not tell us about it?'

Pat dropped her eyes again. What she was about to do was not very nice, and, she knew, was just postponing a much bigger scene, but Gypsy Patience had watched and listened and decided what to say next.

'It's just that I know you don't really like me working there.' She glanced at her mother, and saw her father's eyes follow her own. 'So I didn't want to cause trouble about it.'

She paused, and decided to commit fully to her story. 'And with starting secretarial college I'm going to need new clothes and I wanted to be able to pay myself.'

She let a small crack come into her voice. 'I

wanted you to see that I was taking responsibility.'

There was silence for a moment. Her father cleared his throat. 'Well, that's commendable, Pat. More young people should think like that.'

'Stanley!' Her mother's interjection was small but pointed. Her father nodded.

'However, that doesn't excuse telling untruths.'

Pat shook her head. 'I know.'

'In future, if you are working late you will inform us in advance. You will not let work interfere with church or youth group commitments. Is that clear?'

Pat nodded.

'And?' Her mother's tone was pointed.

Her father shook his head. 'I think this matter is now closed.'

'We said you'd pick her up from work in the car to make sure she came straight home.'

Pat watched her father's gaze drop to the floor for a second. Gypsy Patience might have seen that as reluctance. 'I don't think that will be necessary. Pat's explained. I think she's learned her lesson.'

Pat nodded again, quickly before the conversation could be reopened.

Her father cleared his throat again and nodded towards the clock. 'Well, time is getting on, but I really do need to pop back to the shop.' He smiled brightly.

'At this time? It is getting quite late.' Her mother's tone was equally bright.

Stanley shrugged his shoulders. 'Just a few things to check on. I won't be long.'

'Very well.'

'You don't need to wait up for me. I'll try not to wake anyone up.'

Stanley strode out of the room and a second later they heard the front door close behind him. Pat stood up.

'Wait. We haven't finished.' Her mother stood, putting her hand on the table to steady herself. She blinked and waited for her eyes to focus from the new position. 'Your father's not right.'

'About what?'

'That café. It gives boys ideas.' Her mother took a gulp from her cup, which Pat realised didn't contain tea. Lilian must have been drinking in front of her husband. That was a new development. 'All parading yourself around like that. They'll take you for a trollop.'

Pat didn't respond directly. 'I'm going to go to bed.'

'I know, you know.'

Pat stopped in the doorway. 'Know what?'

'About what you girls get up to these days. I see the television.'

'I don't know what you mean.' Pat ran out of the room and straight upstairs. She sat down on her bed and forced her breathing into a calmer rhythm. Her mother didn't know anything. She didn't know about Charlie. She didn't know about the baby. She was just a tired old drunk. Let her worry about her own secrets. Pat closed her eyes and thought of Charlie. She needed him here now. She lay down on her back on the bed and let the sense of displacement envelop her. She'd read books where people missed each other so much they described it as a physical pain. She'd thought that terribly overdramatic. She'd been wrong. Her arms ached to wrap around his body. Her senses felt empty for the lack of the scent and taste of him. She felt as though her whole self was out of place, set at the wrong angle to reality, and only his presence could set her right again.

There was a change coming. She thought back over the conversation she'd just had with her parents. She'd lied. Straight away she'd lied. She wouldn't be able to lie for much longer. Her belly would swell. She stroked her tummy and tried to picture the life growing inside. She had no idea how big it would be at that moment. No idea whether her baby would be a little boy or a little girl, but it would be her baby. Hers and Charlie's. And she was going to fight for it.

49

Marnie was already sitting on one of the brown plastic chairs in the shared kitchen at Grace's student hall. She looked up as Leo came in. 'Do you know what this is about?'

Leo shook his head. 'Didn't you organise it? To tell her about us.'

'Nope. She just phoned and demanded I come here.'

He pulled out the chair next to his wife. 'Where is she?'

'Bathroom.'

They fell into silence. Leo watched his wife pull her phone from her bag and busy herself staring at the screen. There were grey hairs in the roots at her temples. He wondered when they'd first appeared.

'Hi.'

Marnie jumped up from the table to greet her daughter. Leo hung back. He wanted to know what was going on. He wouldn't put it past Grace to be staging an intervention to save her parents' marriage by reminding them of the impact on their innocent child. She'd inherited her mother's tendency for drama.

She pulled herself out of Marnie's embrace. 'Oh God.'

'What's wrong?' Now Leo was paying closer attention. There were circles under his little girl's eyes and she wasn't wearing make-up. Leo didn't think he'd seen Grace without a full face on in the middle of the day since her secondary school gave up the losing battle to force her to clean it off every morning.

'Nothing. It's incredible.' Grace's hands were shaking. Leo stood up and walked her to his chair.

'Tell us what's going on, Grace.'

She shook her head. 'I was going to take you out somewhere, do it somewhere special.' She turned her head, staring at the drab surroundings. 'I can't wait though.'

He watched Marnie lean towards their daughter. 'Then tell us, darling.'

'It's Olly.'

Leo's stomach had turned to lead. Something was very very wrong. 'What about him?'

'He got in touch.'

Leo shook his head. Grace didn't know about that, did she? Olly had made contact at Patrice's show, but he hadn't told her. Would Marnie have? He didn't think so, but even then that didn't make sense. Grace was supposed to have something to tell him. 'What do you mean?'

'He emailed me. Well, he emailed and then phoned.'

Leo folded his aims. 'Someone's winding you up, sweetheart.'

Grace shook her head.

Marnie hadn't moved. Her hands were locked around her daughter's. She was still half-standing, leaning towards Grace's chair. Leo walked around her and put a hand on her shoulder. 'Marnie! You know Olly is dead. This'll be another con. Remember?'

When Olly was first missing they'd had contact from a host of people claiming to know what had happened to their son, even from a couple claiming to be him. According to the police that was quite normal for a case that made the papers.

'You talked to him?' Marnie whispered.

Grace nodded. She lifted her face and looked straight at her dad. 'It's really Olly. He's alive.'

50

1967

'What are you doing here?'

Charlie leaned on the wall at the entrance to Pat's gypsy booth.

'I haven't seen you for days.'

'I'm sorry.' She glanced back at the door. 'But I can't talk to you here. I'm only supposed to do ten minutes per customer.'

'So?'

'Paying customer!'

Charlie came properly into the room and dropped a couple of coins onto the table. 'Ten minutes then. Are you avoiding me?'

'No! No. Sorry. My parents have been . . . '

He took two steps forward and put his arms around her. 'That's okay. So long as it's not me?'

'No. You're . . . ' She stroked his face in place of finding the words and smiled.

He kissed her and grinned. 'So are you. So what's wrong with your parents?'

She pulled out of his grip and sat down. 'They caught me working late when I was supposed to be at a church thing and now they're checking my movements.'

He moaned. 'All right. Well, we'll have to find ways of meeting up that they can't disapprove of then.'

'Like what?'

'Well, what are you doing tomorrow night?'

'Youth group barbeque. It was postponed from last week. I have to go.'

'All right. Youth group barbeque it is then.'

'You can't come!'

'Why not?'

There ought to have been a thousand objections, but Pat couldn't think of one. 'I don't know.'

'Well then.' He grinned at her from under his hair. 'Let's not waste any more time talking about it.'

He looked at his watch. 'How much of my ten minutes is left?'

'About seven.'

'Great.'

★　★　★

It felt strange standing outside the manse, readying herself to ring the bell for admittance to the barbeque. Her church and home clothes were a costume. Her costume, and her secret stash of gig clothes, stowed in Charlie's digs, felt more and more like reality. Fred, the youth group's pink-faced leader, greeted her like a lost sheep returning to the fold. Perhaps that was what she was.

'Come and meet Charles,' he declared, guiding her through the manse and into the garden. 'Charles is just here over the summer, but he's very keen to get involved in our little group.'

Fred's trust was absolute. Nothing about this

leather-jacketed stranger wanting to spend his evenings talking about the Bible and the proper morals for a Christian young person struck Fred as odd. In the garden, Charlie was sitting, surrounded by the rest of the group, drinking lemonade.

'I think we met, when Charlie, erm, Charles, came to church.'

She didn't add that they'd walked here together, and she'd only let go of him at the end of the street after they'd agreed that arriving together was pushing their luck.

'That's great.' Fred pointed her towards a chair opposite Charlie. 'Apparently, you've met Pat.'

Charlie nodded and turned to face her. 'You were supposed to be showing me around.'

'I'm sorry. I've been busy.'

'Maybe this weekend?'

She nodded.

'I mean, with anyone else who wants to come along too, obviously.'

'Of course.'

'I'm sorry. I didn't mean that to sound forward.'

People giggled awkwardly around them. Pat could feel her cheeks colouring. 'That's all right.'

'Good.' He turned his attention to the people sitting next to him. That was what they'd agreed. Charlie would be friendly to everyone. He had to be accepted. He had to be reported back to adults as a nice young man, a respectable young man, a boon to their little group. He couldn't be the teenager from out of town who rode in and set his sights on poor young Pat. That would never do at all.

Pat leaned back in her chair and watched Charlie talking to Eileen. Ronnie was leaning proprietarily across his girl, marking out his territory with his body. Pat would normally have laughed at his behaviour, but tonight she had a flash of understanding. She didn't want to be sitting watching Charlie charm anyone else. She wanted him all to herself.

She turned her head away from the scene and saw Fred starting to load the first sausages onto the barbeque. She breathed the smell of the coals and dripping fat and felt her stomach lurch. Her skin went cold and a thin film of sweat covered her face. She put her hand out to her side, knocking Denise on the arm.

'I don't feel very well.'

Denise peered at her. 'You've gone all white.'

'I think I'm going to be sick.'

'Oh.' Denise leaned away from her, unhelpfully focused on keeping her own distance.

Pat stood up and swayed unsteadily. She'd been to the manse before and tried to remember where the toilet was. Upstairs, she thought. She walked as elegantly as she could back into the house, and ran up the stairs, slamming the bathroom door behind her. She knelt in front of the toilet bowl and retched.

The vomit burnt her throat and her eyes filled with tears. She knelt up and reached to pull the chain to flush the toilet and then sat back on the floor, leaning against the cold wall. She tried to breathe but every breath caught in her raw throat. She pulled herself up to her feet and scooped some water from the tap into her hand to rinse her mouth.

'Pat!' There was a knock at the door. 'Are you okay? Denise said you weren't feeling well.'

'I'm fine.' Pat didn't want to be subjected to one of Fred's concerned talks. Another wave of nausea passed over her and she retched again over the bowl. Grating, dry retches as her already empty stomach spasmed again.

'Are you sure you're all right?'

Pat stood up. Flushed the toilet again and gave her mouth another rinse out. She opened the bathroom door and tried to smile. 'I'm fine.'

Fred had his features arranged into his special understanding face. 'It's okay, Pat. If there's anything you want to talk to me about though. I know it's hard, but I'm here for you to talk to about, about whatever you're going through . . . '

Pat went cold again. Did he know? He couldn't. She definitely wasn't showing yet. She felt her hand twitch and consciously stopped herself from letting it drift to her belly.

'Pat, if it's drink or you've been experimenting with anything like that, you know you can tell me?'

She stopped herself laughing. 'No. I'm fine. I think it's probably just a bug.'

'Well, you'll have to go then. We don't all want to catch it.'

Pat glanced towards the voice and saw Eileen standing on the bottom step, backed up by a gaggle of young people.

Fred waved his hand at them. 'Come on. If Pat's not well, we can't very well send her away, can we?'

'I could make sure she gets home.' Charlie's offer sounded nonchalant, almost disinterested.

Fred shook his head. 'I'm sure Pat wouldn't ask you to do that.'

Pat leaned back against the wall and sighed. 'Well, I probably should go home.'

'And we shouldn't make her walk on her own,' Charlie chipped in from the bottom of the stairs.

Fred looked momentarily lost. 'Perhaps one of the girls could . . .'

He tailed off as Eileen and Denise looked at the floor. Clearly neither of them wanted to get stuck leaving the party early with the sick girl.

'I don't mind. Really.'

'Okay then.' Pat moved quickly past Fred before he could think of a further objection. She guessed he felt that it was probably part of his role to discourage girls from heading off with unknown young men, but at the same time, she didn't think he'd want to appear an old fuddy-duddy by insisting on it. 'It's only a few minutes to my house. I'd just prefer not to walk on my own.' She sighed loudly. 'I really don't feel that well.'

Charlie was already pulling on his jacket and opening the front door. They were into the street before another word could be said. Once they were out of sight of the manse Pat slowed her pace. 'I actually really don't feel well.'

Charlie put an arm around her and pulled her close. 'Were you sick?'

She nodded. 'I don't know why. I've not eaten anything weird.'

He stopped and stepped in front of her. 'You're joking?'

'No?'

'You really don't know why you were sick?'

'No.'

'Pat, you're pregnant. Morning sickness?'

'It's not morning.'

He took a breath. 'You've not got any younger brothers or sisters, have you?'

She shook her head.

'And no little cousins, nieces, nephews?'

'No.'

'Right. When my sister was pregnant she was sick all the time for about a month.'

'That's not funny.'

'It's not a joke.'

'Oh.'

'Yeah.' He put his arm back around her and they started walking again.

'People are going to notice if I'm sick all the time.'

He nodded.

'We're going to have to tell them soon, aren't we?'

'I think so.'

'Who should we tell first?'

'I don't know.'

'What will your parents be like?'

Charlie shrugged. 'Not happy. Yours?'

'Same.'

'We could run away.'

They'd joked about the idea before, but this time Charlie sounded like he meant it. Pat tried to picture it. Packing a bag secretly, sneaking out. When would she go? In the evening would be easiest, while her father was out and Lilian was busy with her sherry bottle. How would they do it? She could go to Charlie's boarding house and then an early train in the morning, and they'd be away, just the two of them, together making their way in the world. A train to where though? And with what money?

'We have to tell them.'

'My father will try to stop us being married.' Charlie stopped still again. 'He'll say horrible things. He'll probably try to give you money to disappear. He'll say whatever he can think of to make me give you up.'

'But we'll refuse, won't we?' There was the tiniest quiver of doubt under the defiance in Pat's voice.

'Yeah.' He pulled her close to him and let her bury her face into his neck. 'It's going to be okay. You and me and the baby. It's going to be okay.'

They walked slowly most of the way, arms entwined. Pat found herself leaning more and more into Charlie's body. She didn't think she was going to vomit again, but the nausea hadn't subsided, and, from her dizzying, shifting point of view, he felt safe and solid. She pulled away, as she always did, under the tree on the corner.

'I'll see you then.'

Charlie shook his head. 'I'm coming in with you.'

'You can't!'

'I have to. They're going to get told that you were ill. What sort of upstanding young gentleman would I be if I didn't escort you home?'

At the front door his commitment wavered. 'Should I knock?'

Pat shook her head and opened the door with her key. 'Stay there,' she whispered.

More loudly, she added, 'Well, thank you very much for making sure I got home.'

He matched her stagey delivery. 'That's fine. I hope you feel better soon.'

Her parents came into the hallway, Father first, still in his work trousers, but jacket replaced by a pullover and carpet slippers, the spectacles on his nose suggesting he'd been bent over his account books before the interruption. His wife hovered behind him, upright in the doorway. Stanley moved across the hall towards Charlie.

'You're the young man who came to the service?'

Charlie nodded.

'He came to the barbeque. I wasn't feeling very well, so he walked me back. It was just because I wasn't very well. I . . . ' Pat forced herself to stop talking. She was blathering. *Don't blather.* That's one thing she'd learnt as Gypsy Patience. Don't go on too much. It makes you sound less confident.

'Pat was taken ill. I offered to walk her back. Everyone else knew each other, so I thought it would break up the party less if I came.'

'Right.' Stanley looked from Charlie to Pat and back again to Charlie where his gaze lingered a moment. The young people didn't make eye contact. 'Well, that's very good of you.'

51

The restaurant was perfectly decent for what it was. One of those chain Italian places with delusions of class. Leo ordered the penne arrabiata because the waiter asked and he knew he was supposed to order something. He couldn't imagine eating. He couldn't imagine ever being hungry again. His body had shut down all its systems so that he could be purely concentrated on the questions that were streaming through his brain. His initial scepticism was waning. After they'd managed to get Marnie to stop shrieking, and their daughter had shaken her head, quietly but definitely, at her mother's plan to book tickets to New Zealand right that very second, Grace had explained that she'd talked to the man claiming to be Olly at some length, over a period of time that Leo suspected was significantly longer than she was letting on. When they arrived at the restaurant — his penniless student daughter was very clear that, family crisis or not, she still needed to be fed — Leo had asked her when Olly had first got in touch. She'd prevaricated, avoiding the question and wondering aloud whether she would order wine when both her parents, she presumed, would have to drive later.

Olly was alive. At first that was the only thought he had space for, but quickly others barged in. Where was he? Where had he been?

283

Why hadn't he been in touch earlier? Leo's imagination leapt to fill in the gaps. A horrendous accident. A kidnapping. A bout of amnesia.

Grace swirled the wine in her glass — she gone for the house red — ordering it with a confidence that reminded Leo of the teenage Marnie. 'I think Olly might have had some problems.'

'What sort of problems?'

His daughter stared at her glass. 'Like mental problems. A sort of breakdown maybe.' She looked at her mother. 'What is it soldiers get?'

'PTSD.'

Grace wrinkled her nose.

'Post-traumatic stress disorder.'

'Yeah, maybe, after the landslide.'

Leo wished he was drinking too. Just a small one. A brandy maybe — that was what they gave people for shock, wasn't it? 'Just tell us everything. From the start.'

He leaned back in his seat and listened. The first part of the story they already knew. The camping trip. The sudden landslide. Leo tried to stop himself imagining the terror of waking to find the ground rolling beneath you. According to what he'd told Grace, Olly hadn't been asleep when the landslide had hit. He didn't know what had woken him. He'd seen Nick get out of the tent, and then he'd felt the ground shift. He knew he'd started to get out of his sleeping bag and had stuck his head out of the tent to see what was going on. After that, things were a blur. He remembered being thrown down the hillside, and then there was a blank before he remembered finding himself lying at the foot of the hill. Somehow he'd been thrown clear of the tent. He'd broken his wrist and badly bruised his ribs and shoulder but he could walk.

The waiter interrupted Grace's story, putting plates of pasta and pizza in front of them. Grace twirled spaghetti round her fork and stared at her lunch. 'And that's about it.'

'It's incredible.' Marnie's leg was twitching against Leo's thigh. It always did that when she was nervous or excited. It had driven Leo to distraction for nearly thirty years. His wife turned towards him. 'It's a miracle. We're going to get him back. Everything will be like it was before.'

That was the dream, wasn't it? Olly would come home. Whatever tragedy had befallen him would be put aside. Their family would be made whole, and Marnie would love him again. Time would rewind to a point when they were happy. It didn't work like that. Grace was still twirling her spaghetti and studiously avoiding her parents' gaze.

Leo swallowed. 'That's not everything though, is it, Grace?'

'What do you mean?'

He tried to marshal his disparate thoughts into words. Something wasn't there. The journalist in him was pushing for answers. The father desperately wanted to look away. 'Well, that was four years ago. Why didn't he call an ambulance or the police? Or us? You said he wasn't badly hurt, so that means . . . ' Leo didn't want to say what it meant out loud. 'That means he chose not to come home. He could have come back, but he didn't want to.'

Grace chewed her pasta.

Marnie shook her head. 'No. Something must have happened to him. Tell us, Grace.'

'I don't know.'

'What do you mean you don't know? What did he say?'

'I think he saw it as a chance to get away.' Grace still wasn't meeting her parents' eyes. 'You know he struggled at college.'

Marnie's voice rose a notch. 'He was doing fine. He was happy.'

'No. Why do you think he deferred his final year?'

Leo heard the shrillness in his wife's tone. She'd waited a long time for her happy ending; she wasn't going to like Grace trying to rewrite it. 'He wanted some time off. That was all. Something else must have happened.'

Leo tried to think. Who had his son been? He remembered the boy they'd constructed — the photograph Marnie had given the police — the picture of the perfect smiling black-haired boy. He thought about the boy he'd described to Louise. The joker. The athlete. Had he always been like that? Was he like that right up to the end? Images of his son danced through his mind, but refused to settle. What did he remember? Who was Olly? He'd not been academic, but he loved sport. That was what he'd been focusing on at college. Leo swallowed. 'But what about his cricket?'

Grace put down her fork and leaned back. 'What about it, Dad?'

'He loved cricket.'

She shook her head. 'Well, I love doing my nails.' It was true. Grace was currently sporting zebra-print talons. 'I wouldn't want to do it competitively. Or as a job. Some things are supposed to be fun.'

'But he wouldn't have run away.' Marnie was definite, like she'd been definite all these years that Olly was alive, like she'd been definite that Leo and she should marry, that they should live in Manchester, that he should write for a living.

Grace drank some more of her wine, and paused, waiting, Leo suspected, until she had the full attention of both her parents. Then she bit her bottom lip. 'Well, I'm only telling you what he told me.'

'He wouldn't have just gone.' There was a quiver in his wife's voice now that Leo had only heard a few times before. She'd always been utterly certain that something had happened to Olly. Some misfortune. Some dark force had stopped her raven-haired boy from coming home.

Grace nodded. 'But now he's back. Well, not back.'

Every answer raised a thousand more questions. 'Where is he then?'

'Still in New Zealand.'

Something didn't add up. Think like a journalist. What had changed? 'So why get in touch now?'

Grace took a gulp of her drink. 'He's getting engaged.'

287

Leo gasped. He saw Marnie open her mouth.

Grace didn't let her get another question out. 'And his fiancée is having a baby. You're going to be grandparents.'

Olly was alive. Not just alive, but from the sounds of things, thriving. Grace pulled her handbag onto her knee and delved inside. She pulled out a piece of paper with an email address written on it. 'He'd like you to get in touch.' She paused. 'If you want to.'

Marnie grabbed the slip of paper from the table, and pulled out her phone. 'I'll do it now.'

Leo lifted the phone from her fingers. 'Wait. I think we should think about what we want to say.'

'What do you mean? We want to tell him to come home.'

That was the obvious thing, but it wasn't right. 'Let's think about it for a minute. This isn't the teenager who you drove to the airport with his backpack. This is a young man. Practically a father himself, and we don't know anything about what he's been doing for the last four years. We can't steam in and expect him to be exactly like we remember.'

Across the table he saw Grace nod. She wasn't who he thought she was either. In his mind, she was still a teenage princess, but here she was, apparently respecting her brother's wishes, making decisions about how to affect this reunion, holding back as much as she was telling them. 'Thank you, Grace.'

'What for?'

He sighed. 'I'm not sure. For handling this.

For not scaring him off again.'

For a second the little girl he remembered reappeared in front of his eyes. 'I want him to be okay too.'

'I know.'

Leo's phone vibrated against his thigh. He shook his head. Not now. He pulled out the phone. *Barney*. He hit reject. Work could wait. He stopped. Work. Patrice. Patrice had told him Olly was dead. She'd stood on a stage and told him — not just him, a whole theatre full of strangers — that his son was gone for ever. She'd made it okay for him to insist once and for all that Marnie was wrong. She'd lied about the most important thing in the world.

'Dad?' Grace was leaning across the table. 'Are you okay?'

He nodded without really looking at her. His brain wasn't in the room anymore. He'd let himself get used to not feeling anything too deeply. He could see it now. When Olly went, he'd closed down. Marnie had clung to hope. Grace had been angry and attention-seeking. Leo had held things together. He'd held things together when his mum died. He'd held them together through counselling. He'd held them together when Patrice had told him that he wasn't her son. He'd even, somehow, managed to start an affair without embracing the passion or the guilt that he should have been overwhelmed by. But he was feeling something now, and it was incredible.

He pushed his chair away from the table. 'I have to go.'

'What?' His wife's face was incredulous. He was doing the wrong thing. He was letting her down again, but he had no choice. He could taste the anger and it wasn't as he'd imagined. He didn't feel raw or out of control. The anger was cool, but it was definite and it was urgent and it demanded to be used.

Marnie's mouth dropped open. 'Where? Now?'

'Patrice. She told me . . . '

Marnie's face hardened. 'She told you she'd talked to him.' For a fraction of a second, his wife looked at him with something he hoped might be understanding in her eyes. 'And then you'll come back?'

Leo hesitated and nodded. 'As soon as I can.'

52

1967

Pat stared out of the window of the bus. Rain hammered against the glass. She felt Charlie's fingers wrap around her own. This was the day. They were going to tell her parents everything. It had to be now. Exam results had come in. Applications for secretarial college were being finalised on her behalf. Things had to change.

They walked up the street together and to the front door. Pat wondered about that. Charlie was a guest. Her parents would be mortified at the thought of her traipsing him through the kitchen. She turned her key in the Yale and pushed the door.

'I'm home.'

'Pat!' Her mother's voice ran out from the kitchen.

Pat turned to Charlie, letting her head rest for a second against his chest. 'Are you ready?'

He nodded and squeezed her hand.

She took a breath. 'Charlie, Charles is here.'

Both her parents appeared in the hallway, her mother from the kitchen and her father from the dining room.

Pat headed off their questions. 'We've got something to tell you.' Gripping Charlie's hand, she led the way into the lounge and settled herself in the middle of the good settee. She'd

291

picked the good lounge on purpose. It made things formal. It pulled them all out of the everyday business of family and made what was about to happen that little bit less real.

'Whatever is this about?' Pat's father followed them into the room and took a seat on the armchair, followed by Lilian, who had discarded her apron.

'We weren't expecting company, Patience.'

'I'm sorry.' Charlie mumbled the apology and glanced at Pat. 'Do you want me to . . . ?'

She shook her head. 'We have some news.' She'd thought about how to put this, about what to lead with, and she'd made a decision. 'Charlie has asked me to many him, and I've said yes.'

Lilian reacted before her husband. 'Don't be ridiculous.'

Charlie cleared his throat. 'It's not ridiculous. I love Pat very much, and — '

Pat's mother snorted. 'Love? Love won't get you very far. When Patience gets married, it will be to a man who's able to support her. She barely knows you.' She paused for a second. 'When did you meet anyway? A month ago? Not even that.'

Pat glanced at the floor. This was one of the things she hadn't really worked out. Was it better for them to think it was a whirlwind romance, or to know that it was serious but that they'd been lied to for weeks?

Her father swallowed. 'Make some tea, Lilian.'

'Tea? We're not offering this . . . this . . . ' She gestured at Charlie, apparently unable to find a word to describe the horror in front of her.

'Lilian, we have a guest.'

Pat watched as her mother composed herself. The flash of emotion and outrage from just moments before disappeared as quickly as it had arrived. 'Very well.'

The remaining trio sat and listened to the ticking of the clock on the mantel. Stanley pulled a cloth from his breast pocket, removed his spectacles and started to clean the lenses. Pat opened her mouth. 'We really are very much — '

Her father held up a hand. 'We'll discuss it when your mother comes back.'

Charlie shifted on the sofa next to her. What was he thinking? The clock ticked on.

Lilian reappeared with tea on a tray. The normal cups, not the good set, Pat noticed. Her mother poured tea and milk, and offered sugar. No cake or biscuits. Stanley sipped his tea before returning the cup to the saucer. 'So how long has this been going on?'

Pat swallowed. 'Since we first met really.' It was the Gypsy Patience answer. Not technically a lie, but vague.

'And it's serious?'

Pat and Charlie nodded in unison.

Stanley took another sip. 'You're only sixteen.'

Pat nodded. 'So we need your consent.'

Lilian muttered something to herself. Pat's father ignored her. 'And what prospects do you have, young man?'

Charlie sat up straight. 'Well, I'm working with a band, a group of musicians, at the moment, so I'm probably going to do something like that?'

Lilian winced. 'You're going to support my

293

daughter by playing in a band?'

Charlie shook his head. 'No. By managing bands and tours and that.'

'You don't have a university degree then?'

Charlie shook his head again. 'I'm only eighteen.'

Stanley glanced at his wife. 'It seems to me that getting married at this point would be unnecessary. If you secure proper employment, we can discuss the possibility of you continuing to spend time with Pat. But no. You are both simply too young for marriage.'

Pat closed her eyes for a second. What could they do? They could run away to Scotland. You could get married there at sixteen, but then what? She took another breath. 'No, Daddy. We have to get married.'

'What do you mean you have to?'

Pat could feel her cheeks colouring. At her side, Charlie was staring straight ahead, fingers still gripping her own.

Across the room, Lilian's cup and saucer wobbled for a second in her fingers before crashing to the floor. The noise cracked through the silence. Lilian watched them for a second. The brown mark spread across the carpet. 'Fetch a cloth, Patience.'

Pat pulled her hand out of Charlie's and ran to the kitchen. She grabbed the first cloth she saw and dashed back to the lounge. She couldn't leave him alone to face the music. Together. That's what they'd agreed. They would do whatever it took to persuade their parents to consent, but they would do it as a team. She knelt at her mother's feet, pressing the cloth against the wet carpet, waiting for somebody to speak. Her mother broke the silence. 'You don't mean . . . ' Pat watched her turn her head to her husband. 'She can't mean . . . Pat's not that sort . . . '

Not that sort. That summed Pat up, didn't it? Not the sort to disobey her parents. Not the sort to dress up as a gypsy every day and pretend to tell fortunes. Not the sort to have a boyfriend. Definitely not the sort to go all the way. She swallowed. 'Mummy, Daddy, I'm expecting a baby. Charlie's baby.'

And the silence ended. Lilian, who Pat suspected had raised a glass or two to the parson already that afternoon, let everything out. This was, apparently, all Stanley's fault for being too soft with the girl, for letting her work at That Place where she was bound to be exposed to layabouts and loose-moraled boys like this one.

Eventually Stanley spoke. 'Then you're right, Pat. You'll have to get married.'

Lilian opened her mouth to start again. Stanley interrupted her. 'What choice do they have?'

He turned back to the young lovers huddled together on the settee. 'What do your parents do, Charles?'

'My father has a shop.'

'What sort of shop?'

'An ironmonger.'

Stanley's lips pursed.

'He's done well though. He wants me to go to university.'

'What were you planning to study?'

Charlie swallowed. 'I'm supposed to be doing law.'

There was a pause. 'That might be the best plan.'

Pat shook her head. 'Charlie doesn't want to go to university.'

Her father had turned to her mother and was talking more quietly now. 'If his parents are willing to help . . . '

Pat watched them carve up her future in polite whispers.

'I need to telephone your parents.'

Charlie shook his head. 'I was going to talk to them.'

Stanley pursed his lips again. 'I'll deal with this now. I think it's best if you go. I take it Pat knows where we can contact you.'

Charlie looked to Pat for guidance. She didn't know. It seemed like she might be allowed to get married, but somehow, even though she was getting what she wanted, everything had flown out of her hands. She didn't want to let him go. She wanted to keep him right wherever she was, fingers eternally entwined in hers until the signatures were dry on the marriage certificate and nobody, not her mother nor her father nor their polite friends nor a polite god, could rip him away. In the end, she shrugged, opened her hand, and let him drift away and out of the door.

53

Louise understood what to expect this time. She took her seat and fiddled with Leo's recorder while she waited for Patrice to gather herself. She was a calming presence. Apart from Leo, she was the only person Louise had met since Kyle had gone who was comfortable talking about death. She didn't tell Louise to get over it or to move on. She accepted exactly where Louise was and what she needed.

Patrice smiled across the low table at her while Barney poured tea into the cups in front of them, before making his excuses with a promise to be back a little later. 'I'm quite tired today, dear. Sometimes the spirits don't come as strongly if I'm not feeling quite tip-top.'

Louise didn't reply. Kyle would come. She knew he would come. The reading started much like the first one. Patrice had a sense of Kyle in the room, and he was safe now and he was happy. Louise let the sense of his closeness wash over her. 'Can I talk to him?'

Patrice nodded. 'He can hear you.'

Louise expected her tongue to fly. She told him that she missed him and that she loved him and then . . . what? She used to tell him funny stories about the old boys who came into the chippy, but she didn't go there anymore. She used to get on at him about cleaning his room or emptying out his sports bag or spending too long staring at a screen. None of that mattered now. She used to ask him questions about college, about his mates, about the video games he played and the TV he watched. He used to bring life into her world. She stuttered to a halt. 'Just that I love him.'

Patrice seemed to nod slightly, but didn't reply.

Louise needed more. She needed Patrice to keep telling her about Kyle. She needed that sense that he was right alongside her. 'Is he still here?'

'Oh yes. He's saying he's at peace. He's not in any pain now.'

That was good. She hated the idea of him hurting. She was scared of the answer, of the reality of him lying there bleeding and screaming in pain, but she had to know. 'Was there pain though? When it happened?'

Patrice frowned, and then turned towards a sharp knock at the door. 'I'd better see who that is.'

* * *

Leo was bouncing from foot to foot outside the door. As soon as she swung it open, he was past her, barging into the room. Patrice closed the door slowly, taking as much time as she could. Was Leo supposed to be here? She thought maybe he was, but if it was just a normal appointment why was he huffing and stomping about? Maybe he wasn't supposed to be here. Maybe she'd been supposed to meet him

298

elsewhere. It was possible. So little seemed certain anymore.

'You lied.'

Patrice dropped her gaze to the floor in case any hint of the horror inside her head was showing on her face. She walked back to her chair. That girl — the dowdy girl with the dead son — was still sitting on the sofa. Patrice steadied herself on the chair arm before lowering herself into the seat. How could he know? Inside her head, she knew, Patience was coming, ready to grab hold of him and explain herself and beg him for forgiveness. But not. Not here. Patrice swallowed, and then furrowed her brow ever so slightly. Genuine confusion. Not fear. Not anguish. That's what she needed to show him. 'What do you mean?'

'You know what I mean.' He was pacing now, up and down along the four feet of clear carpet between the wall and the bathroom door.

She watched him for a second. His shock of black hair was grey around the temples. Was that what Charlie would have looked like now? Could she see Patience's perfect baby in the man in front of her? She shook her head hesitantly. 'I'm not sure I understand.'

He stopped still, turning sharply to face her. 'You said you talked to Olly.'

Olly? Names and faces swum in front of her — from this world and from the other one that she was trying to hold at bay. 'I'm sorry?'

'My son. You said you'd talked to my son.'

Of course. Another black-haired boy. 'I remember.'

'But you lied.'

Patrice almost laughed. That was the thing. You couldn't guess. That wasn't what this life was. It wasn't guessing. It was researching and watching and thinking. You never let what you wanted interfere. You worked out what they wanted. Of course Leo wasn't thinking about the mother he'd never had; he was wrapped up in the son he'd lost. 'Sometimes messages from the other plane are unclear.'

He shook his head and stepped towards her, leaning down over her chair. 'But it wasn't unclear, was it? You knew about the accident. You knew how it all happened. And I know he didn't tell you. He didn't reach out to you from beyond the veil or whatever it is you say. You didn't talk to him.'

Patrice thought she probably ought to turn towards him, look her son in the eye at least, but somehow her neck didn't want to turn. She moved to fold her hands neatly on her lap. Her left arm stayed stubbornly where it was. No matter. She needed to say something. She just needed a moment or two to work out what.

'What do you mean?' The voice wasn't Leo and it wasn't Patrice so it must, she supposed, be the dowdy girl.

'I mean she's a fraud. She makes it up. She's not talking to anyone.'

'No. She talked to Kyle.' Now the woman was leaning over her too, right in her face, hands grabbing her by the shoulders. 'Tell him. Tell him it's true.'

Patrice tried to nod. Of course it was true.

Fifty years. Thousands of happy customers. Thousands of spirits at peace on the other side. Maybe it was inevitable that one day it would all fall down. She'd known it was coming, but she'd thought it would be Patience breaking out to get her baby back. She didn't think Patience's baby might come back and do the job himself. It was appropriate, she supposed.

Somewhere outside of her head, she was aware of Leo pulling the girl away from her. Then it was his hands on her shoulders. 'Patrice! Patrice! Are you okay?'

He was shouting now. He hadn't shouted before. He hadn't needed to. She'd felt his rage burning ice cold through the quiet.

'Go get Barney.' He shook her by the shoulders. 'No. Get an ambulance.'

He was leaning towards her again, his face inches from her own. It was all falling away. She opened her mouth and tried to tell him but the words wouldn't come. They spun around her head, trapped inside her failing body. *I'm sorry.*

54

Twelve noon. In thirty minutes, Charlie and his parents would arrive for Sunday lunch, over which, Pat had been told, the adults would sort this whole thing out. The plan was that she and Charlie would marry as soon as possible, hopefully before the university term started next month. Charlie would then go to university as his parents expected. His parents and hers would support them to find married couples' accommodation and she would be a model housewife and, sooner that anyone would like, a mother. Their baby, like so many others, would be a little honeymoon miracle.

This was not Pat's plan, but for the moment it would do. She was in a strange and unexpected state, being prepared to be launched, suddenly, awkwardly, into the adult world. She was going to be a wife and mother. In time, she'd be a respectable solicitor's wife, with her own good china and her own bottle of sherry hidden under the sink. She pushed the image out of her mind. She was going to be Charlie's wife, the mother of Charlie's child, and Charlie loved her. Patience sat absolutely still in the good lounge. She'd sat in here every day since she told her parents she was pregnant. She hadn't been to work. She hadn't been to youth group. She hadn't been to church. It ought to be a privilege. It wasn't. It was her holding pen, while the grown-ups worked out what to do with her.

A car pulled to a halt in the street outside. A man Pat didn't recognise walked past the window to the door. Something was wrong. This couldn't be Charlie's father, because he was bringing Charlie with him. They were all meeting together and they were going to talk about the wedding and everything that was being planned for them after that. Pat's fingers twisted around a corner of one of the good cushions, the pale yellow ones that were surreptitiously pulled away from small children or shaky-handed pensioners for fear of spills. Pat gripped the fabric. Everything was decided. It was all wrong, but it was all decided.

Her father answered the door, and a second later the adults paraded into the room. The stranger took a seat on the best armchair. 'Right. I'll say what I came to say.' He looked at Pat. 'Charlie's coming back to London with me.'

Pat opened her mouth, but whatever words there might have been sat tight in her throat.

Her father shook his head. 'We discussed this on the telephone.'

The man nodded. 'I'm sorry, but I know my son, and I don't know this girl.' He waved a hand in Pat's direction. 'I've only your word that she's in trouble, and only hers that Charlie had anything to do with it. So that's that.'

Pat stared at the stranger who purported to be beautiful Charlie's father. There was nothing of his son about him. His face was ruddy and pockmarked. His hair was held flat with a thick layer of grease. He had a big gold signet ring on his fat little finger. She found some words. 'What did Charlie say?'

He shook his head. 'That's beside the point.'

'What did Charlie say?'

The man turned his head away. 'Charlie will see the sense of this once he's home.'

That was it, wasn't it? Gypsy Patience looked past the slicked-back hair and the fat piggy face. He wasn't sure. That was enough for Pat. She jumped from the sofa and ran out of the front door. The car was sitting at the end of the driveway, and there he was. Charlie stared at her from the back seat. His door opened and he stepped out. She stopped a yard away from him. 'He says you're going back with him.'

'I don't want to.'

'Then don't.'

Charlie's eyes flicked to the ground. 'He said it might not even be mine.'

A wave of nausea swept through Pat's body. He couldn't believe that. He couldn't think he hadn't been the only one. Charlie had known her completely. 'You know it's yours.'

He didn't meet her eye. The adults caught up with her. Pat felt her mother's hand on her arm. It was an unusual feeling. 'Come inside, Patience.'

She stared at Charlie. There had to be something she could say. There had to be something she could do that would make this right. 'It doesn't have to be like they're planning. We could move somewhere together. I can get a job, until the baby comes. You can still work with the band.' She was shrieking now, babbling in desperation, saying anything in the hope that something would be the thing that made him stay. She sniffed hard to stop snot streaming down her face.

Charlie still wasn't meeting her eye. 'I don't know . . . ' He shrugged.

'Get in the car, Charles.'

'Wait.' Pat's voice was ragged but definite. She needed to get them all back to where she'd thought they were. 'Charlie knows it's his baby.'

Her mother's hand on her arm again. 'Patience. We're in the street.'

Pat didn't care. She kept her attention fixed on Charlie. 'You know. Don't you?'

He gave the faintest hint of a nod.

'So we're getting married? Like we planned.'

She watched her lover keep his gaze pinned down to the ground. His father stepped between them, his bulky, sweaty body eclipsing Charlie's slight frame. 'We're going.'

'But . . . it was agreed. You can't make him go if he doesn't want to.'

Charlie's father didn't budge. 'Look, I don't want to get physical with a young girl.'

'Dad!' Charlie stepped up next to his father.

The older man turned, his face now just a couple of inches from his son's. 'What?'

Charlie stood his ground. 'Maybe we should talk to them.'

The older man edged forward. 'So she can talk you round? We're getting in the car. We're going home and you're going to university like you promised.'

Pat cleared her throat. 'He's just suggesting that we have a talk.'

305

Charlie's father didn't react. He stayed stock still staring at his son. 'Get in the car.'

The words weren't shouted but they carried across the quiet street like a scream.

Charlie didn't move.

His father raised his voice. 'Get in the car.'

Pat watched. It was going to be all right. Charlie had said that his father would be horrible. He'd said that he'd try to tell lies about her, and he'd promised that it wouldn't work. He'd promised that he'd stand up for her and for their baby.

The final time the words were yelled, sending flecks of spit into Charlie's face. Pat watched him blink against the onslaught. 'Get in the car.'

And this time he crumbled. She saw it in his posture before the acquiescence reached his face. The tension that had been holding him to the spot seemed to dissipate all at once. His shoulders slumped and his head dropped. He nodded briefly. His father stepped back, marching quickly to the driver's side door.

Pat screamed, not words, not arguments, just horror pouring up from her gut. Her mother grabbed her arm more forcefully this time. 'Patience! People will be watching.'

Pat didn't care. The howl subsided, but the feeling wouldn't go away. She'd lost. They'd lost. It was over. She watched from the pavement as Charlie did as he was told, and the sleek black car rolled him away. Her father clapped his hands together. 'Well, best get back inside.'

So this was it. This was the moment Pat was going to be trapped in for ever.

55

1968

Time passed. Summer turned to autumn and then to winter. Christmas came and went in awkward silence. January came, and snow sat resolute on the freezing ground outside, not that Pat went outside much anymore. She was six months gone and life had shrunk to her bedroom, and the dining room for meals. Her parents were hiding her from the world, and she was hiding herself from her parents.

Stanley was out at the pharmacy, and Pat sat in her bedroom and listened to her mother answering the door. Pat wasn't seeing anyone. That was what her mother thought was best. She'd stopped going to church when her blouses started to strain across her tummy. She'd stopped going to work as well. Apparently, Mr Stefanini had been told that she needed to concentrate on her studies, but there were no studies. There was the house and her parents and the silence.

She listened to the voices at the front door, quiet at first and then raised, and then a distinct yell of 'No!' from her mother before footsteps stomped through the house, and eventually onto the stairs.

'Pat!' The voice had reached the half-landing. 'Pat!'

Pat climbed off her bed and opened the door to her room. She watched Hester stop dead and stare from her face to her stomach and back to her face. 'Shit, Pat. What happened to you?'

Lilian bustled up the stairs. 'As I said, Patience is unwell. She's not to be disturbed.'

Hester snorted out a laugh. 'She's not unwell. She's up the sodding duff.' She turned to Lilian. 'And I'm her friend and I've come to see her. All right?'

Pat watched her mother step back from the lacquered and mascaraed vision. When she spoke it was straight past Hester towards Pat. 'Patience, you know our rules about guests. I shall be calling your father.'

Lilian stalked back down the stairs. Hester shrugged as she pulled off her coat. 'I don't think your mam likes me. I've telephoned you know. She just says you're unwell.'

Pat frowned. She hadn't been told about any telephone calls. If Hester had been phoning, maybe he had too.

Hester shoved past her, dropped her coat on the floor and flopped down on the bed. 'So how far gone are you?'

Pat closed the door. 'About six months.'

'So it's Charlie's?'

Pat nodded.

'And he's buggered off?'

Pat couldn't bring herself to concede that point. 'His parents took him away.'

Hester shook her head. 'He buggered off then.' She looked around the room. Pat followed her gaze. What did this room look like to Hester?

The counterpane was blush pink and worn at the corners. The dresser had been her grandmother's, and was covered with trinkets and a silver-handled mirror and hairbrush. She pictured Hester's bedroom. Clothes strewn across the floor probably. Make-up piled up on every free surface. Anywhere Hester lived was instantly soaked through with the spirit of Hester. Pat's room could be anyone's. Hester was staring at the bump. 'So what's it like?'

'What?'

'Being pregnant. Can you feel it moving around?'

Pat nodded. 'She's started sort of hiccupping.'

'Ew.' Hester pulled a face. 'Is it doing it now?'

Pat shook her head. 'I think she's asleep.'

'It's a girl?'

'I don't really know. I imagine it is.'

Hester widened her eyes. 'Then it must be. You'd know.'

'What?'

'It must be a psychic vision. That's amazing.'

Pat didn't answer.

'I missed you at work. I looked you up on the payroll to find your address. Stefanini closed the gypsy booth for the winter, but I reckon he'll get someone new for Easter. Unless you come back. Will you have had it by then?'

Pat shook her head. Easter was in the middle of April. She'd still have another two weeks to go, and then she'd be a mother. A single mother. A fallen woman.

'You should have told us about the baby though. I'll tell everyone now. We'll have a whip round for you. That's what we did when Moira had the twins. And a party. We should have a party.'

'I don't think Mother wants people knowing.'

Hester pursed her lips. 'What's it got to do with her?'

'They're my parents.'

Hester shrugged. 'They're worried about what people will think. It's 1968. Nobody cares about that stuff anymore.'

Pat didn't reply.

'You want it though, don't you? I mean, you'd have taken care of it if you didn't.'

'What?'

'Like drinking gin or leeches. I had an aunt who did leeches.'

Pat's hand instinctively moved to her stomach, stretching across her body to protect the precious miracle inside. This was her baby. Hers and Charlie's. She wasn't something to be taken care of.

56

The girl with the dead son was shouting in her face, and then Leo, and then Barney, and then a man she didn't know with a bright yellow jacket and a green jumpsuit. And then they were lifting her into a funny three-quarter chair thing that didn't seem to know whether it was a seat or the other thing. Patrice waited for the name of the other thing to pop into her mind. Lying-downy thing. For sick people. The poorly lie-down thing. It was no use; she didn't know what it was called. The jumpsuit man asked her to tell him her own name. She couldn't reply. What was she supposed to say? It was a very complicated question.

Patrice closed her eyes. She wasn't in this hotel room anymore. She was somewhere else, back where all of this had begun. The shouting people yelled for her to open her eyes, but she didn't think there was any point. She'd held her off as long as she could, but now Patience was coming. Leo had broken down the final wall inside her head. There wouldn't be any stopping her anymore. Patrice rested her head on the thing that was somewhere between a stretcher and a . . . What was it? A sitting thing. She rested her head and accepted her defeat.

57

'So tell me about yourself?'

The matron peered at Pat from across the desk.

'I'm Patience. I'm seventeen.' She rubbed her hand across her stomach. 'I'm expecting a baby.'

The matron rolled her eyes. Next to Pat, Lilian shifted in her seat. 'Patience understands that this is the best place for her.'

'I'm sure. And what about the father?'

Pat swallowed. What about the father? 'Charlie. Charles. He's not involved with us anymore.'

'Surname?'

'Bickersleigh.'

The woman shook her head. 'The father's surname?'

Pat paused. Charlie was just Charlie. She looked at the matron. She needed an answer. What would Gypsy Patience do? Give her what she wanted. 'Smith.'

'Charles Smith?'

Pat nodded and the woman noted the name on the forms in front of her. She turned to Lilian. 'And you've been visited by the moral welfare worker at home?'

Lilian nodded.

'And you both understand the choices? To

either raise the baby yourself, Pat, or give it up for adoption?' The woman's voice was official, business-like.

Pat nodded.

'And we all agree that adoption is best?'

Pat didn't reply.

The matron continued. 'Best for baby, that is.'

That was what the moral welfare worker had said too. Best for baby. What was best for baby was a proper family with a mother and a father and a house. Pat was a child herself. She wasn't what Charlie's baby needed. She nodded.

The matron smiled. 'Very good. So say goodbye to your mother then, and I'll show you around.'

Lilian stood up and patted her daughter on the top of her arm. 'Well, I'll be off then.'

She hesitated, as if she knew she ought to say more, but couldn't quite think what. Pat nodded and followed the matron out of the room without saying another word.

The tour was brief and to the point. Shared bathrooms with a sign-up sheet where you could book a time in the big bath. One large common room for recreation time and visiting, which was permitted on Sunday afternoons after church but before supper. The kitchens, where all food was provided but the girls were expected to cook and clean up after meals. And finally the bedrooms. Pat found herself in a small dormitory with four beds, two apparently empty and two occupied. Matron gestured to an empty bed underneath the window. 'That's yours. You'll keep your own area tidy. The cupboard has a key.

I'd advise you lock it. I take a dim view of stealing but I can't be everywhere and some of these girls didn't bring anything with them but the clothes they stood up in.'

Pat nodded.

Matron looked at the watch on her chest. 'No chores today but you'll be on the rota with everyone else tomorrow. You've got six weeks to go?'

'Yes.'

'So it'll be full chores for the next month and then light duties for the last two weeks. Everyone pulls their weight here.'

Pat nodded again.

The matron pointed at a bed on the far wall. 'I'll ask Susan to come up and show you the ropes. It's her third time here so she knows what's what.'

The woman turned to walk away.

'What about . . . '

The matron stopped. 'Spit it out.'

'What about after I . . . ?'

The matron shook her head. 'You'll stay here for a month or so, until it's time for the adoption and then you can go home.' She stepped away from Pat. 'It doesn't do to think about that too much.'

Pat sat on her own in the unfamiliar room. Her bag was on the bed beside her. Such a small bag, but she had so few clothes that fit her now, and her mother had refused to be seen out in town buying more maternity things. Two months she'd be here. And then she was to go home as if nothing had happened. Presumably she would go to secretarial college a year late and life would

314

simply go on as planned. Nothing would remain of her baby, nor of Charlie, beyond memories.

'Are you Pat?'

The woman in the doorway was probably no more than a year older than Patience, but her face had a hardness Pat hadn't seen before. She'd thought that being Gypsy Patience had meant she'd seen all the different looks and demeanours that were out there, but this was different. This was a face without hope. Pat nodded.

'I'm Susan. I'm supposed to bring you down for supper and explain about chores for tomorrow.'

Pat followed her new guide along corridors and down stairs. The building was old and had more of the feel of a rundown stately home than a hospital.

'How many people are there here?'

Susan shrugged. 'There's six bedrooms. Space for three or four girls in each.'

'Matron said you'd been here before?'

Her guide stopped and turned. 'Do you always ask this many questions?'

Pat dropped her head. 'Sorry.'

Susan carried on along the downstairs corridor. 'It's stew tonight. It's always stew. Do you like stew?'

Pat nodded.

'Then you'll be fine.'

The dining room was plainly decorated with two long trestle tables squeezed into the space. Susan directed her charge to an empty seat on the long side of the nearest table. Pat opened her mouth.

315

'Sshhh. Grace.'

At the end of the room the matron cleared her throat. The pregnant girls fell into silence.

'For what we are about to receive may the Lord make us truly thankful.'

'Amen.'

'May he also forgive our sins and — '

A pained squawk came from the girl sitting straight opposite Pat.

'And lead us from this time of trial.' The matron ignored the interruption to complete her prayer.

'Amen.'

'Now what seems to be the matter?'

The girl's hands were pressed down onto the table top and she was breathing heavily. 'I think I'm having a contraction.'

The matron let out a sigh. 'Did your waters break?'

The girl shook her head. 'I don't think so.'

'And when's your due date?'

'Another two weeks.'

'Eat your dinner then. Let us know if they start coming more often.'

Pat stared at the plate of greying stew in front of her. The girl across the table was crying. Next to her Susan was tucking into her dinner.

Pat leaned forward. 'What's your name?'

'Nancy.'

'I'm Pat.' She didn't know what else to say. She hadn't thought much about actually having her baby. She'd assumed that there would be doctors and people around, but somehow in her imagination when the time came a curtain was pulled across the image and then, some time later, the curtain was drawn back and the baby was there. Labour was not something that happened at the dinner table. 'Do you think you're having your baby?'

'I don't know.'

Susan shook her head. 'Nah. It's her first, isn't it? First babies take for ever. Even if you're having contractions it's not gonna come till tomorrow.'

Nancy paled even further. Susan pointed at her plate. 'Are you going to eat that?'

★　★　★

Pat knelt on the floor outside the delivery room, and dipped her sponge in the bucket. Floors had to be cleaned. Clothes had to be washed and dried and mended. Meals had to be prepared. Tables had to be set and cleared and set again. Cleanliness wasn't next to godliness in this place. Cleanliness was everything. It wasn't clear whether the constant chores were intended simply to keep them busy or as a form of penance for their sins.

The door to the delivery room was ajar. When Pat had started on this floor, she'd been able to hear Nancy's screams inside the room. It was a noise you couldn't block out. She sat up on her heels as best she could. It was more comfortable, at least, than bending forward over the mass of her belly to scrub the floor.

It was quiet in the delivery room now. Too quiet. The screams had stopped, but there'd been no baby's cry. The door swung open, and Sister wheeled Nancy out. The chair clicked periodically as they went down the corridor. Pat dropped her eyes and pushed her soapy brush further across the floor.

A few moments later Sister returned. She stopped. 'How long have you been there?'

Pat shrugged.

'Say something, girl.'

'A few minutes. Did Nancy have her baby?'

Sister pursed her lips before giving a short, curt nod. Pat watched her bright white shoes disappear into the delivery room. She couldn't resist crawling closer to the door and listening. There were voices, low and muffled. Matron muttering something Pat couldn't make out, and then Sister, louder and more definite. 'It's just one of those things, Enid. You did everything you could.'

★   ★   ★

Visitors' day. Three weeks since Pat arrived at Foss Moor. There wouldn't be anyone for her. Lilian had made it quite clear that she and Pat's father considered it better that she be left to deal with this whole thing on her own. The other girls had spent the hour after lunch doing their hair and make-up in advance of receiving their guests. Most were expecting their parents. Some were excited. Others grew quieter as two p.m. approached. Even Susan seemed on edge.

'Are you having a visitor?' Pat asked.

'My Gareth.'

318

'Is he ... ' Pat gestured towards Susan's growing belly. 'Is he your boyfriend?'

'Fiancé.'

Pat was confused. 'You're engaged? But you're not keeping it?'

Susan paused in front of the mirror. 'Gareth wanted to.' She shrugged. 'I don't want babies.'

Pat lay on her bed while the other girls trooped down to the lounge. She'd never heard of a woman not wanting babies. Babies were part of life. You got married and you had children. It was what people did. It was what everyone did.

She rubbed her hand over her tummy. She was almost due. In a few more days, she'd get to drop down to light domestic duties. No more kneeling with a scrubbing brush. It couldn't come soon enough. Everything ached. Every movement needed planning in advance. She rolled onto her side and wedged her pillow under her stomach in an attempt to get comfortable. Her crochet things lay on top of the cupboard by her bed. She ought to be getting on with that. Mittens and a bonnet for the baby she would never take home. Girls with no visitors were expected to spend their afternoon in an appropriate activity. Lying on one's bed could hardly be deemed an activity.

'Pat!'

She rolled herself awkwardly to face the voice in the doorway.

'Your visitor's waiting.'

Pat shook her head. 'I'm not expecting anyone.'

The girl shrugged. 'Well, you've got someone.'

Charlie? It could only be. Her parents

319

wouldn't have come. Nobody else knew she was here. The voice in Pat's head pointed out that Charlie didn't know she was here either. Pat heaved herself off the bed and shuffled along the corridor and down the stairs. She hadn't done her hair or her makeup. That was silly. She'd never done her hair or her makeup when they were together. She'd always been absolutely herself. It hadn't been enough. She turned into the lounge and scanned the room for the mop of dark hair and the bright blue eyes. He wasn't here. She looked again. In the furthest corner, a hand rose and waved at her. Pat's heart leapt and crashed to earth. She forced a smile onto her face. It didn't do to be rude. Hester shoved her way through the bodies and the worn out wingback chairs, and threw her arms around Pat's shoulders. 'You're massive.'

'Thanks.'

They negotiated their way back to two free seats in the corner of the room. 'How did you know I was here?'

'Your mum told me.'

That didn't seem right. 'When did you see my mother?'

'I went round your house.'

'And she told you where I was?'

Hester grinned. 'When I stood in the street screaming about you being up the duff she did.'

'How was she?'

Hester glanced at the floor.

'It's okay.'

'She was drunk.'

Pat nodded. 'Was my father there?'

A shake of the head.

That made sense. Lilian drunk and Stanley absent. A normal evening in the Bickersleigh household.

'I talked to Levi.'

Levi was the drummer in the band. Levi knew Charlie. Pat gulped.

'He's back with his wife.'

'Charlie?'

'Don't be daft. Levi.'

'I'm sorry.'

Hester shrugged. ''S'okay. I'm seeing Pete now. He's the manager at Stefanini's new bowling alley. He lets me bowl for free, and he reckons he's going to get a motorbike.'

It was another world.

'What about you?'

'What about me?'

'Well, you're gonna have the baby and then what? Are you gonna come home?'

Pat nodded. It was out of her hands. Everything since the moment Charlie had been driven away in the back of his father's car was out of her hands.

'Cool. And you'll come back to work? The woman they've got doing fortunes is useless. She said I was going to end up travelling the country.'

Pat shrugged. 'Well, maybe she's right.'

'Don't be daft. I'm with Pete now.' She paused. 'Levi said he'd seen Charlie.'

Another lump rose up Pat's throat.

'Says he's at university now.'

Pat nodded. It's what she should have expected. 'Cambridge?'

Hester shook her head. 'Didn't get in, Levi said. That's what I wanted to tell you. He's here.'

The baby in Patience's tummy squirmed. 'Here?'

'York.' Hester grinned. 'So you could go see him.'

She could. The thought danced across Pat's mind. She could see him. If she could talk to him without his parents there, then maybe she could make him see that it was all still possible. The two of them and the baby.

'He'll be on holidays at the moment though, won't he? They have stupid holidays, students.'

Pat almost laughed. It would be funny if it wasn't real. Hope soaring for a moment and then squashed by mundanity. She'd have time to think about it now, time to come up with all the reasons not to go to him, time to convince herself that what had been decided was best for everyone, time to realise that there wasn't going to be a happy ending.

They fell into silence. 'So you're going to come back to work?'

Pat shook her head. That wasn't what was going to happen, was it? Charlie. Hester. The summer. The band. The gigs. The freedom. It had all been a dream. She was going to do exactly what Charlie had done. She was going to wake up and get back to the life she was always going to have.

'Up to you.' Hester idled away the rest of the visit with gossip about the girls in the cash office and cow eyes over Pete. When it was time to go she stopped. 'Well, if you need anything . . . '

Pat nodded. She didn't need anything though. Everything she could need had already been planned and decided in advance.

58

Louise stood outside the main entrance to the hospital. It had changed since the last time she'd been here, when Kyle was twelve and broke his wrist, falling off the wall at the back of the flats. Then it had been a single set of swing doors onto a beige reception. Now there was a sort of glass entry way bit leading onto an atrium, and an official smoking shelter, packed full of patients wheeling drip stands behind them as they huddled outside in their dressing gowns.

Somewhere inside was Patrice Leigh. Louise expected her legs to carry her straight through the doors and march her around the hospital until she found the right ward. Her legs had carried her here, after Barney had pulled her back from the door of the ambulance, but now her legs had lost heart. She shuffled over to a woman in a pink towelling robe. 'Can I have a fag?'

The woman shrugged, and handed over a cigarette. Louise bummed a lighter off a skinhead and took a deep drag. She didn't smoke very often. She'd told Kyle she'd kill him if she caught him doing it, so she could hardly take it up herself. Was that even true? She remembered hearing Kyle tell one of his mates that his mum would kill him if she caught them smoking, but she didn't remember ever saying that herself.

This was it. It was happening. He was slipping away. She must have done something to deserve it. Patrice had said Kyle wanted to make contact, but somehow she hadn't been there at the right time, or done the right things, or wanted it enough, and so Kyle couldn't get back to her, and she couldn't hold onto him. She leaned against the Perspex wall of the smoking shelter. What could she do? She could do what she'd come here for. She could march into that hospital, find Patrice Leigh and demand that she bring Kyle back. Still her legs didn't move. She wasn't stupid. She'd heard what Leo had said. She'd heard the paramedics. She'd seen the way Patrice slumped in her chair. Her legs wouldn't take her to find Patrice because her brain was afraid of what she might find. But what other choice did she have?

She couldn't let Kyle slip away. She was his mum. She had to hold on, so she couldn't go home. Kyle wasn't at home. He wasn't at the bus station. He wasn't going to stroll around the next corner. He wasn't going to go to college or get married or have grandchildren. But he was out there somewhere. Whatever Leo thought, Patrice had proved that. She'd talked to him. Louise's brain whirred and raced out of her control. If Kyle couldn't get back to Louise, then maybe she could go to him. Then they'd both be at peace.

At peace.

That was what Patrice had kept saying. Louise closed her eyes for a second. At peace, back with Kyle, where the endless screaming silence in her head would stop — that was what she needed.

Louise started to walk. She knew where she was going. It was where people around here always went. It was imprinted on her imagination since childhood: Croft Bridge, the high road bridge just the other side of town, which carried traffic over the river that flowed down to the sea. When she'd tried to get out of trouble at school by saying Donna Whitlock had made her do it, the teacher would parrot, 'And if Donna Whitlock told you to jump off Croft Bridge, would you?' And then, a few years later, Donna Whitlock's brother had disappeared and people had muttered, 'Croft Bridge,' under their breath and teachers had stopped mentioning it out loud. But it was always there, in whispers, in the local paper, inside her head. If you wanted to just let go, Croft Bridge was where you went.

It was a long walk, but she didn't care. She knew Kyle was out there now, and she knew how to reach him. It was all so clear now. She crossed the road by the roundabout and rounded the bend to see the bridge in front of her. At some point, there'd been a half-hearted attempt to raise the fence, but it looked easy enough to climb up and over. She marched to the middle of the bridge. She didn't know why. It just seemed like the right place.

She leaned over the barrier and gazed out. Out. Not down. She wasn't thinking about her body falling. She was thinking about her spirit soaring. She stepped onto the first rung of the barrier, and caught a glimpse of the river and road below. Of course her body would fall. She screwed her eyes closed. That wasn't the point. She was going to Kyle, and there wasn't anybody left here to miss her.

Apart from her own mum.

That thought was pushed aside as best she could. Kyle. Kyle was all that mattered now. She stepped up onto the next rung.

'Are you all right?'

Louise turned her head towards the voice.

'Kyle?' It was unmistakeable. He was here. He'd seen that she was coming and he was here to meet her.

She kept one hand resting on the barrier and reached the other out into the distance. 'I'm coming.'

Next to her, her baby shook his head. 'Please, don't do that. Just come down onto the pavement.'

'Why?' Why didn't he want her to come?

'I'm sure there's people who need you here.'

'Mum?'

'Right.'

'You don't want me to jump?'

'I do not.'

'Because of Mum?'

'That's right.'

That made sense. He was a good boy. He wouldn't want his nan upset. 'And you're all right?'

'I'm good. I just want you to let go of there and come down.' He was holding a hand out towards her.

'Let go?'

He nodded.

Louise released her fingers from the barrier and clasped his hand. Then she let her feet reach backwards for the tarmac and allowed her whole body to crumple down onto the ground. She looked up. It wasn't Kyle anymore. Of course it wasn't. This man's skin was darker, his hair braided back, not shorn short like her son's, and he must have been twenty-five at least. But Kyle had been here. She was sure of that.

She closed her eyes and let the voices all around her drift away. She could hear sirens and shouting and people asking if she was okay. She opened her eyes and nodded when it seemed like she was supposed to, and told a nice policeman in a high-vis jacket that her name was Louise. She ignored the grey-haired woman who stumbled into them muttering about 'her Dennis'. None of it mattered. She'd seen Kyle. She'd talked to Kyle. She wasn't going to see him again, but knowing that didn't feel like a knife in the guts anymore. It was an ache. Unwelcome, uncomfortable, but not enough to make her curl up into a breathless ball. She let the policeman take her to the car and she sat on a plastic chair at the station until her mother was shepherded through to collect her and take her away.

59

The voices wouldn't stop. They were a long way away, far enough that they shouldn't really be bothering her, but they were. Every noise was like fingernails scraping across the inside of her skull, and the noise never stopped. It kept pulling her back. Patrice didn't want to be pulled back anymore. She wanted to drift.

There were hands on her, touching her face, shining light into her eyes. Who could it be that dared to put their hands on her? Not Georgios. Georgios would pat her shoulder, but never anything more. Not Charlie. Charlie was here though. She was sure of that. Maybe her father. She tried to imagine her father's hand on her cheek, but she couldn't remember his touch. Maybe she'd never felt it to start with. She couldn't recall him embracing her, or her mother. There was the man in the church car park. With the Brylcreem and the trenchcoat. Her father had embraced him, hadn't he?

Then there was the baby. She remembered his touch. Her beautiful baby boy. Charlie's baby boy. Patience's baby boy. Patience had wanted him, and Patrice had given him away. Now Patience was exacting her revenge.

60

1968

'Here he is.'

Matron put the tiny bundle into Pat's arms. She was tired and sore and desperate for sleep. She didn't want to hold the tightly wrapped parcel. She wanted to be wheeled away. She wanted to rest and forget.

'You need to bond with him so your milk comes in.'

Pat felt her eyes widen. 'I have to feed him?'

'For the first few weeks. Until he goes to his family.'

Pat had seen babies lots of times when they had christenings at church. She'd held babies during coffee time after services. She'd never appreciated the sublime littleness of a newborn. She stared straight out at the wall in front of her, not shifting her gaze down to the face in her arms.

She didn't want to look. She didn't want to see his eyes, or his nose, or his tiny fingers. She wanted him to stay vague, just an idea that she could simply let drift away. The bundle huddled against her chest let out a gurgle. Pat screwed her eyes shut.

She imagined that he'd have Charlie's eyes, maybe his hair. Or would he be completely bald? Some babies, she thought, were born with thick hair and then it all fell out. Would he look like her? Pat swallowed. She had to look. She had another month of feeding and bathing this little person. She opened her eyes.

He didn't look like her. He didn't look like Charlie. He looked utterly and entirely like himself, like the most unique and perfect person that he was intended to be. Pat gasped. She'd experienced a shadow of this moment when she'd met Charlie, when she'd thought that she could just float away into his eyes, but that was nothing. That was like an echo or a memory of this moment right now, insubstantial compared to the real thing.

She scoured her baby's face, drinking in every detail. The dark black eyelashes almost comically oversized for his head. The button of his nose. The crinkle of his brow as he seemed to frown with concentration in his sleep.

Pat pressed her lips to his forehead, before loosening the top of the blanket that held him. A tiny, perfect little hand shot out and waved lazily up at her.

'Have you got a name, pet?'

Pat didn't look up.

'Got to have a name for his papers.'

'Paul.'

'Very nice. Is it after someone?'

Pat shook her head. There was St Paul and there was Paul McCartney, but nobody in particular. He wasn't going to be another Stanley or Charlie, or even Pat. He was going to be somebody new. 'It's not after anyone. I just picked it myself.'

She stared at him again. Paul. Her Paul. Her baby. She traced a fingertip along his perfect cheek. 'Hello, Paul,' she whispered. 'I'm your mum.'

61

Leo strode into the hospital, glancing at his phone. He hadn't ridden in the ambulance. He'd stepped back, not intending to follow at all. It wasn't his place, but Barney had grabbed his arm, insistent that he come to the hospital. He'd procrastinated, walking as slowly as he could back to his car, and then driving the long way round, letting himself get snarled up in roadworks and one-way systems. The text from Barney said they'd taken her straight to High Dependency. Leo followed the blue line on the floor until he reached the nurses' desk. 'I'm looking for Patrice Leigh.'

The woman on the desk nodded. 'And you are?'

Leo hesitated. He couldn't say he was her biographer, could he? That wasn't a thing that gave you visiting rights. 'I'm . . . '

'Are you family?'

He shrugged. 'Not really.'

She stared at her screen for a second. 'Then I'm afraid you'll just have to wait with the other gentleman.' She pointed diagonally across the room, to a huddle of plastic chairs bolted unsympathetically to the floor. Barney was sitting on one, facing away from them. 'Right.

Leo took the seat next to Patrice's manager. 'How is she?'

'Not good. They think it was a stroke.'

Leo wasn't surprised. He'd seen the way her body had slumped and her lips had seemed to sag to one side. He'd been so angry with her. He was still so angry with her. 'Do they know what caused it?' He swallowed. 'Could it have been stress or something?'

Barney shrugged. 'I don't know. I doubt it.'

Leo leaned back in his chair. 'I hate hospitals.'

Barney shrugged. 'Everyone hates hospitals, and every time you're in one, someone says that they hate them.'

Leo almost laughed. 'You're not this sharp around Patrice.'

Another shrug. 'She quite likes thinking I'm incompetent. It gives her someone to blame her little absences on.'

'Little absences?'

Barney closed his eyes. 'I tried to get her to a doctor, but . . . ' He shook his head. 'She insisted there was nothing wrong. I'm sorry.'

Leo could imagine Patrice refusing to see a doctor in the face of any level of insistence from her manager. 'Not your fault.'

Barney walked up to the desk again and whispered something to the woman perched behind the computer. He shrugged as he sat down again. 'Someone will be out to talk to us shortly. Apparently they're very busy.'

'Right.'

'Although really they should be talking to you, shouldn't they?'

'What do you mean?'

Barney shifted in his seat, trying to turn towards him. 'Georgios told me some things before he died. He wasn't always so clear by this point but that day seemed like a good day. Lucid, you know?'

Leo nodded.

'He told me to look out for a man who might come looking for her. A man born in the spring of 1968. To an unmarried teenager.'

The waves of shock and confusion kept hitting. 'You mean Patrice?'

Barney nodded.

'I don't understand.'

Now Barney looked confused. 'Have I made a mistake? It's just . . . this book isn't your usual sort of thing. And your agent said you were absolutely determined to do it, which seemed odd, and then Patrice said you kept asking questions about her family and boyfriends and . . . '

Leo screwed his eyes tight for a second. It was too much. 'And you thought I was her son?'

Barney nodded.

'So she did have a son?'

Another nod.

'She told me she'd never had a child.'

'Then I'm afraid she lied.'

That shouldn't surprise him. Patrice had lied about his son. Why wouldn't she lie about her own? 'I see.'

'So are you?' The question was quiet, hesitant.

Leo wondered how to respond. It was a simple question. It deserved a simpler answer than he'd been given himself. He nodded.

'Should we tell the hospital that?' Barney was frowning. 'It might give you rights or something.'

Leo didn't know.

'I mean she doesn't have anyone else.'

'I don't know if I can.' Leo glanced at Barney. 'She's got you.'

'She thinks I'm incompetent.'

'But you're not.'

Barney's face reddened even more than usual. 'Well, we all have roles we play sometimes, don't we?'

Leo didn't reply. Patrice was in hospital. Olly was alive. Marnie was divorcing him. Louise was . . . actually he didn't know where Louise was. She'd been with Patrice when she collapsed, but what about after that? Leo closed his eyes. So many people. So many competing needs. It was a moment when he couldn't help but feel that the world should be fitted with an emergency stop cord that would allow Leo to force the whole thing to a sudden halt while he stepped off for a moment. He could step out of this waiting room. He could step out of the orbit of Marnie's rage and ecstasy. He could step away from the need to decide what to do about Olly. He could step away from the niggling guilt and feeling that he ought to be calling Louise. He could step away from being next of kin to a stranger who'd denied him, and then lied about the most important things in his world. But none of that was an option, was it? Nobody got to walk away.

He glanced down at his hand, and was surprised to see it balled into a fist. Some people did walk away. Olly had. Leo glanced towards the desk and cleared his throat. 'Did she tell you anything about me?'

Barney shook his head. 'Sorry. I think Georgios knew the whole story, but he only told me what he thought I needed to know.' He clapped his hands together. 'Do you want a coffee?'

Leo nodded. 'I'll get it.'

There was a machine at the end of the corridor but Barney had been holding a branded cup from a proper coffee shop, and that would be further away, more distance to walk without having to deal with anything else. There'd been a sign by the entrance when he'd rushed in. Leo followed the blue line back the way he'd come and found a coffee stand next to the exit to the car park. The customers gathered round the few tables near the counter were a mixed bunch. A heavily pregnant woman had her face in her hands and was rocking with silent sobs, while her partner sat wordless across the table. A few feet away two men in suits pored over a laptop. It didn't seem right that your whole world could fall apart when business was going on as usual just across the room. Leo didn't care if it was a cliche. He really, really hated hospitals.

He collected his coffee and turned away from the counter. A woman was joining the back of the queue, handbag incongruously slung over her shoulder, on top of pyjamas and a powder blue dressing gown. Everything here was upside down. In his pocket, his phone vibrated. He didn't need to look to know that it would be Marnie.

62

1968

'He won't settle.' Pat dropped her toothbrush back into her washbag. It was ten o'clock. The girls were expected to be in their dorm rooms by ten, and lights out was ten thirty. Overnight feeds were done with the bottle by the staff — to get the babies used to it, they said. It wasn't the usual nurse who was standing in the doorway demanding that Pat come and see to her son.

She followed the woman downstairs to the nursery and picked her perfect baby from his crib at the end of the row. The nurse leaned on the wall and looked at her. 'He were mithering, stopping the others from sleeping.'

Pat rocked her boy in her arms. 'He seems all right now.'

The woman shrugged. 'Fine. Not up to me to sort him out though, is it?'

Pat didn't reply. Matron and the regular nurses didn't encourage the girls to spend too much extra time with their children, unless they were one of the lucky few who would be taking their own baby home. Pat didn't know who this nurse was, but from her demeanour Gypsy Patience guessed that she was temporary. She didn't seem to care too much about the normal rules. Baby Paul wriggled in her arms, and then screwed his little face up into a scowl. Pat jiggled him against her breast, but it didn't help. He let out a scream. She tipped him against his shoulder, as if she was winding him, and bounced him gently up and down. Another scream.

The nurse folded her arms. 'See. I bet you'll be glad when they come to get him.'

'Who?'

'His proper parents.'

Pat turned her face away. 'But that's not for another week. Maybe two or three.' She nuzzled her nose against her baby's head. 'Matron said some girls stay seven or eight weeks after their baby's born.'

And some stayed much less. She knew that, but she didn't want to think that. She wanted to think that she still had more time.

'Nah. They've sorted the adoption.' The woman waved her hand in the direction of the nurse's office. 'It's in his notes.' She grinned. 'So it'll be back to normal for you.'

The nurse disappeared into the office. Pat sank into the chair in the corner of the nursery, baby Paul still snuggled against her body. Back to normal then. She couldn't do that. She wouldn't have it. It was what she'd agreed, but that was before Paul came and forced her to fall in love. She was her baby's mother now. That changed everything.

She sat up straight and peered through the window into the office. The nurse had her back to the ward. Straining her ears, Pat thought she could hear the slight hum of the radio on low. If she was very quiet, she could probably . . . Pat couldn't bring herself to finish the thought. It was ridiculous. Everything was planned. She would stay here until Paul's new family came to take him away, and then she would go home. A few months at home with her parents convalescing after the illness she'd unfortunately been struck down with, or maybe a few months resting after the strain of caring for a beloved, but sadly aging, aunt, and then back to life. This would be a forgotten moment — a lost year — never discussed, allowed to simply slip away.

Against her chest, Paul gurgled and thrashed a tiny arm against her collar bone. He was sleeping now, his tiny brow furrowed in apparent concentration — an expression Pat was used to seeing. She was coming to think of him as a thoughtful child, and fighting to stop herself imagining the man he might become — intelligent, watchful, focused. She'd never know, of course. Unless . . . This time she didn't stop to think. She pulled Paul tightly to her breast and tiptoed across the nursery. The nurse in the office didn't budge from her seat, as Pat clicked the door open. Now she had a choice. Back up to her room to get her coat or straight out. She had her cardigan and was still wearing her day clothes. She dropped a hand to her skirt pocket. There were a few coins in there. She made her decision. She turned away from the staircase and along the corridor to the back door of the big house. Around her everything was quiet. Even Matron must have turned in for the night. Pat held her breath as she turned the Yale on the big door, and felt the wood creak towards her on its aging hinges. Still nobody came.

She stepped into the night and pulled the door behind her as quickly as she dared. Her instinct was to run, but the baby clutched to her chest prevented that. In her head, Gypsy Patience chastised her. How would it look if she ran? A young girl, haring down the street clinging on to a baby. That would attract attention. Better to walk, nice and calm, as though she had all the time in the world. She got as far as the next street corner before she slowed down. Where was she going? There wasn't a plan apart from the one her parents had made. But there had been. Before her mother and father and Charlie's father and Matron and the nurses, there'd been a whole other plan. She picked up the pace as far as the main road and looked around for a street sign. The university was near Heslington, she thought. There'd been things in the *Post* about it spoiling the area. If she kept walking and kept on the main roads, sooner or later there'd be a sign, wouldn't there? Or someone she could ask? Pat rocked her baby in her arms. She had Paul. She had the plan they'd made all those months ago. Now she just needed to find Charlie.

★　★　★

It was after eleven by the time she got to the university. An hour walking across town had left her shoulders sore from holding Paul close. She should have borrowed the pram they kept in the corridor outside Matron's office. Her feet ached but she didn't slow down. Charlie was here. Somewhere. She stood at the end of the lane that dropped away from the main road onto the university campus. The buildings sat like grey boxes dropped into the countryside. At the near end, there was scaffolding up and building work was clearly in progress. It was getting cold. She pulled her cardigan around her baby and set off down the path, forking towards the lights and buildings to her left.

She hadn't really thought about how she would find him. How did universities work? Was there a reception she could go to and ask for Charlie? If there was, would there be anyone there at this time of night? Pat pushed the thought away. She'd come this far. If she had to knock on every door in every building, then she would.

The campus was busier than she'd expected. She headed towards the first building with lights on and doors open. Off the main corridor there was a dining room and what looked like a bar, filled with light and people. Pat hovered in the entrance, cradling baby Paul's head against her hand. She scanned the mass of bodies. They were about her age, a year or two older but no more, but their clothes were modern and completely unlike anything their parents would choose. The girls' hair hung loose around their shoulders rather than being primped and set on their heads. Pat found herself flashing back to the first time Hester had talked to her on that bus. She'd thought Hester was from another world, but she could see now: Hester was just like her. She was a girl from nowhere preening herself for a world she didn't know. These people

342

were living in that strange new world all the time. Gypsy Patience wouldn't have known what to promise them. From where Pat was standing, they already had it all.

She peered around the room, not daring to go further in, in case she was hauled away as such an obvious imposter. She couldn't see Charlie. She carried on along the corridor. There were locked doors off at one side leading, she guessed, to the student accommodation. Pat carried on out of the college and across a small paved courtyard into another squat grey building. Here she followed the sound of voices to another packed bar. Another packed bar where Charlie was nowhere to be seen. She made her way back outside. Might she be defeated? She didn't know whereabouts he actually lived. She only had it from Hester that he was here at all. She sat down on a bench at the edge of the lake that seemed to have been penned in by the grey concrete of the university. A single stray swan glided across the water in front of her. In her arms, Paul, who had slept peacefully all the way here, stirred and squawked. She rocked him hopelessly, as he opened his mouth wide into a scream.

'Oh my god. You've got a baby!'

The voice behind her was loud and confident. A young woman appeared beside her. 'Where did you get a baby?'

Pat frowned. 'He's mine.'

'Woah. And you're a student?'

Pat didn't answer. If she said no, would people come and drag her away? She still wasn't entirely sure she was allowed to be here.

'Can I hold him?'

'I'm not sure.'

'I'll be good with him. I've got seven little brothers. Seriously. I'm the only girl. Been comforting babies since I was about five years old.'

The girl pulled Paul into her arms, and he settled instantly. Pat watched this stranger comfort her baby, rocking him, cooing over him, pulling faces and blowing kisses. Some other woman giving him what he needed. The woman stepped back onto the path and turned towards the building. Pat could make out bodies in the distance. The woman called to them. 'Come down here. This girl's got the cutest baby.'

A whole group of strangers followed the woman's call. Three girls, two men and a silent figure at the back that Pat couldn't make out for a second. And then she saw. He walked past the others towards the girl with the baby. 'What are you doing?'

'Just holding him.'

Pat watched as his fingers landed gently on the small of the girl's back. It was such a subtle intimacy, fleeting but confident. Gypsy Patience noticed it. Pat swallowed. 'Whose baby is it?'

Pat cleared her throat. The man turned towards her and, for a second, everything stopped. Those eyes were as deep and all-consuming as they'd always been, but the look he was giving her now wasn't love or joy or hope. It was fear. Pat pulled her gaze away. 'He's my baby. Baby Paul.'

Then she waited. Charlie was staring at the

baby. 'Maybe you should give him back.'

The girl shrugged. 'It's fine. She doesn't mind. You can hold him too if you want.'

Charlie stepped backwards, but the girl's enthusiasm didn't allow for reticence. She fumbled Baby Paul into his arms. Pat's stomach clenched. This was what she'd come for — Charlie holding his son. The baby gurgled contentedly in his daddy's arms. Pat stared at her son and the hands that were wrapped around him. She didn't look into Charlie's face. She didn't want to see the alarm and uncertainty that might be there.

The girl cooed some more over the tiny bundle, but the rest of the group were tiring of the fleeting distraction. One of the lads started to stroll away.

'I thought you wanted to go for toasties.'

The girl nodded. 'Chocolate and banana!'

'Come on then.'

The girl smiled over towards Pat. 'You could come?'

Pat shook her head.

'Right. You probably need to get home.'

Pat couldn't answer. Here was home. Here was where Charlie was.

'Come on then.' The girl followed the rest of her friends along the path.

Charlie stepped forward, stopping a few feet in front of her and leaning down awkwardly to pass Paul back into her care. She met his gaze. He looked away. 'There's a sort of toasted sandwich takeaway place. They'll basically put anything between two slices of bread for you and toast it.

345

Chocolate bars and stuff. Jelly babies, but they just burn your tongue. Savoury stuff too, you know. Obviously. But yeah . . . she likes chocolate.'

Pat hadn't moved. Her heart hurt for what seemed to be about to happen. Charlie was going to hand their baby back to her, and then he was going to follow his friends into the darkness. 'I came to find you.'

Charlie nodded. 'It's just . . . I'm with . . . It's not a great time.'

Pat glanced up the path. The girl had stopped, maybe twenty yards away in the half-light. 'Are you coming?'

Paul let out a screech.

Pat forced a lightness into her voice. Tell them what they want to hear. 'He doesn't want to be handed back.'

She heard an answering laugh in the darkness.

Paul wailed again.

Charlie turned his head toward the girl on the path. 'I guess I'll catch you up.'

'All right.'

As the footsteps got more distant, Charlie took a seat on the bench next to her, angling Paul back into her arms, as soon as he was able.

'Is . . . ' His voice trailed away. 'Is it okay?'

'He's fine. He's called Paul.'

'Right.'

Pat stared at her baby for a second. This was the moment. She'd come here. She'd actually found him. There was a whole future that they'd talked about. This was the moment that she could claim it back. She just had to persuade

346

him that it was all still possible.

'So are your mum and dad helping with him?'

Pat shook her head. 'They sent me to a mother and baby home. He's supposed to be adopted.'

Charlie nodded.

'But I don't know if that's what I want.'

He shrugged. 'It's up to you.'

This was it. She had to try. 'Not just me. I mean, I keep thinking about what we talked about. You and me and him. Just the three of us. We could still do that. We could find somewhere. Or I could come here. Do they have couples accommodation? They must. I don't know. We could find out. Or we could go somewhere new. I could get a job as soon as he's big enough. And . . . '

Charlie stood, focusing his attention away, up the path where his friends had gone.

What could she say? Think about what it is he wants, and then work out how to give him it. That was the trick. That was how it worked. And it did work. Time and time again she sent people away feeling brighter than when they came in. You just had to tell them that the thing they wanted was possible, somehow.

'But the adoption thing. I mean for him, maybe that's for the best.'

Pat could feel it slipping away. She had to find the words that would make him see that it could all still be all right. 'We could try . . . '

Charlie shook his head. 'I'm here now. There's new people.'

A flash of his hand on the strange girl's back. 'Things are different.'

Pat didn't reply. She couldn't promise him the thing he wanted because that thing wasn't her. It wasn't her and it wasn't Paul and it wasn't that future she'd been dreaming of with the three of them far away and safe from everything. He wasn't her Charlie anymore. The realisation jabbed into her gut. He wasn't hers. The dream she'd been holding onto so tightly was nothing. The whole life that she'd been so close to she could almost touch it was nothing at all. 'Right.'

He nodded, apparently relieved that she was seeing sense. 'Good. Do you know how to get back to . . . ?'

Pat nodded.

'All right then.' He stepped towards them and hesitated, rocking backwards slightly on his heels, and then leaning quickly over Paul, touching one fingertip to his cheek. 'I'd better.' He pointed off up the path. 'With the others.'

And he was gone. So quickly. Pat sat in the silence for a second holding her breath, waiting for him to change his mind and come rushing back. He didn't come. His footsteps faded into the darkness.

She couldn't go home. She didn't have money for a hotel and would a hotel even take her with a baby anyway? She couldn't stay here. It was turning colder and she didn't have a spare nappy or fresh clothes. She didn't have a crib to put the baby down.

Pat let the tears come. Normally she tried not to cry. She dug her thumbnail into her palm and screwed her eyes up tight, but now there was no point. There was nobody here to see, nobody to

348

demand she explain. She cried. She wasn't sure how long for. Time drifted away. It didn't matter. The baby pulled close to her breast woke and joined her, sending his own sobs out in unison with her own.

'Are you all right, pet?' The new voice was male with a gentle twang of a Geordie accent.

Pat glanced up before dropping her chin to hide her face. 'We're fine.'

'Ah, you're not. You've got a bairn there needs to be in the warm. Come on.'

She looked up properly. The man was wearing neatly pressed blue trousers and a blue shirt under a dark blue blazer. There was a badge on his breast and epaulettes at his shoulders. 'Are you a policeman?'

The stranger laughed. 'University porter. Come on. I've a got a kettle in the porter's lodge.'

Pat followed the man up the path and into a brightly lit office in one of the buildings. There was another porter already working in there, head bent over papers at a desk in front of a hatch that opened onto the main corridor. Pat sat on a hard plastic chair in the corner while the kettle boiled.

'Now, I don't think you're a student?'

Pat shook her head.

'So where've you come from, pet?'

She hesitated. There was no good lie available to her. 'Foss Moor House,' she whispered.

The porter didn't answer. She glanced up and saw the two men exchange a look. The one at the desk mouthed something at his colleague.

Unmarried mothers.

'Right. So shall we get you back there?'

It was over, wasn't it? Paul was hungry and cold. Pat was exhausted. Charlie was living in a different world. There really wasn't any other choice. Pat nodded. It was time to go back to her real life.

63

The voices were getting more insistent. She could hear specific words here and there. They seemed to be very keen on asking if she knew where she was. Patrice felt sure that she did. She was in the . . . the . . . big house for sick people. Which must mean that she was sick. That made sense. That explained why all the voices sounded so far away.

She opened her eyes, or at least she tried. Her right eye cooperated perfectly. Her left eye seemed to have gone sleepy.

'Hello, Patrice.'

'Yer.' Her answer slipped out of the corner of her mouth. Talking was hard. The man leaning towards her had black hair and glasses. Dark hair like Charlie. She wondered if Charlie wore glasses now. Lots of older men did, and he must be an older man.

'There's a Leo Cousins here and a Barney, who says he's your manager. Is it okay for us to tell them how you're getting on?'

Leo. Leo was like Charlie. More than like Charlie; there was something else. She couldn't remember what else. It probably didn't matter now. Patrice tried to make some more words, to say to the man that he could tell Leo and Barney whatever he liked. Words didn't seem to want to come like they used to though. She tried to nod instead. Her left side felt numb. No. Not numb.

351

It was definitely still there. It just felt like it belonged to somebody else. She managed to whisper another confirmation from the corner of her mouth. The man nodded, and continued talking. She let the words filter over her. Blood clot. Stroke. Scan.

Patrice closed her eyes.

64

1968

Pat sat in the chair in the corner of the nursery. There was no reason for her to be here. She had no baby to feed anymore. No skin against her skin. No brush of soft fluffy hair against her cheek. No tiny fingers that she could simply watch for hours. He'd been her Paul, but now they'd told her that his proper mummy and daddy might change that, so she'd never actually even know his name. That meant that she could never find him. His new mummy and daddy lived in the Midlands. She'd written them a letter explaining his feeding times and how he always wriggled in the bath. Then she'd dressed him in his romper suit and put his crocheted bonnet on his head and held him, watching him frown and grimace in his sleep. She'd held him until the nurse had come and uncurled her fingers from his tiny body, and then she'd sat and held the air where he'd been — the last fading vapours of her son — until now, when she was entirely without him. No more of his mouth at her breast. No more of his fingers between hers. Even his scent in the air had drifted away into nothing.

The nurse appeared at her shoulder. It was one of the regular nurses again. The girl who was on duty the night she'd run away hadn't been seen since, and nobody else had mentioned it. It seemed as though it had been decided that if it was never talked of, then it had never happened at all. 'So are you all packed?'

Pat nodded.

'And do you need to use the telephone before you go?'

That had been the arrangement. She would telephone when she was ready to come home and Father would collect her from the station and this whole horridness would be over and never mentioned again. She'd be Pat who helped out at the pharmacy and went to young person's group and everything would be back to normal. She nodded to the nurse and allowed herself to be led through to the office where the house telephone stood.

'I'll give you a minute.'

Pat picked up the phone. She stopped. The office was cold and bare, like the rest of the house. She glanced around the walls and across the desk. No personal touches. Nothing of the nurse and matron who worked here. It was a shell. It reminded her of her bedroom at home. She hadn't kept hold of her baby. She hadn't kept hold of Charlie. Now she was all that was left. And she was floating. No ties. No tethers. She picked up the phone again and waited for an answer.

'It's Pat. I'm coming back.'

Hester chattered for a moment on the other end of the line.

'Do you think I could stop with you for a while?'

'Of course.'

65

Louise came out of the doctor's office, where she'd been brought by her mother promptly at nine a.m., and into to the waiting room. Her mum popped the out-of-date copy of *Take a Break* back on the table and followed her daughter into the street. 'What did she say?'

'Gave me a prescription. And this.' Louise held out the purple leaflet for her mother to inspect.

'Bereavement support?'

Louise nodded. 'Counselling and groups and that.'

'And will you go this time?'

She nodded again. She thought she probably would. She'd said it hadn't helped before but maybe she hadn't given it a chance. And there wasn't really much choice. Kyle was gone. 'I don't know if I want to though.'

Her mum grabbed her hand. 'I know, but it's not that we're moving on from Kyle. It's just dealing with what's happening now. You gave me a fright last night.'

That was the thing. She'd nearly done to her mum exactly what had happened to her. The police at the door. The news that would have broken her life into before and after. 'Sorry.'

'Well . . . ' Her mum dropped Louise's hand. 'No point dwelling. Best to deal with the here and now.'

In her own brisk way, she was right. The here

and now just kept on happening whatever Louise did to try to stop it.

'You need to start dealing with things. Sort out your money. Talk to someone about the rent.'

'I know. There's something else I've got to do first.'

Her mother's open face closed into an anxious frown.

'Nothing bad. Just someone I need to talk to.'

'Who?'

'Just a friend.'

★ ★ ★

Leo followed Barney towards the hotel lift. They'd come to collect some of Patrice's things. There was no reason for him to be here. Barney had suggested he stay at the hospital but he felt like a fraud. If anyone asked him something about Patrice, he had to check with Barney anyway. Here they were only a phone call and a ten-minute drive away and Leo didn't have to think quite so hard about how he was supposed to be acting.

Patrice's suite had been cleaned since she'd been taken to hospital. Everything was neatly piled or put away. The bed was made. Clean towels had been placed in the bathroom. Leo shrugged at Barney. 'So what do we take?'

'I don't know. Toiletries. Night clothes.' He looked around. 'I don't know if she has a dressing gown.'

Leo peered around the bathroom door. There was a robe bearing the embroidered logo of the

Grand. 'Nick the hotel one?'

Barney smiled. 'I'll go and buy one later. She'll only need that if she . . . when she's well enough to get out of bed.'

Leo was at a loose end as Barney busied himself gathering clothes from the wardrobe and pots and potions from the bathroom. 'Could you check the bedside drawers?'

'What for?'

'Personal stuff.' Barney stuck his head out of the bathroom. 'There's probably not much point keeping the room on if she's going to be in hospital a while. I'll ask the hotel to have her things moved into my room, so, I don't know, check for anything she might not want a stranger going through.'

Leo sat down on the bed and opened the bedside drawer. Empty. He leaned backwards, swung his legs over the bed and opened the drawer on the other side. A Gideon Bible. Obviously. Four different types of painkiller, all half-empty, and an envelope. He pulled it from the drawer and turned it over. Addressed simply to 'Miss Leigh' c/o Barney's office in London. He hesitated. As she'd kept it, it was clearly important, and it was addressed c/o Barney, who was in the next room. Obviously, all he needed to do was hand the envelope back to Barney. But. But, she'd kept it.

Leo peered again at the envelope. There was a scribble of ink next to the L of Leigh, as though the writer had started writing a different name and them remembered themselves and crossed it out.

'I'm just going back to my room to get changed.' Barney reappeared from the bathroom with an arm full of Patrice's things. 'I've got an overnight bag this lot'll go in.'

Leo nodded.

'You okay waiting here?'

'Sure. Actually, wait.'

Barney paused in the doorway. 'What's up?'

'I just wondered. The book. Do you still want me to carry on with it?'

Barney leaned on the doorframe. 'I don't see why not. You must have quite a lot from the interviews now?'

Leo nodded. He actually didn't have anywhere near as much as he should, but with some colour from the shows and a bit more research he could start to build a rough draft.

'Then yes. She was adamant that was what she wanted. And by the time you've got something for us to look at, I'm sure she'll be back on her feet.' He said it with a certainty the circumstances didn't warrant.

Leo waited until the door clicked closed and then he peeled open the envelope. At least now he could tell himself it was for the book. He flipped over the single sheet of notepaper and checked the name at the bottom. Anthony Abbot. It didn't mean anything to him. It hadn't come up in his research, and he was sure Patrice had never mentioned the name. Could Anthony Abbot be somebody to Leo? He flipped the letter over.

Mr Abbot appeared to have been a friend of Patrice's father, and now he wanted Patrice to get in touch with him. Had she? Leo had no way of knowing. It was a brief note, but even so there was no hiding the fact that it was a letter from someone who hadn't seen Patrice in a very long time. He mentioned her father's regrets. He mentioned the disappointment of not seeing Patrice at her father's funeral. And there was something else. At the top right of the letter just below Mr Abbot's own address, there was a phone number.

'Leo!' Barney was at the door to the suite. 'There's a Miss Swift in reception looking for you.'

'That's Louise.'

'Right. She seemed quite distressed when Miss Leigh was taken ill.'

Leo crumpled the letter in his hand, stuffed it in his pocket and followed Barney out of the room.

'Did you find anything I need to clear out before the cleaners get to it?'

Leo shook his head.

⋆ ⋆ ⋆

Downstairs, Leo led Louise into the lounge.

'So how's Patrice?'

He swallowed. 'It was a bad stroke, but she's conscious, apparently.'

'Apparently?'

Leo hadn't slept. He hadn't called Marnie back. And he hadn't been in to see Patrice. The doctors had said they could go in last night and again this morning, but he'd just waited. 'I've not seen her yet.'

Louise nodded. 'I came to see you anyway. I came to say sorry.'

He raised an eyebrow. 'For?'

'I think I used you a bit.' She shuffled in her seat. 'To get to Patrice. To get to Kyle, really.'

Leo didn't reply. It wasn't news. It wasn't another new thing to deal with. It was what it was. 'Yeah.'

'And I think it's probably best if we don't see each other anymore.'

Leo nodded. He didn't know what he was supposed to say. What did people say? They begged the other person to stay. They shouted. They cried. 'You're probably right.'

'Okay then.'

'There's something else.'

She didn't respond.

'You heard what I said to Patrice before . . . before she got ill?'

Louise nodded.

'Well, she didn't really talk to Olly.'

'You don't know that.'

'I do.' He swallowed. 'Olly's not dead.'

'What?'

'He's still alive.' Saying it out loud was still a shock. The last forty-eight hours had been nothing but shocks, and that first massive shock was still raw. 'I found out yesterday.'

He watched Louise's face. He wasn't sure what he was expecting to see — maybe something that would tell him what the right emotion might be. She closed her eyes for a second. When she looked at him again it was with disbelief. 'Then what are you doing here?'

'Well, Patrice . . . '

'But Olly. He's out there. You should go to him.'

360

'It's complicated.'

Louise shook her head. 'No. It's not.'

If she was going to say more, she didn't get the chance. Barney appeared by the table. 'Are you ready to go back to the hospital?'

Leo hesitated. 'I'll meet you there. I need to make a few calls.'

★ ★ ★

Louise stood up and walked out of the hotel with Barney. She should be happy for Leo, but there wasn't room for any more emotion at the moment. She thought she would go back to her mum's like she'd promised. She would try not to get back in bed until after eight o'clock in the evening. She would start reading the jobs page in the paper. She didn't think she'd apply for any jobs just yet, but she'd start reading the page again. She'd read the bereavement support leaflet properly and, she promised herself, she'd make herself go to at least one meeting. She'd write a list of all the phone calls she'd been putting off and the tasks she ought to do. She'd let her mum bring her cups of tea and chivvy her out of bed. She wasn't better. She wasn't ever going to get better, but she would remember that the here and now didn't care if she was better or not. It was just going to keep on happening, with or without her. Other people's lives were carrying on. Leo had a son out there somewhere. And a wife. And a daughter. She couldn't piggyback on his life. She was going to have to find her own.

The woman, a stranger, clattered into Louise's shoulder as she thrust a digital recorder into Barney's face. 'Is it true that Patrice Leigh is dying?'

Barney shook his head. 'She's in a stable condition. We're hopeful that she'll make a full recovery.'

'What about this?' The stranger held a newspaper out in front of them. Louise stared at the headline *Suicide Bridge Death*. Barney pushed the paper away. 'No comment.'

The stranger was marching after them down the street. 'This woman had asked Miss Leigh to contact her loved one many times. Do you think that contributed to her death?'

'No comment.'

'Don't you think it's cruel to tell vulnerable people that you can talk to their loved ones?'

Barney stopped and turned around. 'Miss Leigh has a gift. This woman,' he slapped his hand against the newspaper, 'this woman was clearly seriously unwell and she has my sympathy, but to suggest that Miss Leigh was in any way responsible . . . ' Louise watched him take a breath. 'No further comment.'

He pulled a key fob from his pocket and pressed the button to unlock the four-wheel drive parked at the side of the road. 'Do you need a lift?'

Louise shook her head.

Barney glanced from her to the still-loitering reporter. 'It's fine. Get in the car.'

The reporter hadn't quite finished yet. 'This woman just wanted to talk to her loved one.'

362

'Her loved one was a Pekinese.' Barney slammed the door as Louise climbed into the passenger seat. He started the engine and pulled away. 'Where do you live?'

'I'm stopping at my mum's. I can get the bus from the hospital though.'

They drove in silence through the town centre traffic.

'She's for real, isn't she?'

At the wheel, Barney frowned.

'Who?'

'Patrice.'

'Of course.'

Louise knew she should let it go. If Patrice was for real, then everything was as she thought and nothing had changed. If she was a fraud, then she hadn't talked to Kyle, but then Louise had seen him herself, so that didn't matter. Did it? The delicate resolution she thought she'd found was in the balance. 'Who was the woman in the paper?'

'Some local crazy.'

'But she came to see Patrice?'

Barney shook his head. 'She came to a show.' He paused. 'A couple of shows maybe but Miss Leigh's connection is with humans on the other side. There was nothing she could offer.'

'Did she try?'

'Of course.'

Again, this was the moment to stop. This was the moment to accept that what she'd experienced had been real and to stop asking questions. 'What about Olly?'

'Who?'

'Leo's Olly. She said she was talking to him.'

'Yeah.'

'But he's still alive.'

Barney didn't take his eyes off the road, but Louise couldn't pretend that she hadn't seen the frown fly across his face. 'Well, I'm not an expert, but I understand that messages from the other plane can be confused. It's possible that Miss Leigh misinterpreted a message that was meant for someone else.'

They pulled into the hospital car park. 'You're sure you can get home from here?'

Louise nodded. 'But, what about — '

Barney twisted in his seat. 'What do you want me to say?'

'What?'

'Do you want me to say she's a fraud? Do you want me to say that there's nothing out there?'

'I don't know.'

'Well, what do you think? Your son . . . '

'Kyle.'

'Right. Kyle. Do you think he's out there somewhere? Do you still talk to him? Do you still think about him, dream about him? Is he still part of you?'

Louise nodded.

'Then what else do you want me to tell you?'

Louise shook her head. She'd been right before. She'd hold on to what she thought she'd seen. She would go back to her mum's. She would let her mum take care of her, for now, she would try to let that be enough.

★ ★ ★

364

Leo stared at his phone. There were too many options. Too many calls he just had to make. Marnie. Grace. The hospital to check on Patrice. But he had to know. He'd started this whole thing because he thought Patrice was his birth mother. And then he'd thought she wasn't. And now he thought she was, but that she might never tell him the truth. He needed to talk to somebody who might know. He pulled the letter from his pocket, smoothed it out on the table and dialled Anthony Abbot's number.

66

Leo picked up a coffee on his way back into the High Dependency Unit. Barney was gathering his coat and case from the corner of the waiting room. 'You're going?'

'Just to get something to eat.'

'How is she?'

Barney shrugged. 'In and out. They said you could go in.' He paused. 'Or not. Up to you.'

Leo put his coffee cup down on the floor next to a chair. He would go in. He was starting, at least, to understand who he was going to see. 'Right. Well, can't put it off for ever.'

'First bed on the left then.'

He pushed through the swing doors into the unit. The corridor ran between bays partitioned off, with windows running along the top half of the partitions. He peered through at Patrice's bed. Patrice on stage was polished, always well made-up, neatly turned-out, hair just-so. The woman in the bed was a decade older at least, skin tired and grey and hair limp against the pillow.

'You can go in.'

He turned. One of the unit nurses was nodding enthusiastically towards Patrice's bed.

'She's sleeping a lot, but that's to be expected. The consultant will be round later. All being well, they'll arrange for her to be transferred to the stroke unit.'

Leo nodded without taking the details in. The woman in the bed was a stranger. She was barely the Patrice he'd met. The nurse was still talking, ' . . . so that'll be something to discuss with the stroke team down the line.'

'Sorry?'

'Whether you want your mum nearer you. I mean, she's not ready for discharge yet, but the long-term care won't be hospital based.'

'Right.' Leo left the nurse still muttering about care plans and discharge social workers, and sat down next to Patrice's bed. Patrice needed him. No one else did. Grace was a young woman. Olly had made his choice. Marnie had made hers.

The woman in the bed opened her eyes. Her mouth listed slightly to one side as she tried to talk. 'Char . . . '

'Sorry?'

'Charlie . . . '

Leo shook his head. 'I'm not Charlie.'

Patrice's eyes drifted closed again.

Leo sat for a few minutes watching her chest rise and fall. Anthony Abbot had been kind, surprised to hear from him, even more surprised by who Leo thought he was, but willing to talk. He'd suggested Leo come and meet him in person, but had confirmed that yes, Patrice Leigh was Patience Bickersleigh, or at least she had been in some previous world. Leo wandered back through the waiting room and onto the main corridor before pulling his phone from his pocket and switching it on. Missed call and text notifications from Marnie and Grace scrolled across the screen. The phone buzzed violently in his hand. Marnie again. Time to stop hiding.

'Hello.'

'Where are you?'

'Still at the hospital.'

Marnie didn't reply.

'She's sleeping a lot but conscious, so that's good I suppose.'

No reply again.

'What?'

'I just . . . '

The tension between them rose, as it always did, when they tried, and failed, to talk.

'I don't understand why you're there.'

'She's my mother.'

There was silence for a second. Marnie would be choosing her words, deciding which issue to focus on.

'Dinah was your mother. She brought you up and did your laundry and helped you with your homework and goodness knows what else. This is just the woman you think gave birth to you.'

'That's not fair.'

'No, and it's not fair to tell someone their son is dead when he's alive and well and living in New Zealand.'

There was real venom in her voice now. Leo swallowed. He'd been so sure that Olly was gone. 'I didn't mean to — '

'I don't mean you. Her. She said she'd talked to him from the other fucking side.'

'I know.' The anger was still there, but it had softened a little at the edges, become more complicated in among all the other things he was allowing himself to start to feel. 'It's what she does. But she's still my mum. Sort of my mum.' He walked along the corridor to a quieter corner and leaned on the wall. 'I don't know why she does what she does, but . . . ' He could stop now. He could avoid the risk of saying what was on his mind. He didn't have the energy. 'But I don't know why Olly did what he did either. He's still my son.'

'That's different.'

'Yeah.' Because it was. Olly had given them nearly twenty years of himself before he ran away. Patrice was all but a stranger, and, although she hadn't planted the idea of Olly lying under the mud of that landslide, she'd watered it and watched it grow. And then, trusting what she'd told him, he'd done the same to his wife. 'I'm sorry.'

Marnie was quiet for a second. 'Olly is still your son though.'

'Of course.' Some things weren't changeable. 'I'll always be Olly's dad, and Grace's dad, and your . . . ' He stopped himself.

'When are you coming home?'

'Where's home?'

She didn't answer directly. 'When are you coming back here? We need to talk.'

'About Olly.'

'About everything.'

That was a lot of things. 'I really am sorry.'

'You said.'

'But about other stuff as well.'

'Me too.'

Leo swallowed hard. He wasn't going to cry in the corridor of some hospital fifty miles from home. He wasn't going to cry for everything he'd messed up.

'Have you talked to him yet?'

'You said to wait.'

He was surprised. He thought of Marnie as certainty made flesh, not as someone who waited for anyone's opinion or help. Maybe that hadn't been true for a long time though.

He heard his wife's voice soften a little. 'I want us to do this together.'

Leo exhaled. 'So do I. I'll ring you when I'm on my way home.'

He ended the call and walked back to Patrice's bedside. The old woman was asleep. He sat on the chair and leaned towards her. He didn't have the words. The counsellor had said he needed to work on expressing his emotion, but when it came down to it, that wasn't who he was. He was quiet. He was an observer. He'd had his moment of anger at the hotel and somehow that had ended up here. Marnie was the one who grabbed moments by the scruff of the neck and wrung the emotion out of them — the necessary yin to his yang. What would Marnie say? He started tentatively, quietly. 'You lied.' That was it. He kept going. 'You lied about Olly, and you lied when I told you who I was. You lie in every show and every reading and I think you've lied so much that you don't care what's true.' Leo sighed. He'd come looking for something real. There was nothing real here. 'So I'm going now. My family need me. I might come back later. I don't know.'

He stood and took the three steps to the

entrance to the bay. There should be more to say. There should be something else, something final, something that would release him from the confusion. 'I forgive you. But I have to go.'

He walked away. It was just words.

★ ★ ★

You lied . . . I forgive you . . .

The words bounced around Patrice's mind, settling here and there, before sliding away into the darkness. Everybody lied. Her mother with her bottle under the sink. Her father with his Brylcreemed man, who lived above the shop. Charlie, who was going to stay with her for ever and raise their baby. Everybody lied.

And Patience had lied. Patrice opened her eyes. She was in . . . oh, those words again . . . She was on the special sleeping thing at the hospital, she supposed. This must have been what Patience wanted all along. She wanted Patrice brought low so that she could take her mind back. Patrice closed her eyes. Well, tough luck, Patience. Patrice wasn't done yet. A smile half-tugged at one corner of the woman's lips. She hadn't stolen anything from Patience. She'd tried so hard, but she'd simply failed. And then, Patience had decided. She looked at going home and she'd looked at being Gypsy Patience for ever and she'd made her choice. Patrice remembered. She'd made her choice.

371

67

1968

'So why should I give you your job back?'

Pat took a deep breath. 'Because I was really good at it.'

Mr Stefanini leaned back in his big chair behind his big dark wooden desk, but he didn't argue the point. That was good. He could argue with you from a position of whole-hearted agreement, if the mood took him. He must be feeling benevolent.

'You were, but then you buggered off.'

'That won't happen again.'

He didn't reply. He didn't need to. It was obvious she was going to need to provide some evidence of her reliability. What should she say? Work out what they wanted and give them it. That was the rule, but this was Mr Stefanini and it was his rule. What did he want? He wanted to make money. That was obvious. What else? She thought back. He'd been good to her when she'd worked for him before. He'd bunged a bit extra in her pay packet, which she hadn't asked for, when she'd moved from the café to the gypsy booth. He'd given her more hours. What else? He'd tolerated Gypsy Nadia doing God knows what with God knows who in her gypsy booth, but he'd been livid when he'd found out that she'd had her hand in the till. He wanted loyalty, and where he saw it he rewarded it. Georgios Stefanini looked after his own. So how did she convince him that she was one of his own? Sometimes the best lie was still less useful than the worst truth. 'I got pregnant. My parents sent me to the mother and baby home in York and they made me give him up for adoption. I'm back now.'

She watched his eyes widen just for a second but she didn't drop her gaze. This was her new life. No sitting in silence and ignoring awkward truths. No pretending. She was acting confident, more confident than she was feeling.

'Right.'

'Nothing like that will ever happen again.'

'I know it won't.'

She frowned.

'I know it won't because getting yourself pregnant once is unlucky. Twice would be stupid. I don't think you're stupid. Are you, Pat?'

She shook her head.

'I'll not be giving you your job back though.'

Pat's mood sank. She'd thought she was getting somewhere.

'I promised it to this new lass and it's not right to chuck her out because you've turned up with your tail between your legs.'

Pat nodded. It was fair enough.

'It's summer coming though, so you can do some evenings as extra cover.'

'Thank you.' She picked her bag up from next to the chair. 'I really appreciate it.'

'Where are you going?' He fixed her in the seat with a stare. 'I've got other plans for you. Lady at that party evening you did last year told me you could talk to dead people.'

Pat felt her cheeks colouring. 'Well, no. I can't. I mean . . . '

He shook his head. 'Never tell anyone you can't do that. Ever. Do you understand?'

Pat nodded.

'You have a gift, lass. A gift that needs to be nurtured and brought before the public in the proper way.'

'What sort of way?'

He paused. 'I'm not sure yet. We'll probably start with the churches. Spiritualist meetings and that. But then . . . ' He shook his head.

'Then what?'

'Then we'll see. You need a proper story though. Being Gypsy Nadia's niece and happening to fit in the costume won't cut it anymore.'

'What sort of story?'

'We'll think of something. Smoke and mirrors and all that.' He leaned forward, steepling his fingers in front of him. 'You've got to decide though. What I'm thinking, it's more than just a gypsy headdress and bit of hoo-hah with your crystal ball. You'd have to listen, and learn. It wouldn't just be a story. We'd be making a character that you'd have to be the whole time.'

Patience didn't answer straight away. He said those things like they were a warning. To Pat they sounded more like a promise — a get-out-of-jail-free pass to a whole new Pat. She swallowed. 'But it won't be real.'

Mr Stefanini shook his head. 'Real's what you make it, pet. Now there's your first lesson.'

374

Acknowledgements

Thank you — yes, you, right there — for reading. That's the most important thing by a very long way. Writers need readers, so please allow me to shake my metaphorical cheerleader pompoms vigorously in your direction. There are some other acknowledgements I ought to make as well, dear lovely reader, but just remember that all the time I was writing them I was secretly still thinking about you.

I do have to thank the fabulous people who helped me get *All That Was Lost* from half-formed idea to messy manuscript to finished book. Huge thanks to everyone at Legend Press, especially my brilliant editor, Lauren, but also Tom and Imogen for all their work and support. And thanks to my lovely agent, the incomparable Julia Silk, for seeing something in this book that I didn't quite know was there myself, and for believing in that something every step of the way.

Thanks also to my writing support network — the RNA, the ADCs, everyone who helped with the research, particularly Anne Harvey for her incredible generosity, and last, but never ever least, the glorious, opinionated, supportive, magnificent, frequently drunk women of the very naughtiest of kitchens.

Next, massive thanks to my family, especially mum and dad, for not batting an eyelid at my novel about a girl growing up in a chapel-going family in a northern seaside town. Particular thanks for not being even slightly like Lilian and Stanley.

And finally, as always, thanks to EngineerBoy, for mortgage paying, washing-up, and general all around husbanding, in support of me spending my days corralling the made up people into some sort of narrative sense.

Thank you. I salute you all.